Bring It On Home

A Misfit Inn Novel

Kait Nolan

Bring It On Home

Written and published by Kait Nolan

Cover design by Najla Qamber

Copyright 2019 Kait Nolan

AUTHOR'S NOTE: The following is a work of fiction. All people, places, and events are purely products of the author's imagination. Any resemblance to actual people, places, or events is entirely coincidental.

A Letter to Readers

Dear Reader,

This book is set in the Deep South. As such, it contains a great deal of colorful, colloquial, and occasionally grammatically incorrect language. This is a deliberate choice on my part as an author to most accurately represent the region where I have lived my entire life. This book also contains swearing and pre-marital sex between the lead couple, as those things are part of the realistic lives of characters of this generation, and of many of my readers.

If any of these things are not your cup of tea, please consider that you may not be the right audience for this book. There are scores of other books out there that are written with you in mind. In fact, I've got a list of some of my favorite authors who write on the sweeter side on my website at https://kaitnolan.com/on-the-sweeter-side/

If you choose to stick with me, I hope you enjoy!

Happy reading!

Kait

To the steadfast and true

Chapter One

"In conclusion, I think we can all agree that Aponyx will be in good hands."

A single pair of hands began to applaud. "You nailed it."

Satisfied, Maggie Reynolds nodded at her audience of one, her administrative assistant Alyssa. "I think I did. Now let's just hope the real presentation goes off without a hitch."

"You're due in the conference room downstairs in—" Alyssa checked her watch. "—ten minutes."

"No time to lose." She shoved up from the chair behind her desk and her stomach pitched as the room made a slow revolution.

"You okay?"

Fingers gripping the edge of the desk to keep from sinking right back into her chair, Maggie blinked and waited for the world to right itself. "Yeah, I'm fine. I just stood up too fast."

Alyssa looked askance in her direction. "Are you sure? Have you eaten today?"

Had she? "I grabbed a pastry on my way into the office." *Or was that yesterday?*

"That was six hours ago."

Convinced her legs would hold her, Maggie began to gather up her presentation materials. "We'll get a celebratory meal after the contracts are signed. Seriously. I'm fine. I just need another cup of coffee."

"Already on it." Alyssa thrust a travel mug into her hand.

"You are a goddess." Even as Maggie sipped, she wondered if Blood Coffee Level was a thing. If so, hers was well over the legal limit. But it was the only way she'd been able to function the past few weeks. Okay, months, if she were being honest. She'd been working too hard because work kept her from thinking. That was par for the course and what she'd done for the past twelve years when September rolled around. A part of her was afraid of where her mind would go without the distraction of contracts and mergers and the endless minutiae of being right-hand to one of the most powerful women in the country.

But this year had been worse than usual. Ever since her mother died in a car accident and she'd been pulled home to Tennessee to help her sisters deal with the estate and the aftermath, it had just been one thing after another. A lot more travel to settle things, a lot of legal stuff Maggie had been the natural choice to take on. A lot of reconnecting with her sisters. Which was good, so good. Mostly. But it was bringing up memories she'd done her best to forget.

Instead of a few weeks of overwork distraction in September, she'd been at this for more than a year. She'd been doing double duty for somewhere around eighteen months, keeping herself too busy to be overwhelmed by things she'd rather not remember. She couldn't deny it was taking a toll. Her body was drained, and all the caffeine had her pulse skittering so she felt simultaneously edgy and dull. Maybe she should take a little time. A long weekend to catch up on sleep. Maybe she'd find a spa up in Sonoma and get pampered.

Later. After the anniversary.

Palming the flash drive with her presentation, she moved around her desk. "Let's do this. Do you have the copies of the contract?"

"Right here. Sticky-tabbed, exactly as you wanted."

"Perfect. You're a lifesaver."

Reviewing the details of the final pitch, they headed down the hall toward the elevator that would take them to the conference room on the forty-second floor. The merger with Aponyx was all but locked in. Its owner, Roman Lewis, just had to sign on the dotted line.

Maggie's phone began to vibrate. Seeing her sister Pru's name flash across the screen, she stopped dead. The baby. Thirty-seven weeks. Her mind spun through all the prospective complications, everything that could go wrong. Preeclampsia. Preeclamptic seizure. Placental abruption. What if Pru had gone into pre-term labor? What if the umbilical cord had wrapped around the baby's neck?

A cold wave of fear swept over her skin, leaving a dewy sheen of sweat in its wake. "Let them know I'll be there as soon as I can. I have to take this." Peeling off, she strode back to her office, punching answer as she went. "What's wrong?"

"Do you want to tell me why there's a $700 stroller in my foyer?"

Mind still trapped in the horror of *what if*, it took Maggie a few moments to register the tone of mild interest underscored with just a hint of exasperation. "I...what? Are you okay? Are you having contractions?"

"I'm fine. The baby's fine. I'm just trying to figure out why you sent me the Cadillac of baby strollers."

Reassured everything was okay, Maggie released a controlled

breath and wrangled her emotions back in line. She couldn't afford to be rattled for this meeting. "Because you're going to need it in a few weeks." Of course she would. Because her pregnancy had been textbook perfect so far. There was no reason to expect anything else. But that didn't stop Maggie's brain from reminding her of the possibilities. She knew better than many that textbook-perfect could turn into a nightmare in a heartbeat.

"We already had a stroller."

"Yeah, but this one reclines to become an emergency bassinet. And it has a two-way facing toddler seat, an adjustable handle-bar, a temperature-regulating bamboo insert to keep the baby from getting too hot in the summer, and a massive, extendable canopy with UPF 50+ to protect the baby from sun. It's very well-rated." She'd researched every model on the market before settling on this one.

"I'm sure it's wonderful, but honey, it's too much. You already gave us the Pack 'n Play, the BabyBjörn, a DiaperGenie, and enough clothes to clothe the kid until he or she is four. It is not on you to outfit us with every baby accessory known to man."

It was the only way Maggie could think of to make up for the fact that she'd been slowly pulling back as her sister's pregnancy progressed. She hadn't known it would be this hard, watching Pru and her besotted husband, Flynn, prepare for their new arrival. The baby had been a surprise—a good one. Everyone in the extended Reynolds family was beside themselves with excitement. Not at all how anyone had reacted when it had happened to her. There was no comparison to their situations, but still, Maggie had struggled with feelings she'd thought long buried. She'd sooner streak naked down Rodeo Drive than have Pru realize she was anything other than ecstatic about this baby.

"Are you seriously going to rain on my doting-aunt-to-be parade?"

In the beat of silence, she imagined Pru closing her eyes and praying for patience as she rubbed the mound of her belly. "No. And thank you for your generosity. But seriously, you have to stop. We've got absolutely everything we need. We don't have *room* for anything else."

"I suppose I could return the cute little giraffe onesie."

"Giraffe?" Pru didn't quite manage to hide the interest. She had a weakness for all things animal. The nursery had been done up in a Noah's Ark theme and already held more stuffed animals than FAO Schwartz.

"Mmhmm. It says 'You bet giraffe I'm cute.' But it's still got tags on. I can take it back."

"Don't you dare."

Laughing, Maggie felt the last of the tension dissolve. "I put it in the mail yesterday, along with a box of those bonbons you like."

Pru groaned. "I'm going to be big as a cow before this baby comes."

"Give them to Ari. I'm sure she'd be happy to take one for the team." Her teenaged niece had a major sweet tooth.

"Over my dead body."

"That's the spirit. Listen, I've got to go. I've got a meeting to run. I'll check in soon. Love to everybody."

"We love you back. Come for a visit when you can. I miss your face. We got used to seeing more of you over the past couple of years."

Maggie swallowed back against the lump in her throat because that, too, had been harder than she'd expected. There'd been a reason she'd run from Eden's Ridge when she'd turned eighteen. She hadn't been the only one, but at this point, even Athena, their youngest sister, the award-winning chef, had moved home. That left her the odd sister out, way out here on the West Coast.

"I miss y'all, too. Talk to you later."

As soon as she hung up the phone, the warm glow she'd felt

talking to her sister faded. Did Pru suspect she wasn't being completely honest? Did she and the rest of the family realize that Maggie had been burying herself in work and sending endless baby gifts as an excuse not to be directly involved? She'd been in Los Angeles for five years, rocketing up the ranks at Invation. That had involved plenty of backbreaking work. She hoped they just thought she'd been making up for all the time she'd taken off to come home since Mom died. The alternative—that they'd look at her in pity and realize she wasn't made out of titanium like she pretended—that was unthinkable.

Shutting it away, she hurried down the hall toward the elevators. Halfway there she staggered, pressing a hand to the wall for support.

What the hell is wrong with me? Did I pick up some kind of a bug?

Vowing to take the rest of the day off as soon as the meeting was over, she straightened, squaring her shoulders and pinching her cheeks so she didn't look as worn out and ill as she felt. Yeah, she shouldn't have had that last cup of coffee.

The conference room was full when she stepped inside, mask firmly in place.

At the head of the table, Genevieve Kessinger, Maggie's boss and head of Invation was deep in conversation with an older man whose silver-shot brown hair swept back from his face in thick waves. Roman Lewis had crinkles around his eyes and mouth that told her a smile was his default expression. Or maybe he spent a lot of time outdoors in the sun.

"—sure you're ready to hand over the reins?" Genevieve asked.

"Definitely. Aponyx is no longer an infant company. It's not even a toddler anymore. And that means it's time to pass it on to someone who can grow it into something more robust and mature. My passion is in the development phase. Seeing innovation at the ground level and finding a way to make it a reality."

"You like incubation," Maggie observed. All eyes turned to her. "So sorry to have kept you waiting."

"Gentlemen, you remember my number one, Margaret Reynolds."

Roman beamed. "Pleasure to see you again, Miss Reynolds. And you're absolutely right. Aponyx is ready to leave the nest, and that means I can turn my attention to finding something new and different to invest in.

"A worthy goal, certainly."

"I like to think so. Let me introduce you to the rest of my team."

Maggie shook hands, trying to match the names and positions she'd seen on paper for weeks with the faces in front of her, but each one seemed to flow into her brain and out again. She was maxed-out on information. Praying she didn't mix anyone up, she moved with careful deliberation to plug her flash drive into the laptop hooked up to a projector. Obviously noting her unusually slow pace, Genevieve frowned, a question clear in her eyes.

Maggie just shook her head and called up her PowerPoint. "We're here today to go over the final details of the merger between Aponyx and Invation. You each have a copy of the latest contracts in front of you."

As she spoke, she thanked God for all the practice runs. It made it easy to slip into autopilot. Sweat broke out along her spine. The thermostat had to be set too high. Feeling her skin flush, she fought the urge to unbutton her suit jacket. The excessive heat was making the dizziness worse.

Pausing so Genevieve could answer a question, Maggie edged over to the water service that had been set up on the credenza. She'd just pour herself a glass. Her throat was so parched.

The hand that curled around the handle of the pitcher shook and the edges of the glass began to blur.

Dehydrated. I must be dehydrated.

Fighting for control, she lifted the pitcher, sloshing water as she tried to pour. The pitcher clattered against the rim.

"Margaret?"

She tried to turn, to speak, but the moment she shifted, the room tilted. She was dimly aware of someone shooting up from their chair before everything slid into blackness.

"You ready for this?" Porter Ingram studied the woman across the desk, taking in that oh-so-familiar face—the straight, dark hair and big brown eyes, and that crook at the corner of her mouth, always ready to twitch into a full smile. A smile that was about to be a part of his future.

"To hitch my wagon to yours? Bring it on."

He shoved the paperwork over and handed her a pen, watching as she scrawled her name—Mia Whitmore—on all the relevant lines. When she finished, she beamed a smile at him. "That's it then. It's official."

Porter grinned back. "Welcome aboard—partner."

He considered himself a lucky man. The business he'd built from the ground up had gotten big enough, successful enough, that he both needed and could afford to take on a partner. And he'd found a good one in the woman he'd worked side-by-side with on a series of restoration projects down in Gatlinburg. They'd kept in touch after, and when she'd expressed a desire to make a change and relocate, he'd invited her up to Eden's Ridge for a job. She'd loved the town, the people, so before they'd gotten more than halfway through the second phase expansion at The

Misfit Inn Spa, he'd asked if she'd be interested in making it permanent. A few of her crew had decided to make the transition as well, and Mountainview Construction had officially expanded as a family.

"This calls for a celebration," Mia declared.

"Drinks and pizza at Elvira's?" Not that there was really anywhere else to celebrate in their town of less than three thousand people, unless you wanted pie at the diner.

"Meet you there."

Ten minutes later, he strode into the controlled chaos of Elvira's on a Friday night. Bodies were packed on the tiny dance floor, kicking and stomping to some upbeat country song, and the space around the bar was three patrons deep in places. That he didn't recognize a fair chunk of them was proof that the tourism push was doing some good. Behind the bar, Denver Hershal worked the taps, a towel draped over one shoulder and the sleeves of his henley shoved up to his elbows. Business was booming, but the furrow between his brows was sign enough that he was frazzled.

Porter made his way through the crowd, until he'd managed to belly up to the bar and catch Denver's eye. "Y'all are jumpin' tonight."

"Kennedy picked a helluva time to leave me to go work full-time at the inn."

Kennedy Reynolds—Kincaid now—had been a fixture at Elvira's since she'd returned to Eden's Ridge eighteen months before. With her eldest sister in an advanced state of pregnancy, she'd finally called it quits on her second job in favor of taking over more duties at their family business, The Misfit Inn and Spa.

"Pru's only a few weeks from popping. Doctor's orders that she cut back."

"I know, I know," Denver grumbled. "Doesn't mean I have to like losing my best bartender. What'll it be?"

He'd beaten Mia here, but given how busy the place was, Porter figured she'd forgive him for ordering for her. "Two of the IPA you've got on tap."

"You got it."

Propping an elbow on the bar, he scanned the room, wondering if Mia had scooted past him.

"Well, hello handsome." The redhead's tilted blue eyes skimmed down his face to check his left hand.

Porter resisted the urge to shove it into a pocket and simply nodded politely. He wasn't here for flirtation.

"You a local?"

"I am."

She leaned next to him, mirroring his position. "Cute little town. I'm passing through on my way up to Virginia for my next job and ended up stopping for a couple days to try out the hiking. But what's a girl to do at night around here?"

Porter recognized the flirtation and the implied invitation. She wasn't unattractive, but he just wasn't interested and didn't quite know how to make that clear without being rude.

"You're pretty well doing it. Other than Elvira's we tend to roll up the sidewalks in time for supper."

"That can't be all there is to do around here on a Friday night."

"This time of year, most folks are up at the high school for football. But it's an away game tonight."

"Pity. Where do you take your dates?"

He was still searching for a polite brush-off when Mia strode up, faintly breathless.

"Sorry I'm late. I had to run by the house to feed Leno."

The redhead lost her flirty demeanor as her gaze shifted between the two of them. Color rose in her cheeks and she backed away with a muttered, "Sorry."

Mia watched her go. "Aw, I ran her off. Damn. Sorry about that. I'm a shit wingman."

"I'm not looking for a wingman. You did me a favor." Porter scooped up the beers Denver delivered. "C'mon, let's see if we can find a table."

They lucked into one of the high-tops toward the back as a trio of women, clearly out for girls' night, vacated.

Mia took a stool and sipped at her drink. "You know, I haven't really seen you interested in anybody since I moved to the Ridge."

"I could say the same about you." Mia worked like a dog and loved to hang out with friends, but she'd shut down the handful of guys who'd shown interest in her over the past few months.

"My relationship status is permanently set to 'It's complicated.' What's your excuse? Have you got some ex in your closet who scarred you for life?"

"No." He'd never actually been with the woman he couldn't get out of his head.

"A secret long-distance relationship?"

I wish. "Nope."

"Do you secretly swing the other way? Because it's cool if you do."

He huffed a laugh. "Not that either. There's just no one here I'm interested in."

Her gaze sharpened. "Which begs the question of whether there's somebody somewhere *else* you're interested in."

That was a can of worms he wasn't willing to open. "I want to talk about that about as much as you want to talk about that ring you wear around your neck that you think nobody knows about."

Her hand reached up reflexively to check the chain, her good humor fading. "Yeah okay, we're not here to talk about our love lives. Or lack thereof."

"This is about business and partnership." Porter lifted his pilsner glass in a toast. "To our future success."

"Fine, fine. Be that way." Mia grinned and lifted her own glass. "To our future success. With the resort contract, that seems in the bag."

The Paradise Mountain Resort was the biggest construction job to hit Stone County in...maybe ever, and Mountainview had been first in line to bid on the job. "I was beginning to think it was a pipe dream, as long as it's taken to get off the ground." There'd been one delay after another with the proposal to the city, and Eden's Ridge had already missed the window of prime opportunity to easily siphon off some of the tourist trade after the Gatlinburg fires. Gatlinburg had already rebuilt—Porter and Mia had been a part of that—and here the powers that be were still waiting to break ground.

"Bureaucracy. Slows things down the world over," Mia declared. "But it'll be good to have solid work for the crew through fall and winter."

"True that. But I won't feel totally relaxed about it until after the meeting with the mayor in a couple days." Porter hid a scowl in his beer. He'd have to be on his best behavior around Mayor Bradley Danforth.

Mia circled a finger in his direction. "What is this face? You're fine with meetings."

"I am not a fan of Danforth."

"Why?"

"There's...bad blood between our families."

"What kind of bad blood? Like a Hatfield and McCoy sort of feud?"

Under the circumstances, he owed her some kind of an answer. "His family is about as close as you can get to Stone County royalty. They go back generations, and they're the type that walks around acting like their shit don't stink and that they're better than everybody else. Danforth senior wasn't one for keeping it in his pants. He habitually strayed on his wife." Dropping his voice low, despite the din of the bar, he leaned closer. "One of those affairs was with my mother."

Mia's mouth dropped open, her eyes going wide. "Shit."

"The details aren't widely known, so keep that under your hat. Anyway, my dad found out, my parents split, Mom left town, and Dad fell into the bottle—bad."

"That's how you ended up in the system?"

Porter nodded. The fact that they'd both grown up as foster kids was one of the things he and Mia had in common. But she hadn't been lucky enough to find an amazing foster mother as he had. Joan Reynolds had made sure he hadn't followed the same path as his father.

"So you basically hate the family on principle?"

"Something like that. Our illustrious mayor doesn't fall far from the tree, as it were. That's always rubbed me the wrong way." It was a partial truth anyway.

"Is that gonna be a problem for you?"

Porter shrugged. "I can be a grown-up about it. I may think it's laughable that he's the guy elected as our leader, when he's about as far out of touch as it is possible to be with what life is like for normal people here, but he's the one in charge, so I'll make nice. This is just business. The meeting shouldn't take long, anyway. It's just a formality to sign off on the contracts." There was no reason to think the project wouldn't be rubber-stamped. It wasn't like there was another construction company in the area who could take on this project. For all he despised Danforth, the man did believe in keeping labor local.

The phone in his pocket began to vibrate. Sliding it out, he caught sight of Maggie's name on the screen, and his pulse leapt with anticipation. Stupid. They were friends. Had been since they were kids. But she'd been giving him heart palpitations since he was fifteen, and no amount of time or distance seemed to dim the sensation. No matter what, no matter where, he'd always stop what he was doing to answer her call.

"Hey Maggie."

Across the table, Mia arched a brow, and too late he realized he hadn't managed to school the tone of his voice.

"Is this Porter Ingram?" Another woman's voice. Definitely not Maggie.

Unease began to unfurl in his gut. "Yes. Who is this?"

"My name is Genevieve Kessinger. I'm a friend of Maggie's."

Kessinger. Friend and boss, he remembered. "What's going on?"

"I'm calling because she passed out at work today and is in the hospital. I know you're not her next of kin, but I didn't want to call her pregnant sister, and you were the next most frequent contact—"

For one stunned moment, his mind simply blanked. Then his heart began to pound. Maggie in the hospital? She hated hospitals. As far as he knew, she hadn't been in one since senior year of high school. Certainly not as a patient. She had to be fucking terrified.

Already sliding out of his chair, he demanded, "Where is she?"

Genevieve named the hospital. "We haven't been here that long, but she's been admitted and they're running tests."

He was aware of Mia trailing him to the door. "I want to talk to her."

"You can't. As I said, they're running tests. I practically had to threaten her job to make sure she agreed to them."

For a few heartbeats he squeezed his eyes shut and saw her face at seventeen, ashen, terrified, screaming as they wheeled her through the double doors in the ER, away from him.

Willing back the old, helpless rage, he shoved open the door with more force than necessary, surprising Jolene Lowry and her husband Curt. He waved an apology and made a beeline for his truck. "I'm on my way. I'll be there as soon as I can."

"I'll have a private jet on standby in Johnson City."

His hand stilled on the door handle. "You...really?"

"She's one of my best friends and money is not an issue for me, Mr. Ingram. I don't know what they're going to find, but I think she needs someone from home here for her. I'll text you the address of the airstrip."

"Thank you." As soon as he hung up, he yanked open the driver's door and finally glanced back at Mia. "I'm sorry, I have go to."

Expression dialed to concern, she crossed her arms. "What's going on, Porter?"

"A friend is in the hospital. I have to get out to Los Angeles."

"By friend you mean Maggie Reynolds."

"Yeah."

"Why did they call you instead of her sisters?" Mia might not have been in Eden's Ridge that long, but she'd already met the rest of the Reynolds sisters.

"Because Pru is more than eight months pregnant. Maggie wouldn't have wanted her to have a shock." She'd been going overboard on the worry and caution the entire time. It had been driving Pru nuts, but she knew what Maggie had been through, knew the obsessive research and concern came from a place of love, so she tolerated it with her usual good grace.

"Aren't you going to tell Kennedy or Athena before you go?"

"No. Not until I can give them some definitive answers about what's going on. And neither will you if you run into them on-site at The Misfit Kitchen while I'm gone."

"Fine. But what about the meeting?"

"I'll probably be back by then. And if I'm not, it's nothing you can't handle. I'm sorry to bail on you, but this is important."

After a moment's hesitation, she nodded. "I've got your back. I hope Maggie's okay."

"Me too."

She'd be all right. She had to be. Anything else was unthinkable.

Chapter Two

"I can't *believe* they had the nerve to say nothing is wrong with you." In the backseat of the town car, Genevieve fumed.

Maggie didn't know how she had the energy. They'd both been up most of the night. Too exhausted to work up much of an argument, she rested her head against the seat, staring out as the quiet streets of L.A. slid past. She wished she could just fall into sleep and avoid all conversation, but the edgy restlessness told her sleep would be a long time coming, if it came at all. And she was afraid of what dreams would bring when it did.

"I told you, I'm fine."

"You're *not* fine. You passed out in the middle of a presentation."

Humiliating. Roman Lewis had apparently been the one to catch her, just before her head cracked against the floor.

"Which they concluded was from low blood sugar, lack of sleep, and excessive caffeine. Not a brain tumor or whatever else you made them test me for." She'd lost track of the number of scans and blood draws she'd been subjected to. "And can we talk about how we're going to salvage the mess I made of the merger?" Anything to avoid further discussion of her health.

"You didn't make a mess. We postponed the meeting and no one is upset about it. Everybody just wants to know you're okay."

"Which the doctors say I am." And okay, yeah, she was grateful she had that confirmation, even if she did still feel like warmed-over death.

Genevieve snorted. "Narrow-minded, old-school blowhards. You totally have adrenal fatigue."

This again. Genevieve had already argued this with the attending physician—for half an hour.

"The doctor said that's not actually a recognized diagnosis."

"Oh bullshit. They said fibromyalgia wasn't a real diagnosis for decades until somebody finally figured out how to prove it existed."

"Why are you so convinced this is a thing?" Maggie had never even heard of it.

"Because I know half-a-dozen people who've been through it, and both my acupuncturist and naturopath have been warning me for years that I'm skating the edge. Why do you think I have that weekly massage and take all those hot yoga classes? You think I actually *like* all that crunchy granola health food stuff? I love pastry and French fries with a religious fervor, but it's not great for my health, so I drink the damned wheat grass."

"Gag me."

"Same. Every morning. But either way, just because Western medicine hasn't caught on to the fact that there is actually a middle ground between normal adrenal function and failure doesn't mean the rest of the world missed the memo. You have almost all the symptoms." She started ticking them off on her fingers. "Chronic fatigue, brain fog, lightheadedness, depression, moodiness and irritability, problems with your sleep, hair loss, decreased libido—"

Maggie interrupted the recitation. "All of which have a multitude of other potential causes."

"Adrenal fatigue, burnout—whatever you want to call it—the root of all of it is stress."

"On that we can agree."

Genevieve's voice went soft. "You've had a helluva couple of years, with your mom dying, your niece's adoption, Kennedy and Pru's weddings, and starting the inn and spa, and running the financial side of that from here, on top of your normal duties. It's a lot."

Not looking away from the window, Maggie shrugged. "It's life. I'm dealing with it."

"You can't keep going on like this. If you don't get your health under control, next time it *will* be something even more serious."

"I'm dealing with it," Maggie repeated. Dealing with whatever came up was simply what she did. It had taken everything she had not to collapse into a whimpering puddle of anxiety when she'd woken up at the hospital, but she'd dealt with that, too.

"You're not dealing with it, not really. But you will."

The seriousness of Genevieve's tone roused her enough to look at her friend. "What's that supposed to mean?"

"Hold that thought. We're here."

The town car pulled up in front of Maggie's building, and the driver came around to open the door, offering a hand to help her out.

"Thanks for the ride, Carlos."

The older man nodded. "Miss Reynolds. I hope you feel better soon."

What else could she say? "Thank you."

"I'm walking her up. I'll be back down in a little while," Genevieve told him.

"Yes, Miss Kessinger."

Neither of them spoke as they crossed the lobby, and that was good. Maggie had to concentrate hard to stay vertical. Each step felt like dragging her feet through molasses. Even if she couldn't really sleep, she couldn't wait to get horizontal. She was so damned *tired.* It had taken so much to combat the renewed sense of helplessness and all the memories of fear, confusion, and powerlessness to stop whatever the hell was going on. To pretend she wasn't freaking the hell out on the inside so they'd let her simply go. All she wanted was the chance to fall apart in the sanctuary of her own home. Was that too much to ask? Maybe she'd have a nice soak after she kicked Genevieve out. That might unwind her enough to manage a nap.

When they were finally shut into the elevator, Genevieve crossed her arms. "It's partly my fault you're in this condition. I suspected you were pushing yourself too hard, working too much, and I let it slide. You're so damned good at your job, I didn't realize it had gotten this bad. That's on me for not pushing, not asking questions. But I'm not gonna let you work yourself into an early grave on my behalf."

Maggie curled her fingers around the rail as the car moved smoothly up to her floor. "What are you saying?"

"I'm saying you're going to make some serious changes. Starting with taking forced vacation. None of this day or two here every few months. A real vacation. Where you sleep and rest and *relax.*"

Genevieve rarely played the boss card, so it wasn't as if Maggie had a leg to stand on to argue. She'd already been thinking of taking time herself, but having it handed down as a dictate rankled. "Fine. I'll take a week—"

"You'll take until the end of the year. At least."

In the mirrored walls, Maggie saw her own mouth gape open like a fish. "That's more than three months! I can't not work for three months!"

"You'll be paid."

That was a concern, certainly, but that wasn't her primary issue. Work was her coping mechanism. The thing that kept her sane. If Genevieve took that away, what would happen? "What the hell will I do with myself for that long? More to the point, what the hell will you do without me?"

The elevator doors slid open, and they stepped into the quiet hall. "You have a painfully efficient administrative assistant. Alyssa is as much your right hand as you are mine. We'll manage. As to you—why don't you go home and spend some time with your sisters? Be around for the birth of your new niece or nephew and get your dote on?"

Because I don't know if I can survive it.

But she wasn't about to mention that to Genevieve. She'd never told her friend about her miscarriage. That pregnancy had changed the course of her whole life, forever branding her in Eden's Ridge as "that girl who got knocked up in high school." The boatload of academic accolades and professional accomplishments she'd racked up in the years since then meant exactly nothing in her hometown. Nobody saw the successful business-woman she'd become, only "that poor Reynolds girl" who'd suffered the same fate as her birth mother. Was it any wonder she'd run to the opposite coast to make a life far from rumor and speculation? No, she couldn't go home for that long. Not now.

"I can't just go home for months. I have obligations here. To you, if you'll remember. I'm in the middle of at least seven different negotiations that I can't just walk away from."

"We'll handle it. None of them are worth your life."

Maggie slid her key into the lock. "You are out of your mind."

"I knew you'd be stubborn about this. So I brought in some backup. If you won't listen to me, maybe you'll listen to him."

Beyond irritated, Maggie shoved open the door. "Backup? What are you talking about?"

"Maggie."

At the sleepy male voice, she shrieked and slapped on the overhead light.

Shielding his eyes, the intruder straightened to sitting on the sofa, sandy hair tousled, clothes rumpled, as if he'd been up all night, as they had. "Sorry, sorry. It's just me."

His familiar drawl cut through her instinctive panic, but still she stared, because there was no way he was really here. She was hallucinating. Had to be. There was no other good explanation. But God, if anybody could make her feel better about all this, it was him.

"Porter?"

* * *

"The super let me in."

It was probably a dumb response to her shock at seeing him, but Porter wasn't at his sharpest. He'd travelled more than half the night to get to California. By the time he'd landed—hours earlier than if he'd had to arrange his own flight, thank God—Genevieve had texted he should go straight to Maggie's place because they'd be releasing her shortly, and he wouldn't make it all the way to the hospital before then. The news had relieved a little of the sick worry that had gripped him all the way from Eden's Ridge. If they were releasing her, it couldn't be that bad. Could it?

But looking at Maggie now, seeing the dark circles under her eyes, the paler-than-usual skin, she seemed so very fragile. Worse, even, than when Joan had died. Lines of strain bracketed her mouth and eyes, and he recognized the toll the night had taken. She was barely holding it together. He wanted to wrap his arms around her, fold her in and keep her safe from whatever it was she'd been facing alone.

But this was Maggie Reynolds. She faced everything alone.

So he held himself still, drinking in the sight of her until a slim woman with honey-brown hair strode through the door with all the command of a model on a catwalk.

"Excellent. You made it. It's nice to meet you, Porter. I'm Genevieve Kessinger." She offered her hand, effectively breaking his paralysis. Her grip was firm, businesslike, as if she were ready to run a board meeting, even in the middle of the damned night.

"Likewise. Thanks for the transportation assist."

"It was nothing. Anthony didn't kick up a fuss about letting you in?"

"No." And he'd wondered about that. About whether the guy would let just anybody in to anybody's apartment.

"Owning the building has its advantages," Genevieve moved into the kitchen. "Maggie, come sit the hell down."

Maggie still hadn't moved from the entryway, still hadn't taken those exhaustion-bruised eyes off of him. "What are you *doing* here?"

He didn't know what to say. *I thought you needed me.*

But he'd expected to find her in a hospital bed, facing God-knew-what health crisis and the specter of horrific memory. He hadn't thought beyond that.

Fortunately, Genevieve leapt in to explain as she banged around Maggie's kitchen, putting on a kettle to heat. "You needed someone other than just me. I knew you'd have a fit if I called any of your sisters and it got back to worry Pru, so I called your next most frequent contact."

He was her number two? Or was it four, after her sisters? He was too damned tired to math, and it was taking everything he had not to march over and scoop Maggie directly off her feet. Why didn't she sit down?

She kept her gaze on his. "And you just dropped everything and came?"

Porter couldn't tell whether the idea of that pleased or annoyed her. "She said you were in the hospital. Of course, I came." Because he knew what it must've done to her to be there.

Her face flexed with emotion before she managed to get her expression under control. "Well, since they let me go, I'm sorry you made a wasted trip."

To his mind, the chance to see her was never a waste. And she *did* need him—or someone, at least—whether she was willing to admit it or not.

"I told you, I called in backup." Genevieve poured water into a couple of mugs and stabbed the buttons on the microwave to set a timer before she shifted her focus to him. "I need you to convince her to go home to Tennessee for a few months."

That shocked him enough to pull his attention away from Maggie. Had hell frozen over? "Beg your pardon?"

"I'm putting her on forced vacation. She's burned out, and if she doesn't get some radical R and R, she's going to work herself into the kind of health crisis that doesn't mean getting out of the hospital in under twenty-four hours."

What the hell did that mean?

Maggie grumbled something under her breath.

"I love you, but if I see you at the office before January, you're fired." Ignoring the death glare Maggie shot in her direction, Genevieve hugged her. "Tough love, cupcake. You need it. Drink your tea, have a good vacation, and take care of yourself or you'll be hearing from me."

And then she was gone.

"Is she always like that?" Porter asked.

"It's rarely directed at me." Maggie shut the door behind her, then simply stood there, palm pressed to the wood.

Moving slowly, he closed the distance, until he stood just behind her. "How bad was it really?" he murmured. He didn't need to explain himself. It was just them now, no more reason to hide.

The hand against the door flexed and began to shake as the tension of truth grew between them. He expected some dismissal. A shrug. A flip remark that downplayed whatever she'd gone through these past hours. Instead she turned into him, sliding her arms around his waist, pressing her cheek to his chest, and he understood she was at the end of her reserves. So he gave in to the urge to wrap her up, hauling her tight against him as if he could shield her from her demons.

"It's okay. I've got you. You don't have to be strong for me."

"I'm not—I just...need a minute." Her voice against his chest was muffled and full of strain.

"Take as long as you need."

He felt it as she let the panic come. Shudders wracked her body, and her breath wheezed. He wanted her to burrow in. To hold onto him as she once had. But she only leaned a little, the dammed up tears never falling. Because even now, with him, she wouldn't let herself break. And maybe that was why, since he was the only person to ever see her do it. The only one who truly knew she wasn't made of titanium. When the timer went off, she pulled away and walked into the kitchen to deal with the tea. He worried she might fold into a heap right there. He wanted to curl up on the sofa, with her in his lap, and hold her until she actually rested. But that wasn't going to happen.

"What's really going on, Maggie?"

She sipped at the tea before answering. "I've been burning the candle at both ends since Mom died. Apparently you can only do that for so long before you run out of candle, so Genevieve is playing hardball to force me into dealing with it."

"Shit timing for you." The anniversary of her miscarriage was just around the corner.

Her eyes shot to him in surprise.

"Did you think I'd forget?" He'd been there that day. Every moment was as indelibly carved into his brain as it was in hers.

"No," she whispered. "No, you never have."

Porter herded her toward the sofa, plucking the tea from her shaky hands. "Come sit down before you fall down."

She dropped onto one end. Because she was still trembling, he dragged the throw blanket off the back and wrapped it around her. She shifted, putting her back to the arm of the couch and pulling her feet up, neatly carving out her space bubble again. Ignoring the twinge he felt at that, Porter handed the tea back and sank onto the opposite side.

"Before you start the hard sell, I can't go home."

He knew why. But he didn't entirely agree with her, and maybe it was time he nudged, just a little. "You've spent the past twelve years working yourself into the ground to avoid remembering. Did you ever think that maybe facing the grief head-on might be a better tactic?"

Those long, slim fingers clenched white around the mug. "I did grieve. More than any of you could know. And for years I was fine. It's just—watching Pru's pregnancy has been so much harder than I thought it would be. I can't help but play 'What if?'"

Yeah, he'd played plenty of that game himself over the years, when it came to this woman. What if the baby had lived? What if Maggie had said yes? What if he'd admitted how he felt—before the baby? Before He Whom She Never Named? But Porter knew how fruitless that line of speculation really was.

"I know it hurts you. If there was a damned thing I could do to make it stop, I would. But for better or worse, Pru's baby is coming. You're gonna have to make your peace with that. I think the longer you put it off, the harder it will be."

She swallowed. "I'm scared."

Maggie Reynolds didn't admit to pedestrian human emotions

like fear. And that, too, was a sign of how thin she'd spread herself.

Porter couldn't resist reaching out to lay a hand over her slim feet. He just needed to touch her, to offer whatever support he could. "Of what, honey?"

She rested her cheek on her up-drawn knees and let loose a bone-weary sigh. "That I won't be able to take it. That Pru will know and be hurt by the fact that I can't be a hundred percent excited about this baby. That it'll dim any of her joy. She and Flynn deserve to be over the moon about all of this without worrying about me. I don't want to ruin that."

God, it made him ache that she didn't think her own feelings deserved consideration here. "You're not gonna ruin anything."

"Maybe not," she conceded. "But that's not the only reason I've stayed away."

"It's been more than a decade, Mags. There are a whole boatload of newer scandals for people to talk about."

"You and I both know memory runs long in the Ridge. No one's forgotten."

True enough. But hopefully people would have enough sense to keep that shit to themselves.

"So come home and show them what an amazing woman you grew into. Spend some time on-site working on the inn and spa. Hang with your sisters. And you know how much it would mean to Pru if you were there when the baby is born. If it's too much, nobody said you had to stay in Tennessee until Genevieve lifts her ban in January. Hell, she'll probably figure out in a week or two she can't do without you and will want you back. But come home in the meantime. I think, in the long run, you'll be better for it."

Maggie hesitated. "If I go home right now, like this, Pru will know something's wrong. They all will."

"So we'll take a couple days for you to sleep and rest and

pack. Maybe throw in a massage or a facial or something. Then we'll go home."

She arched her brows. "We?"

"I mean, I came all the way out here. Seems a shame not to see something of the city you've been calling home." He gave her foot another squeeze. "I'm not leaving you to face all this alone."

Her lips curved into a real smile this time, albeit a tired one. "You're a good friend, Porter."

He held in a sigh. Here was the reminder of their status quo. Friendship wasn't what he wanted from her. It wasn't why he'd flown all the way across the country at the drop of a hat. But what they'd rebuilt since her mother died was more than they'd had in years, and now wasn't the time to rock that boat.

"Any time. Let's get some sleep."

Chapter Three

Porter had suggested at least a few days of pampering. Maggie took all of one, getting a massage and facial, and having some kind of detox body wrap from Genevieve's cadre of self-care gurus. She needed a lot more, but the process had left her feeling almost human. It was good enough to manage the trip home. What she didn't actually achieve, she could fake with cosmetics. Past that, she'd brazen her way through. She'd had plenty of practice. But this wasn't a boardroom negotiation. This was her family.

They didn't know she was coming. She'd decided surprise was the best option. If they had advanced notice, they might put together some big homecoming party and invite people. The existing Reynolds clan was more than enough to handle as it was, with all three of her sisters, their significant others, and Ari.

"You ready for this?" Porter asked.

She looked away from the sprawling Victorian that had been home for so many years. "Does it matter if I am?"

He caught her hand, squeezed. "If you're really not, you can hide at my place until you are."

Maggie closed her eyes for just a moment, reveling in the feel of his strong fingers curling gently around hers. This man had already given up three days for her, blowing off his own business to make sure she was taken care of. Maggie didn't know what to do with that. The idea that he'd hide her, shield her, was so appealing—and familiar—she forced herself to square her shoulders. She hadn't let him be her shield at seventeen. She wouldn't start now.

Squeezing his hand back, she released it and took a step toward the house. "Thank you, but you and I both know someone would probably look out a window and see before we could make a clean getaway."

As if she'd created a self-fulfilling prophecy with her words, the front door swung open.

"Maggie?"

She'd barely turned toward the voice before Ari was bounding down the steps.

"You're here! You're here!" The girl launched herself at Maggie, wrapping her in a massive hug.

"I am!" Laughing, Maggie returned the embrace, feeling her heart trip at the enthusiastic greeting. "You're taller."

"A whole inch since you were last here. Mom and Dad are taking bets on whether I'm done growing or not." She stepped back, grinning, and Maggie could see some extra maturity in her features, too.

God, she was growing up so fast. She didn't belong to Maggie, but Maggie felt a pang nonetheless. Shoving that down deep, she forced her lips into a smile. "How is everything?"

"Mom is bored to death and tired of having everything but answering phones taken off her plate, and she's cranky and underslept because the baby has decided to tap dance on her internal organs most of the night. But she'll be ecstatic to see you. Come on!"

Before she could blink, Ari was charging back up the porch. She glanced back at Porter. "Into the breach."

He just smiled and followed.

As soon as Maggie stepped through the front door, something in her settled. Even without her mother, even though things were different now that it had been turned into an inn, this was still home. She'd never feel this peace anywhere else.

Tones of argument drew her back to the big kitchen, where her very pregnant sister scowled from her seat at the massive farmhouse table. "I can wash a damned dish."

"Not so long as I'm on duty, you can't." At the sink, her youngest sister, Athena, crossed her arms and scowled right back. "My kitchen, my rules."

Pru glared. "If you think I'm going to say, 'Yes, Chef,' you've got another thing coming."

Maggie stepped into the room. "It's a sign of exactly how bored you are that you're fighting to do dishes."

Everybody started talking over each other.

"Maggie!"

"Holy shit!"

Pru started to shove up from her chair, but Athena got to Maggie first, wrapping her in a rib-cracking hug. "It's so good to see you!"

"Back atcha, baby sis." Maggie moved over to hug Pru, who was still struggling—and failing—to get out of the chair.

"Damn it, my center of gravity is in China. What are you doing here?"

"Well, you did say you missed my face, so I thought I'd surprise you."

"That's wonderful!"

Kennedy strolled into the room. "Am I missing a party? What's all the commotion about?"

Maggie wiggled her fingers in a wave. "Surprise."

A smile broke over Kennedy's face and she jumped in on the hug train. "A helluva good surprise. Welcome home. How long can you stay?"

Reflexively she glanced at Porter, who'd slipped into the room unnoticed in the chaos of greetings. No way in hell was she admitting she had until January. She'd never last that long here, and she didn't want to hurt anyone's feelings. But she'd committed to being here through the baby's birth. Porter was right. She needed to face it head-on.

He offered a faint nod, and his silent, steady support made this a little easier.

"A while. I've arranged to telecommute so that I can help out around here until after the baby's born."

Pru rubbed the mound of her belly. "I'm not due for another two-and-a-half weeks."

"I know. But this is important. You're important. I wanted to be here." Okay, that was mostly true.

Pru's eyes went glassy. "Oh!"

"For heaven's sake, don't cry. This was meant to be a good surprise."

"Shut up. I'll cry if I want to. It's in the Preggo Handbook. I'm so happy to see you, I can't even be angry that you're just gonna be another jailer stopping me from doing *anything*."

"I did say she was cranky," Ari said.

"Are you judging your mother, then?" Flynn Bohannon, Pru's husband, strode into the kitchen, automatically kissing his wife and whispering something in Irish that soothed her ruffled feathers as he winked at Maggie.

Seeing the easy way Pru leaned into him, the way they made such a perfect unit, gave Maggie a pinch somewhere in the vicinity of her heart. She refused to admit it was envy. It was just...longing. Longing for something she'd long given up hope of finding.

Straightening, her brother-in-law crossed to dole out more hugs. "Well, this is a lovely surprise, to be sure."

"I'm hoping it's not a problematic surprise. I didn't check to make sure there's room at the inn, as it were."

"There's always room for family."

After all the isolation in California, the idea of that was soothing.

Maggie found herself shoved into a seat. Athena bustled around, making tea and putting together a tray of snacks, as everyone began to talk. She lost herself in the familiar chaos of family, too exhausted to track more than half of what was said. As she reached for a slice of friendship bread from the tray her sister put out, her hand shook with another of those almost uncontrollable tremors. Hastily, she yanked it back into her lap, glancing around to see if anyone had noticed.

Across the table, Porter was frowning, but everyone else was too busy chatting about Athena's plans for the next few episodes of her web series, *The Misfit Kitchen.* He put a slice of the bread on a napkin and laid it in front of her. Maggie wanted to be annoyed. She wasn't a child. But it was impossible to be angry with him for giving a damn.

"Subscription numbers are on an exponential rise," Kennedy reported. "I don't think we're gonna have any trouble paying off the construction costs of your new kitchen."

"It's not much to see yet, but oh, I can imagine it finished." Athena hugged herself and beamed.

Between the runaway success of her blog and web series and her deepening relationship with Logan Maxwell, the organic farmer she'd been dating the past several months, Maggie had never seen her happier. She was carving out her own niche. Maggie envied that. Since Athena had moved home back in the spring, Maggie had felt like the odd one out. She and Athena had been the city girls. Now it was just her. Her baby sister had been absorbed back into the family in that tight-knit way that could only happen when you were local.

"Framing was done last week. Mia says the exterior walls and roof will be done by end of next week," Athena continued.

"Mia?" Maggie didn't recognize the name.

"She's part of Porter's crew," Kennedy put in.

"Actually, she's my business partner."

Porter had a business partner? A *female* business partner? In all their conversations this past year, he'd never once mentioned her. Not that Maggie talked about all the ins and outs of her job with Invation, but him taking on a partner of any stripe seemed like news he would have shared. That he hadn't brought it up felt...odd.

"Oh, you finally made it o-ohhhh—" Pru's face went slack with surprise.

Maggie had already vaulted out of her seat and circled around to lay a hand on Pru's shoulder, automatically looking down to check for blood. "Are you okay?"

"I think my water just broke!"

For one stunning moment, Maggie gave in to the terror. Then the entire room burst into motion.

"I'll get the car!"

"I've got the hospital bag!"

Shoving back the fear, Maggie helped her sister to her feet. "Well, come on then. It's time to have a baby."

Porter's gaze followed Maggie as she paced the waiting room. They'd been at the hospital most of the night. He'd expected her to volunteer to stay back and take care of things at the inn to avoid going to yet another hospital. But she hadn't hesitated to join her sisters in the caravan to Johnson City. Still, exhaustion and anxiety wrapped around her like trailing blankets. Both arms crossed over her middle, as if she had to physically hold herself together. That just killed him. He wanted to wrap her up, let her lean again. But he knew she wouldn't do that in front of her family.

Did any of them remember that today was the anniversary?

Across the waiting room, Kennedy was asleep against her husband Xander's shoulder. Ari was dozing on the other. Athena's boyfriend, Logan, was slumped in a chair, long legs stretched out, hands folded over his chest as he dozed.

Determined to try again to get Maggie to rest, Porter shoved up and joined her. "Maggie, sit down before you fall down."

She barely spared him a glance. "I can't."

He lowered his voice. "This endless pacing isn't good for you. You're supposed to rest, remember?"

"I'll rest when it's over."

Who knew when that would be? This whole labor business was a long and drawn-out process. The waiting had effectively eradicated the limited good those few spa treatments had done. After another long, restless night, she looked almost as tired and strung out as she had when he'd arrived in California.

Porter opened his mouth to argue, but Maggie turned away from him, toward the echo of footsteps. Athena came down the hall. She'd been taking her shift helping distract Pru. At various points she, Kennedy, and Ari had all gone back during the labor, trading off.

"Well?" Maggie asked.

"Everything's going fine." Athena reported something about dilation and effacing that Porter didn't want to think about, but whatever it meant, Maggie relaxed a little. "The doctor says she ought to be ready to push in another hour or so. Do you want to go back?"

This was the line Maggie couldn't seem to make herself cross.

She shook her head. "I don't want my anxiety about all of this to make anything worse for her."

Porter could feel that anxiety pulsing off her like an electric field, vibrating the air between them.

Athena just squeezed her shoulder before going to wake Ari for another turn.

As the girl disappeared down the hall, Porter tried again. "Honey, at least sit down and stop wearing a hole in the floor."

On a long exhale, Maggie nodded and sank into a seat as far from her family as she could get.

"Hey, you're up on the charger." Athena held up the cord.

His phone had died several hours before, and between the lot of them, they'd only managed to round up one cable. He left the phone charging, and crossed back to sit beside Maggie. She lifted those dark brown eyes to his, looking so tired and wounded, it took everything he had not to cup her cheek.

Keeping his voice gentle, he leaned back in his chair. "Try to rest a bit. Sounds like it won't be too long now."

On another of those soul-weary exhales, she closed her eyes and tipped her head to his shoulder. The light pressure felt like a victory, but he knew it was a hollow one. She'd only capitulated because she was too tired to fight him anymore. As soon as she'd had rest, she'd pull back again. Because that was what she did. She refused help, refused to lean. Because Maggie Reynolds imagined herself an island. It frustrated the hell out of him, not only because he wanted so much more from her than this, but because he knew things would be better for her if she'd just bend a little.

Across the room, Xander arched a brow. Porter just shook his head slightly, because Maggie had finally slid into a doze.

They'd been best friends since they were children, and Xander knew perfectly well how Porter felt about Maggie. How he'd always felt about Maggie. She was the topic they didn't discuss. Not since he'd asked for advice about how to handle the fact that he'd fallen for his foster sister.

Because of his father's alcoholism, he'd been in and out of Joan Reynolds' care all through high school, and his attraction to Maggie had never seemed a thing he could act on. His one attempt—something Xander didn't know about—had been so bound up in the worst time of her life, he'd long ago accepted he'd never get another shot. He'd tried to move on. To distract himself. To forget.

But Maggie was well and truly woven into his heart, and the past year and a half, as they'd become friends again, he'd begun to yearn for the impossible. And Xander, damn him, obviously knew it. Ignoring his friend's assessing cop stare, Porter gently rested his head against Maggie's and let himself drift off.

"It's starting!"

Porter jolted awake to find Ari bouncing into the waiting room. Her proclamation had everybody waking up, stretching. Whatever modicum of relaxation Maggie had managed to capture was gone. She'd gone ramrod straight in the chair.

Kennedy crossed over. "C'mon. Help me get coffee for everybody, will you?"

He thought Maggie might refuse to move, but after only a moment's hesitation she followed her sister out of the room. Good. Maybe Kennedy could keep her distracted for a bit.

Retrieving his phone, Porter discovered several missed calls from Mia, and he remembered the meeting. He'd put the whole thing out of his mind when he'd gone to deal with Maggie. Her voicemail was nothing more than a terse, "Call me." He didn't like the sound of that. But the deal was all but done. Maybe she was just frustrated at having to experience the grade-A douchecanoe that was Bradley Danforth.

As it was far too early to call her back, he spent some time going through email, catching up on what work he could. He'd be paying for all this time off, but as he caught sight of Maggie coming back with her sister, both loaded down with Styrofoam cups of shit coffee, he knew she was worth it.

They'd barely passed out the drinks before Flynn was practically running into the waiting room. "It's a healthy baby girl!"

A cheer went up.

"Seven pounds, one ounce, eighteen inches long. And my wife is the bravest, most beautiful woman on earth."

"She's okay?" Maggie demanded.

He beamed. "She's grand, she is!"

"Oh thank God." She promptly slumped and burst into quiet tears.

As Flynn got lost amid a flurry of hugs and congratulations, Porter made his way to Maggie and slid an arm around her shoulders. She turned into him, wrapping her arms around his waist and holding on. His heart gave a kick before he folded her in. She felt right, here in his arms.

"There now. Everything's fine. Everybody's okay," he murmured.

"Thank you for being here."

"I wouldn't be anywhere else."

She straightened at that, her eyes searching his before she offered a hesitant smile and pulled away. Wiping her eyes, she turned back to Flynn. "When can we see them?"

Of course she'd need to see for herself that mother and baby were truly fine. Everyone seemed to realize that, so nobody challenged her getting to go back first. Flynn laid a hand at the small of her back and nudged her down the hall. They'd only gone a half-dozen steps before he turned back and looked at Porter. "Are you coming?"

He jolted. But nobody seemed to think it an odd request, even Maggie. He wondered how long it would take her to realize that the family had accepted him as her keeper. He wondered, too, when they'd ask him about it.

Pru sat propped up in the hospital bed, a blanket-wrapped bundle in her arms, a mile-wide smile on her face. "Isn't she beautiful?"

Maggie eased one hip onto the bed, peering at the new arrival. The last of the tension visibly drained out of her, and her lips curved into a smile as she reached one tentative finger out to stroke along the baby's cheek. "She absolutely is."

"We decided on Bailey Siobhan. Siobhan is Irish for Joan. So we can honor Mom, but her name is still up for grabs in case anybody else wants to use it."

Maggie sniffed. "Oh, that's lovely."

Porter clapped Flynn on the shoulder. "You did good, man. That's a good lookin' kid." Actually, it looked kinda like an overripe tomato, but he figured being born was hard work, and the kid would be cute later.

Pru angled her arms toward her sister. "Do you want to hold her?"

Swallowing hard, Maggie nodded. She carefully accepted the baby, settling her into the crook of her arms and looking into her tiny face. Bailey's eyes opened and stared into hers.

"Hi. Hi, there. I'm your Aunt Maggie." She cooed and gently stroked.

"Well, let's see her." Porter moved around the bed to get a better look—ostensibly at the baby, but he really wanted a closer look at Maggie.

Anyone who didn't really know her would think there was nothing but joy in her expression. But Porter could see the shadows in her eyes as she looked up at her new niece.

"This is your Uncle Porter." She shifted around so the baby could see him. Could babies even see this soon?

He leaned in anyway, rubbing one knuckle gently over the baby's cheek. "So soft."

Maggie looked up at him, smiling, and for a moment he couldn't breathe as the picture she made, holding a newborn baby, etched into his brain. This was what she'd been robbed of. What they'd both been robbed of.

The pang of fresh loss struck his heart like a fist, making it squeeze. And he realized that he'd been lying to himself that he'd ever move on from her. Because this, with her, was still exactly what he wanted.

Chapter Four

Something came into Porter's eyes as he looked at her. A fierce tenderness that made Maggie's chest ache. She hadn't seen him look at her like this in years. Not since before, when he'd volunteered to sacrifice his own future for her. She'd come so close to saying yes. So close to breaking that personal vow to never, ever be like her birth mother. Because he'd made her feel things. Things she couldn't trust and didn't believe in. But she felt the stirring of those same emotions now as she looked into his blue eyes.

It couldn't work then, and it sure as hell wouldn't work now, for a whole host of different reasons. The last thing either of them needed was to go back to before, so she dropped her gaze, shifting her attention to the baby.

Bailey was so tiny in her arms, but so full of precious life. Her heart sang with a potent cocktail of joy and grief. For so very many years, this day had been a nightmare for her. The anniversary of the day she'd lost her own child. Something she'd tried in vain to shut away. Now, it would forever mean something else. Something good. And at that thought, an overwhelming love drowned out the grief, because this child was family. It was a gift she knew only one way to repay.

Pressing a soft kiss to Bailey's head, Maggie handed her back to Pru. "I want to give you something."

"Oh no. Maggie, we've talked about this. You've given us quite enough already."

"I *need* to give you something." Maggie took her sister's hand and swallowed. "I want you to have the cradle."

Behind her, Porter jolted. She didn't know how he'd feel about her regifting the cradle he'd hand-built for her all those year ago. It was the only thing she had left from that time, something she hadn't been able to part with because of what he'd put into making it. But she knew it was time.

Flynn wore a polite but puzzled expression, obviously not certain what this meant. But Pru understood. Her eyes went misty. "Maggie. It was for—"

"Porter made it for the first Reynolds baby. I'd rather it be a family heirloom than a shrine, so I want to offer it up to be used with all the future Reynolds children, of which I hope there will be many. Bailey is just the first."

Pru's eyes shifted to Porter, then back to her. "We'd be honored."

It was the right decision. Maggie knew it was. But now that the deed was done, she felt the weight of it bearing down on her. There'd be grief to process over this, too, and she needed the space to do it.

With one final squeeze, she stepped back. "There's a boatload of other people who want to see you both, and I'm sure Abbey would appreciate some relief at the inn, so we're gonna go." She probably shouldn't be speaking for Porter, and definitely not as a "we", but he was the only one who could really understand where her head was.

Back in the waiting room, Kennedy and Athena were eagerly

waiting their turn. Because she knew they'd been worried about her, she dredged up one last smile. "She's gorgeous. Pru and Flynn can't wait to show her off."

"My turn!" Kennedy announced. "Xander's gotta get back for work."

As the two of them disappeared down the hall, Athena searched Maggie's face. "You're okay?"

"I'm fine. Just tired. I'll see you back at the house."

Athena looked like she wanted to say something else, but in the end she just nodded.

Ten minutes later Maggie was back in Porter's truck, buckling in for the forty-minute drive back to Eden's Ridge. "Thanks for driving me."

"No problem." He wheeled out of the parking lot as the sun crested the horizon. "Try to sleep if you can. It's been a long night."

Freed of the burden of conversation and the worry that had dogged her for months, she tipped back the seat and did as he suggested.

Of course, she slid into dreams of before.

Maggie laid a hand over the curve of her belly. It seemed impossibly big—as if she was fifteen months pregnant instead of five. A great big billboard announcement of her stupidity. Everybody looked as she walked down Main Street. Some people stared. It took everything she had to keep her head held high. To ignore the gossip she knew followed in her wake. Every time got a little bit harder, and she'd become a master at staring people down in pure defiance.

Go ahead and talk. I won't become my mother.

A dusty truck pulled up to the curb beside her, the window rolled down. "What the hell are you doing walking?" Porter was already parking, opening the door to come around.

"I was headed home from work." She didn't fuss when he

opened the passenger door and nudged her in. Her feet were miserably swollen and her lower back had been aching for a couple of weeks now. She relaxed against the faded bench seat.

Porter slid behind the wheel and glared. "You shouldn't be on your feet this much. Do I need to talk to Darlene?"

His overprotective streak almost made her want to smile. He was the only one who made her even come close these days. "You'll do no such thing. I'm fine, and I need to earn as much as I can." The part-time job after school and on weekends was the best she could do right now. She wasn't about to drop out of high school like her birth mother had. Maybe she'd have to postpone college, once the baby came, but by God, she'd have her diploma.

"Do you want to go home?"

She should. There was homework waiting. And dinner wouldn't be far off. But the thought of sitting around the big farmhouse table with her multitude of siblings left her wanting to hide. "No. Not yet."

"Okay."

Maggie didn't ask where he was taking her. Porter didn't pressure her to talk. He was good about that. He was good about so many things. The hours she spent with him were the only time she still felt like everything would be okay. Like she hadn't completely ruined her life. Somehow, he made her less afraid with his unflappable and unwavering support. She knew he'd put off college a year to stick around and be her support. She hadn't asked—she'd never have done that—but she was so pitifully grateful he hadn't left for Knoxville at the end of the summer.

He drove to one of the scenic overlooks, parking beneath the shade of a big sycamore tree. Because she knew this routine, Maggie stayed put until he came around to open her door, taking her hand to gently help her out of the truck. The feel of his strong, callused fingers closing around hers made her pulse jump and her lungs feel too tight. That had been happening more and more often. She told herself it meant nothing. She was grateful, that was all. Everything would settle once he let her go.

But Porter didn't release her hand this time. Instead, he kept it tucked in his as he led her over to the bench and tugged her down beside him. He was close enough she could feel the brush of his thigh against hers. There was a rip in the knee of his jeans and some kind of...something spattered on the denim from the construction site where he'd been working. Still, he didn't let go of her hand.

She was torn between wanting to rest her head against his shoulder and yanking her hand away to put some distance between them so she could think again. Sitting this close to him made her want things. Things she couldn't have. Not with Porter. He was her foster brother, though, technically he'd aged out of the system. He still had a home with Joan until he got on his feet. A home that put him right down the hall from her and made him one hundred percent off-limits.

"You're a helluva girl, you know that?"

"Am I?"

"Smart as a whip and possibly the bravest, most stubborn person I know."

"I'm just a really good actress. Because I'm scared basically all the time now." *Except when I'm with you.* But she wasn't going to admit that out loud.

He glanced over, a lock of sandy hair falling into his eyes. "Anybody else would've folded by now. Pointed fingers. They wouldn't have thought it worth keeping the secret."

Maggie stiffened. She had an iron-clad reason for keeping the parentage of her child quiet. And if, in the dark of night, she hated herself for agreeing to it, she'd convinced herself that the ends justified the means.

"Don't worry. I'm not about to ask you who it is. That's not why I brought you out here."

Her muscles relaxed. "Why did you bring me here?"

"I've been doing a lot of thinking. This whole single-parent gig is hard under the best of circumstances. These aren't the best of circumstances."

She snorted. "You're the master of understatement."

One corner of his mouth tipped up for just a moment before he sobered again. "You don't have to do all this alone."

"I know Mom and my sisters will help as much as they can, but—"

"That's not what I meant." He laid his free hand over their joined ones and shifted to search her face. "Marry me."

Stunned, she could only stare. "What?"

"Marry me, Maggie. Let me give you both the protection of my name. Let me be a father to this baby. Let me be a partner in this. A partner to you."

"You're serious." It wasn't really a question. She could see it in his face.

"As a heart attack." He reached up to brush the hair back from her face, and his knuckles skimmed along her cheek.

Everything in her wanted to lean into the touch, into the goodness that was Porter Ingram. She wanted to jump at what he was offering. As much time as they spent together, there'd been speculation over whether he was the father already. If she married him, people would assume that was true. No one would ever have to know otherwise. It could be good between them. They were friends—good friends, and these past months had shown the potential for more. Maybe...maybe something positive could come out of all this heartache.

She lifted a hand to his cheek, giving in for just a moment to the desire to rub a thumb over his stubble. She liked the golden shadow of it against his jaw. "Porter I—"

The shock of pain ripped through her like lightning, stealing her breath, doubling her over with a cry.

"Maggie? Maggie!"

"Maggie."

She jolted awake, immediately slamming her eyes shut again at the stab of sunlight. Morning, not sunset. Now, not then. God, the dream had been so vivid. Sucking in a breath, she reached for calm, waiting to speak until she knew her voice would be steady. "Are we back at the house?"

"Not yet." Something in his tone had her opening her eyes again.

The truck was parked beside a low, wrought-iron fence. Beyond it, the rolling hill was dotted with old-growth trees, stretching their branches over neat rows of graves. It was a quiet, peaceful place, with generations filling family plots. Her mom was buried here. And her daughter.

That clench in her heart relaxed. Porter had known. Of course he'd known she needed to visit Jessica today. Reaching out, Maggie squeezed his hand in silent thanks before sliding out of the front seat.

They didn't speak as they walked the path to the tiny grave. She hadn't been here in years. Not even after they'd buried Joan last year. It had been as much about self-protection as knowledge that her loved ones weren't here. The first trace of autumn lingered in the cool morning air. It would burn off in an hour or two, but it was a sign of the changing seasons she'd missed in California. Maggie wondered if she'd still be here to see the changing of the leaves. The grass was just a hair past neatly trimmed, and she liked that departure from artificial regimentation. There was nothing neat and tidy about death and loss.

She stopped beside the little headstone, with the neatly printed name. *Jessica Leigh* and the single date of her death. A teddy bear was etched into the black granite. It was a simple memorial, all she'd been able to manage back then. But she saw now that it wasn't the only thing here. Kneeling down to get a better look, she saw a pair of tiny, carved wooden fawns peeking around a corner. On the other side, a little cat looked like it was about to pounce out of the grass. Beyond that, she could just make out what looked like the tail of a wooden squirrel sticking out of the grass. Each one was carved in exquisite detail, though some showed obvious signs of weathering, as if they'd been out here for a long time.

With a trembling finger, she reached out to trace the ear of one of the fawns. "You made her toys?"

"Yeah." She could hear the shrug in his voice.

"Why?"

"Because she matters."

Maggie's throat closed up, tears spilling fresh down her cheeks as she watched Porter reach into his pocket and pull out another little figure, setting it on top of the stone. An owl, its face comically carved in a surprised "Hoo."

To everyone else, she'd moved on from this baby that never saw life. But Porter knew she hadn't. Because he knew her. In his quiet, steadfast way, he always seemed to give her exactly what she needed. What had she ever done to deserve that? Not a damned thing except run away to save him from his own nobility. And yet here he was, years later, still being what she needed, what she wanted. He'd been a far better friend to her than she to him. And it was time she returned the favor, whether he liked it or not.

* * *

Maggie straightened, turning away from him, and Porter wondered if he'd made a mistake bringing her here. He'd thought she'd need some closure after today. A chance to drop that brittle mask she'd been wearing for months and just feel...whatever it was she felt. To let it go.

Maybe that was foolish. She'd lost a child, and it had changed her whole life. Was that a thing that could be let go? Hell, he was still carving little toys to leave here because he hadn't. But that was more about Maggie than Jessica. Because he hadn't been able to let her or the fantasy he'd woven around her go.

When she finally spoke, her voice held the low thrum of confession. "All these years, I've had so many conflicting feelings about all this. When I found out I was pregnant, I thought my life was over. My birth mother spent plenty of time when I was young telling me I'd ruined hers. I'd vowed to myself I'd do everything differently. I wouldn't be that foolish. And there I was—Maggie Reynolds—first in her class, voted most likely to succeed, the girl who followed all the rules—pregnant at seventeen. I was so scared when I saw those stupid pink lines. I didn't have the first clue what to do. Then I stumbled out of the bathroom, straight into you."

Porter remembered. "You were white as a sheet. I don't think you even knew the test was still in your hand." But he'd seen it, and his world had crashed down on him like a rockslide. The girl he loved had been with someone else. Would forever be tied to someone else. Because it hadn't occurred to him yet that the father wouldn't do the right thing by her.

"You took me up to your room before anybody else could see me, and you held me while I fell apart." Glancing over at him, she frowned. "I never thanked you for that. I never thanked you for any of it."

Uncomfortable with her gratitude, he twitched his shoulders. "You didn't owe me thanks."

"Yes, I did. Do," she corrected. "I wouldn't have gotten through it if not for you."

Well, who the hell else was going to be there for her? The baby's father had refused to acknowledge her, and Maggie had stubbornly refused to ever name him, no matter what hell was lobbed in her direction. "It wasn't a hardship."

"You made the unbearable seem somehow bearable."

"Not everything," he murmured. He hadn't been able to do a damned thing to stop the hurt after her miscarriage.

With a restless shrug, Maggie turned back to the grave. "The miscarriage was..." She seemed to cast around, searching for the right words. "It broke something in me. By that point everyone knew. I'd acknowledged and accepted what I'd done...and I *wanted* her. Then she was gone and it was too little, too late. My reputation was destroyed. And so was my heart. And even so, a part of me was so pitifully relieved. I wasn't ready to be a mother at seventeen. It was going to derail my entire life plan. Rationally, I know I wasn't ready, and I'm grateful I didn't have to give up on my dreams because of a foolish mistake."

Her mouth twisted, her eyes closing for a moment. Was she seeing that mistake? Seeing that jackass who'd used and discarded her? Because Porter wanted to reach for her and didn't have the right, he curled his fingers into his palms.

"I hated myself for feeling relief," she whispered. "Like she was a problem that disappeared and fixed itself. Like maybe I willed her away."

"Maggie." Unable to stop himself, he tipped her face up, until those deep dark eyes, still swimming in so much pain, fixed on his. "It wasn't your fault. The doctors said nothing could have been done, even if we'd been closer to the hospital."

"I know. It's not rational. But there's a part of me that wonders. A part of me that grieves every year. Wondering what she'd have looked like if she lived. Wondering if I would have made a better mother than mine."

She'd never talked about any of this, as far as he knew. Certainly not with him. After her miscarriage she'd shut down, retreating into the controlled, driven persona that had fueled her fast-tracked Ivy League education and subsequent career. This glimpse of vulnerability, of the younger, softer Maggie, fed all his impossible wants.

"You would have made an amazing mother. And if Jessica had lived, you'd have made a new plan." He knew her, knew that was true. She'd already been in the process of that when everything went to hell.

"Maybe. Or maybe I'd have turned out like my mother. Bitter and regretful of everything I didn't get to do."

"You, Margaret Anne, are nothing like your birth mother. Never have been, never will be. Joan saw to that. You're her daughter in more than just name."

Her lips quirked in the ghost of a smile. "That may be one of the nicest things you've ever said to me. Thank you."

"It's nothing more than the truth."

She inhaled a breath and crossed her arms like she was cold, effectively closing herself off from him. Porter dropped his hands, already regretting the loss of contact.

"Either way, I'm tired of living with regrets. The fact is, I wouldn't have what I have today, wouldn't have achieved the things I've achieved if she'd lived. Maybe it's time I stopped punishing myself for that. I dodged a bullet." She gave an awkward laugh. "I guess we both did."

Porter stared at her. She'd never given him an answer all those years ago. They'd never discussed it. But this was the first hint she'd ever given that, had things turned out differently, had she not lost the baby, she might have said yes. And suddenly, he needed her to know the truth. Needed her to know that his offer hadn't been some impulsive, altruistic act.

"I have all kinds of regrets, but asking you to marry me and being father to that child isn't one of them."

She huffed a sound of disbelief. "You wanted to be a teenaged father to a child who wasn't yours?"

"I wanted to marry you. I wanted to make a family with you."

Her head snapped up, eyes going wide. "Why would you want that?"

"You're a smart woman, Maggie. Why do you think?"

She stared at him, apparently at a total loss for what to say, and for some reason, that irritated him. For twelve years—more than—he'd been patient and steadfast, and it was so fucking obvious to absolutely everyone. She had to know why.

Finally, she murmured, "We were kids."

"We're not kids now."

"What are you saying?"

"I'm in love with you. I've been in love with you for fifteen years. And I'm tired of waiting for you to recognize it, so I'm laying it out there."

She looked like she'd been mule-kicked. For a second, he thought she was going to discount his feelings, explain to him how he was wrong or confused. He knew damned well that's exactly what she'd have done twelve years ago.

"Porter, I—why didn't you say anything before?"

"You wouldn't have believed me."

Distress flicked over her features and he cursed himself. "Look, I don't expect anything from you. I'm not going to force anything. I'm your friend, first and foremost, and I know that in a lot of ways, today was absolute hell for you. As declarations go, this was complete shit timing. I'll apologize for that. But I won't apologize for what I feel for you."

He paused, giving her a chance to say something...anything... but she only stared, caught somewhere between stupefied shock, exhaustion, and worry. Sighing, he gentled. This was all too much. He'd known that, and now he'd tipped his hand. But he simply couldn't deal with the status quo anymore. He had to break free of this holding pattern they'd been in for years, either moving forward with her...or without her.

"Come on. I'll take you home."

Chapter Five

Maggie stood there, rooted with shock. What the hell could she say? Porter had just obliterated her belief that he'd been acting purely out of noble intentions all those years ago. It was the thing that had enabled her to walk away. To save him from throwing his life away on her. Because it couldn't have been real.

Except...he loved her. Now. *Still.* For fifteen years. Jesus. She'd have been...fourteen back then. Ari's age. The entire concept of that made her brain implode.

So Maggie didn't dare open her mouth on the short drive home. Porter said nothing, his face settling back into the relaxed, easy-going lines she was used to. As if he hadn't just rocked her world with his declaration and wasn't feeling...*something* about her lack of response. Never once had it occurred to her that it could be a mask. That he'd be that good at hiding his thoughts and emotions.

It seemed there were a whole lot of things that hadn't occurred to her when it came to Porter.

He pulled up by the inn's front steps, bracing his arms on the steering wheel of the truck as she slid out.

She couldn't just shut the door without saying *something*. "Porter, I—"

"Don't." There was no rancor in the word, no heat, but it shut her up nonetheless. "Go get some sleep, Maggie."

Swallowing hard, she nodded and shut the door. He lifted one hand in a semi-wave, then drove away.

Her body weighed a thousand pounds and every step into the house felt like she was wading through quicksand.

Please, dear God, let no one need anything. She wasn't sure she could dredge up a shred of professionalism or hospitality just now.

She nearly went straight up to her room. Except...she didn't know which one that was, and unless someone else had moved them, her bags were still in the kitchen. Mind spinning, she wandered that way.

Athena turned from the coffee pot. "Hey! We figured you would have beaten us back."

Maggie could only shake her head.

Kennedy shot up from her seat at the kitchen table, concern all over her face. "Honey? What's wrong?"

She ought to put them off, go up to bed. Pretend none of this had actually happened. Handling everything on her own was what she did. But when she opened her mouth, she said, "Porter's in love with me."

Athena just continued to pour coffee into the oversized mug she favored. "And?"

The complete lack of surprise jolted Maggie out of her shock. "You knew?"

"Honey, everybody with eyes knew. Except, apparently, you." Leave it to Athena not to sugarcoat a thing. Her little sister's forthright manner was something Maggie usually appreciated, but not so much when it was directed at her.

Kennedy shot an exasperated glare in Athena's direction and nudged Maggie onto the bench. "You want coffee? Tea?"

"I don't know." Maggie rubbed at the headache blooming in her temples. She couldn't think. Her brain was too fuzzy.

"I'm going to make you some chamomile tea." Kennedy squeezed her shoulder and crossed to put on the kettle.

Maggie only barely resisted the urge to drop her head into her hands. "This isn't how it was supposed to work. He was supposed to be over me."

Kennedy froze, a tea bag dangling from one hand. "Over you? You knew?"

"The marriage proposal was a pretty big clue," she muttered. *Oh hell. I didn't mean to say that out loud.*

"Hold the phone. Porter asked you to *marry him?*" Athena exclaimed.

Seeing their wide-eyed shock, Maggie realized she was going to have to explain. "Not today. Before. When I was pregnant."

Her sisters exchanged another look. Kennedy came back to sit down. "Maggie, was Porter the father?"

"No." If he had been, maybe everything would've turned out differently. "No, I didn't see him like that back then. But he was there for me, through all of it. And when the baby's father didn't step forward, didn't stand up, he asked me to marry him."

"Marry me, Maggie. Let me give you both the protection of my name." He'd been so earnest, and she'd wanted so badly to believe that it could work. That this incredibly kind, good boy could and would make a life with her, with her child. That something positive could come out of all the heartache.

Athena's voice was uncharacteristically gentle. "What did you say?"

"I didn't get a chance to say anything. My miscarriage started, and he rushed me to the hospital." She could still remember the sharp stab of pain and the hideous cramping that had taken her to her knees. And the blood. God, the blood.

Swallowing hard against the knot in her throat, she continued, "After...it was a moot point. We never talked about it. Until today."

"Why today?" Kennedy asked.

Maggie held onto the words until she knew she could say them without a waver from the pain underneath. "Today's the anniversary."

Their expressions went stricken, and moments later she found herself in a tangle of arms.

"Christ, I didn't even think. I'm so sorry." Athena held on tight.

"Nobody thought. We were all so caught up with Pru—" Kennedy began.

"As we all should have been. Today was not about me. But Porter remembered. It's why he stuck so close." Maggie hesitated. "Well, part of why. All these years, I thought he was just a really good friend. That he'd offered to marry me out of some misguided good intentions. I knew he thought he felt something for me back then, but it was such an emotionally-charged situation, I didn't think it was real. I never dreamed he really loved me. That he could *still* love me."

Athena eased back. "More to the point, how do you feel about *him?*"

Maggie could only shake her head. "He's one of my best friends. I don't..." She trailed off, unable to push past the shock and exhaustion to find an answer.

Kennedy met her gaze. "What would you have said back then, if you hadn't lost the baby?"

That was a thing Maggie had tried very, very hard not to think about. Because it was a future she'd lost along with Jessica, and she couldn't bear to dwell on that, too. But she was just exhausted enough that she couldn't stop herself from whispering, "Yes." She sucked in a shuddering breath. "I wanted to say yes."

"To shut up the gossips or because you actually felt something for him?" Athena asked.

Maggie shot her sister a bland stare, offended at the idea that she'd use Porter like that. "I think I proved I wasn't going to do anything simply out of a desire to shut up the gossips."

"Fair enough."

"He was my rock. He didn't have to be. The baby wasn't his. But for all those months after I found out I was pregnant, he put me first. No one but Joan ever did that. Of course I felt something for him."

Kennedy laid a hand over hers. "And now?"

Maggie couldn't even consider the question. She was too terrified of the answer, when he'd just upended one of the few truly stable things in her world. "I don't know. I...he...Christ, how can he just dump this on me? Why now? I live in California, for God's sake." She was already dealing with so much, feeling the bone-deep exhaustion of the adrenal fatigue that had sent her home in the first place. How could he pile this on her, too?

She knew she should tell her sisters about her health, but that was a conversation she simply wasn't up to dealing with yet.

Athena picked up her mug. "So now what?"

"I don't freaking know. The only reasonable answer to that question is tequila or sleep, and it's too damned early for tequila." More was the pity.

"Sleep then," Kennedy declared. "The guests are taken care of for now. We'll reconvene later to sort out a new rotation for that to work around Bailey."

Maggie retrieved her bags and headed for her assigned room. She felt a little lighter, if no less confused, having brought her sisters into her confidence. But as she made her way up the stairs, she wondered if she'd just lost one of her best friends.

* * *

Porter spent the drive back into Eden's Ridge castigating himself. Why had he opened his big, fat mouth? Why *today* of all days? Frustration simmered beneath his skin—with himself for pushing Maggie. With her for not being in a place where she could admit there was more between them than friendship. Maybe he was fooling himself believing that was true. Maybe it was exhaustion dimming his good judgment and intuition when it came to her. But there was no calling the words back, no undoing what he'd done.

He just wanted to go home and fall face-first into bed and forget about all of it for a few hours of oblivion. Was that too much to ask?

The ringing of his phone said it was. Seeing Mia's name flash across the screen, he remembered her messages. Guilt prickled that he'd forgotten about them. Again.

"Morning."

"Where the hell have you been?" she demanded. "I've been trying to reach you since yesterday. Tell me you're not still in California."

Porter winced. "No. Sorry. We got back yesterday, but Pru went into labor."

"We?" He could practically hear her going brows-up.

"Maggie came back with me."

The weight of Mia's curiosity carried over the line. "Let's put a pin in that and come back to it later."

Let's not. "We were at the hospital all night. Baby Bohannon was born at 5:26 this morning. A girl. Bailey Siobhan."

"That's great. When are you coming into the office?"

"I was planning on getting a couple hours of sleep first."

"Yeah, you may want to put a pin in *that*, too. We need to talk about the meeting with the mayor."

Unease whispered through him. "Listen, I'm sorry I left you to handle Danforth alone. If he was a sexist asshole—"

"No. I mean, he was, but it's not that." She sucked in a breath. "We don't have a contract."

"Excuse me?"

"There is no contract."

The surge of fury struck him like a wave. *That son of a bitch.* "What, exactly, did he say?"

"Not a damned thing directly to me. I got stonewalled by the secretary and told that there were no contracts to be signed at this time and that the mayor would be in touch. Which, of course, he hasn't. The whole damned thing feels like a big brush-off to me."

He was already changing directions. "I'll find out what the hell is going on."

At this hour of the morning, he didn't have to fight for parking on Main Street. He strode straight into the three-story brick building that housed the city and county offices.

"Mornin', Porter." Mel Jackson, one of the cadre of veterans who rotated serving as security, lifted his hand in a wave.

Taking a firm grip on his raging temper, Porter managed a nod. "You seen the mayor yet this mornin', Mel?"

"Sure did. Headed up about half an hour ago."

Then he'd be able to beard the lion in his den. "Thanks."

Porter resisted the urge to take the stairs two at a time. The door to the outer office of the mayor's suite was open, and the no-nonsense twang of Danforth's personal assistant floated out into the hall. Gladys Meckler had been at the periphery of city government as long as Porter could remember. She'd been the administrative assistant for every mayor for the past forty years. As institutional memory, no mayor had ever dared fire her. Everybody in town kept wondering when she'd retire, but when asked, she just laughed and said she liked to keep a finger on what was going on in town.

She was on the phone when he stepped into the office, her back to the door. Taking advantage of her momentary inattention, Porter stalked by her desk and threw open the door to the mayor's office. Bradley Danforth himself looked up from his desk, one sandy brow arching.

"Porter Ingram. Well, you look like you slept under a bridge last night."

He was too tired and pissed off to beat around the bush. "You already gave my business partner the runaround. I'm here to find out what the hell is going on."

There was the clatter of a phone behind him as Gladys came hustling in. "Mr. Mayor, I'm so sorry. I didn't let him back."

Danforth waved a hand. "It's perfectly fine, Gladys. Please see that we aren't interrupted."

Huffing a little, the older woman shot Porter a filthy look before shutting the door behind her.

The mayor waved a hand. "Sit down, Porter."

Porter wasn't about to let this man do anything else to control him. "I'll stand."

"I presume you're here about the resort. Frankly, I expected to hear from you sooner."

"I've been out of town." Prowling forward, he pressed both fists to the top of the desk and leaned toward Danforth. "We had a deal. I realize you get off on jerking me around, but I was under the impression you actually gave a shit about this town. How dare you go with some outside contractor."

"I didn't."

The flat denial took Porter by surprise. It wasn't like Brad not to gloat at putting one over on him. "Then why the fuck don't we have a contract?"

Something flickered over his face, marring that perfect politician's mask. "Because Faber Development pulled out. We no longer have investors for the resort."

That made absolutely no sense. The city had been courting Faber for months. He'd met with the developer himself. They were excited about the project. "Why would they pull out?"

Brad shoved a hand through his hair in an uncharacteristic show of irritation. "I don't know. They didn't give an explanation, just pulled out of the deal. So unless they change their minds or we find new investors, the resort project is dead in the water."

And if the resort project was dead in the water, his business was in serious trouble. Porter laced his hands behind his head and paced a tight circle. "Fuck."

"My sentiments exactly."

There had to be a solution to this. "Are there any other possibilities for investors on the horizon?"

"I've put out some more feelers, but these things take time."

The thing that he didn't have. *Shit.*

Brad studied him, amusement curling his lips. "Did you really think this was about you?"

That supercilious expression rolled over him like a swarm of fire ants, pricking at his pride, but damned if he'd let it show. "It seemed like something you'd do."

Leaning back in his chair, Danforth steepled his fingers. "Contrary to what you might think, I don't run this town or my life with an eye toward fucking you over."

They both knew that wasn't true, but planting a fist in his face wasn't going to help matters, so Porter held his tongue and his body still.

"Look, I know you hate me, but I do have the best interests of this town at heart. I promise I'm still looking for investors and when and if the project proceeds, I intend for Mountainview Construction to get the contract."

Porter didn't trust that conciliatory tone for a second, but at this point he couldn't do anything else. His employees were counting on him to keep them in work, so he didn't have the luxury of telling Danforth to fuck off. With them in mind, he bit out, "Thank you. Keep me posted."

"Of course."

Without a backward glance, Porter stalked out of the office, wondering what the hell he was gonna do now.

Chapter Six

The problem with being a workaholic on forced vacation was that there was far too much time to think. Even with the extra duties she'd taken on around the inn and spa while Pru was on maternity leave, Maggie was desperate for something to distract her. Because the downtime meant far too many chances for her brain to replay every interaction she'd had with Porter for *years*, seeing them through the lens that his feelings for her were real. And that led to a very dangerous game of What If.

What if she'd believed in what he felt back then?

What if she'd said yes?

What if she hadn't made assumptions because she'd lost the baby?

It all led to visions of a possible future she'd destroyed by walking away. Because no matter that he was still here, that he still loved her, no matter that she felt more for him than she wanted to admit—it couldn't work. Even without the geographic distance between them, she wasn't fit for a relationship. The last decade had more than proven that, and he deserved better.

But she didn't know if they could go back to being friends. Too terrified of what that could mean for them, Maggie retrieved her laptop and brought it out to the spa, where she was manning the front desk. She'd just check in with work. Nothing strenuous. Some emails. Maybe some notes on the contracts she'd walked away from. See how things were going and who had been tasked with picking up the reins on various projects she'd had cooking.

But her login credentials weren't working. She tried them four times, even attempting to reset the password. No dice. She couldn't access anything on the network drive, couldn't even get into her work email. There'd either been a catastrophic hacker attack on Invation or Genevieve had terminated her access.

It was one thing to choose to take time off. But being deliberately blocked like a former employee was something else entirely.

Maggie checked the clock. It was still early out on the West Coast. Only seven-thirty. Genevieve shouldn't be in meetings yet. She dialed, grateful for the presently empty reception area.

Genevieve answered on the second ring. "Good morning, Sunshine. How's Tennessee?"

At the sound of her cheerful voice, Maggie couldn't repress a scowl. "Don't you 'How's Tennessee?' me."

"Ah. You tried to log in. Props. You lasted a whole three days longer than I was betting you would. I owe Alyssa a latte."

"What the hell, Genevieve? Why would you block me from the servers?"

"Because the doctor said you need rest and if you have access to work, you won't do it. Really, I'm saving you from yourself."

"As if I'm some kind of recalcitrant toddler, incapable of making my own decisions?"

Genevieve snorted. "Hardly."

"I just wanted to check on—"

"Doesn't matter. Every bit of it has been reassigned. It's being handled."

She'd known that was Genevieve's intention, but a part of her had expected to be called any day now for a consult or transition notes. If someone could so easily come in and take over everything she'd been doing…Insult and fear made a noxious brew in her belly. "I've been replaced, then."

"Don't be ridiculous. You're irreplaceable. As soon as you're medically cleared in a few months, your office and job will be ready and waiting for you."

And what happened when they realized in those months that they didn't need her after all? What then?

Oblivious to Maggie's turmoil, Genevieve rolled on. "In the meantime, I expect you to take this whole rest and recovery thing as seriously as you would any other work duties. Right now, this *is* your job. That and helping out with your family's inn, I assume? How's your sister?"

"Tired and happy. They just came home with the baby yesterday. A girl." She reeled off the expected stats.

"Oh! Then you were there for the whole thing. That's wonderful! See? Aren't you glad I forced you to take time off so you didn't miss that?"

"Don't change the subject. I'm mad at you."

"You can be as mad as you want, as long as you rest and recover."

"I'll be no good to you if I've gone stark raving nuts by the end of this whole thing."

"I know it's hard right now. But you've just forgotten *how* to relax. After a few weeks, you'll figure it out."

"That seems unlikely. I basically haven't relaxed since my junior year of high school." Not since before the pregnancy. Before her life changed forever.

"Then it's high time you had a refresher course." Her voice turned sly. "Maybe Porter will help you out with that."

"What are you talking about?"

"I'm just saying, he seemed pretty eager to spend time with you."

His voice echoed in her head. *"I'm in love with you. I've been in love with you for fifteen years."*

Nope. She wasn't thinking about that right now. "We're friends." Maggie hoped that was still true. She hadn't seen him since he dropped the bomb.

"If you say so."

"What is that supposed to mean?"

"Just that he was in an awfully big hurry to get to you."

"You told him I was in the hospital. Of course he came. That's what friends do."

"Then you have better friends than most of mine."

For just a moment there was something in her tone, a wistfulness and yearning Maggie wasn't accustomed to hearing from her friend. She was one of the most powerful women in the country. It was odd to realize that for all her wealth, all her assets, there were still things she didn't have. And that was a humbling thought.

"Listen, I have to go," Genevieve said. "But touch base again when you can. And seriously, *relax*, woman."

Then she was gone and Maggie was left staring at the phone.

As abruptly as the temper had come, it waned, leaving her drained and yearning for a nap. Before eleven in the morning. God. It was ridiculous. She'd been sleeping more since she'd gotten home, and it was as if, now that her body was finally getting more than four or five hours at a stretch, it was starving for more. She'd slept nearly fourteen hours straight the other night.

Maggie told herself that was just catching up from being awake all night at the hospital—for the second time in a week. But what if it wasn't? What if she'd done some kind of permanent damage? What if she slowed down these next few months and then couldn't get up to speed again when she went back to work?

She'd legitimately been working her ass off since her senior year of high school. First to make up for time lost to the pregnancy and miscarriage, ensuring the grades that would take her to the next level. Then to keep up with her coursework at Brown for undergrad and Yale for law school. Then hopscotching her way up the ladder at Invation. She didn't *know* any other way. She couldn't imagine being satisfied in a life where she wasn't achieving things. Because if she couldn't point to her accomplishments, what was left? Just Maggie Reynolds, that girl who got knocked up in high school.

She'd done too much, worked too hard, to backslide into being that girl again. So if Genevieve wanted her to treat this recovery like a job, that's exactly what she'd do. She needed a plan. A schedule. And probably a list of all those things people called "self care" that she'd considered excessively self-indulgent and told herself she didn't have time for. She would actually use the services of their spa. Surely that counted as market research? She'd be better able to write advertising copy if she experienced those treatments first-hand.

She'd gone well and truly down the rabbit hole of planning by the time the bell to the outside door chimed softly. Looking up from her fourth page of notes, Maggie summoned a smile. "Welcome to the Misfit Spa. How can I—Dahlia?"

The brunette offered a tentative smile. "Hey Maggie." She gestured in the direction of the house. "I stopped by with some taco soup for the freezer and to see the new arrival. Pru mentioned you were in town and said I could find you out here."

Maggie hated the reluctance in her tone, her expression. Because Dahlia Atwood had been her best friend—before. Unlike most of her other so-called friends, Dahlia had stuck by her. But after the miscarriage, Maggie had pulled away, shutting herself off from everyone because getting close meant too great a temptation to reveal the truth, and the consequences for that would be far too high a price to pay. It was long past time to apologize for that.

Moving around the desk, she mustered a genuine smile. "It's really great to see you." Uncertain of her welcome, Maggie held back from going in for the hug.

Dahlia didn't. At Maggie's smile, she opened her arms wide and flexed her hands. "What are you doing? Bring it in, girl." She squeezed extra tight, and something in Maggie's chest snicked, like a lock popping open after years of being rusted shut. She squeezed Dahlia back.

"Listen, I owe you an apology. Our senior year, I didn't treat you right—"

Dahlia pulled back just far enough to give her a little shake. "Stop being ridiculous. You went through hell, and I understood why you needed some distance. Sure, I missed you, but I never blamed you for any of that. We're fine."

And Maggie understood that for her, it was simple as that. She'd missed Dahlia's unqualified loyalty and kind heart. It was so different from most of the people she dealt with in California. If she could reconnect and reestablish this friendship while she was in Eden's Ridge, that would make the stay more than worthwhile.

"Well, thanks for that. I've missed you."

Dahlia gave her one more squeeze for good measure. "I know you probably don't have a lot of time before you have to go back, but I'd love to catch up while you're here."

"I'm actually going to be in town for a little while, helping out around the inn and spa while Pru's out with the baby."

"Really? That's wonderful!" She beamed. "If you're gonna be in town on Saturday night, and you're not tied up with the inn, you should totally come to the artisan supper."

"Has Athena been cooking something up I didn't know

about?" As far as Maggie knew, her sister was spending most of her time on her web-based cooking show.

Dahlia laughed, a bold trill of sound that buoyed Maggie's spirits. "Good guess, but no. Misty Pennebaker—she owns Moonbeams and Sweet Dreams—"

"The florist. We used her for Kennedy and Pru's weddings."

"Right. Well anyway, you probably know she carries a lot of work from area artists and artisans. Once a month, she organizes a pot luck dinner and an informal showcase for them to show off their wares. It's good food, good people. There's usually music—sometimes Flynn gets in on that. You should come."

It sounded like some of that living she was supposed to be doing, and maybe it would serve as the distraction she needed. "Of course, I'll come."

"Wonderful! You'll get a chance to meet Landon."

"Boyfriend? Husband?" Maggie was appalled to realize she had no idea whether her friend had gotten married.

Dahlia's cheeks flushed, even as she beamed a megawatt smile. "Boyfriend with serious potential for husband material. He's great."

That pinch in her chest was *not* envy at her friend's obvious happiness. She wasn't that petty. "I look forward to meeting him."

Dahlia took a step toward the door. "I need to be getting on. I just stopped in to say hello. But I'll see you on Saturday!"

"Wouldn't miss it."

* * *

"So...the situation isn't good." Porter leaned back in his chair, wishing the spreadsheet in front of him told a different story. "Once we finish building Athena's new kitchen facility out at the inn, all we've got on the docket are a couple of residential new construction projects and an assortment of renovations. The bottom line is, without the resort project, there isn't enough on the schedule to get us through to spring."

Mia dropped her head in a slow thump against the wall. "Shit. That is...not what I was counting on." She grimaced. "I guess it's awful that I was hoping he was just being a sexist pig and wouldn't deal directly with me."

"A job from a sexist pig is still a job. Principles don't get the bills paid." Which was the only reason he'd gone out for the job in the first place. Much as he'd rather eat rocks than work for Bradley Danforth, the resort would have meant unparalleled security for his crew.

"Truer words."

Porter hesitated. "Listen, this is not what you signed on for. When you agreed to partnership, the financial future of this company was a lot more solid. I'll understand if you want to reconsider."

Mia stopped beating her head against the wall and gave him the side eye. "Porter, you're my friend, and I love you, so I'm gonna pretend you didn't just insult me by saying that."

"I just don't want you to feel obligated—"

She held up a hand. "Stop. I didn't sign on as your partner because you had a ready-made cash cow here. I mean, sure, the resort job was a helluva sign-on bonus, but part of what I agreed to when I signed that contract is to put in the work to continue to build the business beyond what you've already managed. I'm in it, come hell or high water, so you might as well get used to me. Besides, Leno has a yard here, with a pretty Labrador retriever next door that he's madly in love with. He'd never forgive me if I took that away."

Equal parts amused and relieved, Porter couldn't quite hold back a smile. "Okay then."

On a sigh, she flopped into the chair opposite his desk. "So what are we gonna do? We can't just wait around for the mayor to find new funding."

"No, we can't. I can beat some bushes for some more local work, and if we have to, we can bid on some jobs further afield. It wouldn't be the first time." But it wasn't what he wanted. Not with Maggie home. Although maybe she'd prefer it if he wasn't around. He hadn't heard a word from her since he'd made his declaration—something he'd been trying hard not to think about.

"What about asking Maggie?"

Was there a neon sign above his head flashing that he was thinking about her? Jerking his attention back to the conversation, Porter tried to keep his tone casual. "Asking Maggie what?"

"You've said she's one of the smartest business minds you know. Maybe she'll have some ideas."

"Maybe," he conceded. And if nothing else, it was an excuse to go talk to her that would maybe get them past the elephant he'd plonked down between them.

It was nearly lunch by the time he got to the inn. The trucks of his crew were parked around back, and he heard the steady whine of saws and nail guns. Instead of going to check on the project, he went straight to the office, expecting Maggie to be sequestered there. Instead he found Kennedy scrambling off her husband's lap.

"Dude, do you knock?" Xander demanded.

"Sorry. I was looking for Maggie."

Kennedy and Xander exchanged a look, then fixed expectant gazes on him.

Porter sighed. "She told you?"

"Well, she told me. I told Xander."

Of course she had. This week just kept getting better. But he couldn't quite stop himself from asking, "How bad did I fuck up?"

"You shocked the hell out of her. I can't say whether that's a good or bad thing."

"You're the one closest to her. Seems like you ought to know that," Xander observed.

Porter scowled. "Anybody ever tell you that you're no help at all?"

Kennedy winked and pecked Porter on the cheek. "Well, *I'll* help by saying she's manning the front desk at the spa, and I'm on your side."

"Thank you." He turned toward the door.

"Good luck," Xander called. "You're gonna need it."

Porter shot up his middle finger and got a rumbling chuckle in return.

Maggie was head-down, feverishly writing in a notebook when he walked into the spa. He didn't even think she'd heard the bell over the door. For a moment, he just stood there, drinking in the sight of her. The khaki pants and button-down shirt were far more casual than the suits she favored, but her posture was all business as her pen flew over the paper. The pale blonde hair she so often wore in those fancy, professional twists was swept back into a simple ponytail that hung over one shoulder. Was it as soft and silky as he remembered? As he watched, she bit one corner of her mouth, narrowing her eyes in thought. He wanted to kiss that spot, soothe the little hurt she'd wrought on herself. He wanted to kiss and love all her hurts away.

When his brain promptly supplied an image of him boosting her onto the desk and stepping between her thighs, Porter gave himself a hard mental slap. Nope. Not happening. He didn't have the right to any of that, and the last thing he needed was to pop wood right when he was trying to get things back on some kind of even keel with their friendship.

Wiping the want off his face, he stepped closer. "Hey Maggie."

She yelped, the notebook landing on the floor with a thwack. "Porter! You scared the life out of me."

"Sorry." He automatically skirted the desk, bending down for the notebook at the same time she did. They each grabbed one end and lifted, freezing as their eyes met. Hers were troubled, wary.

Shit. He'd done this. He'd gone and made things weird between them. It was on him to get things back on track. Somehow.

Letting go of the notebook, he straightened. "Can we talk?"

For just a moment, she clutched the notebook to her chest like a shield. "Of course." She pushed to her feet, swaying a bit.

He reached out to steady her, curving one hand beneath her arm.

"I'm fine."

Porter wasn't at all sure that she was. Her hands had that jerking tremor again. Something was wrong. Letting her go, he trailed her into an empty treatment room and shut the door. "Look, at the risk of being a jackass, because the answer is probably me, what's wrong?"

Her mouth dropped open. "I don't know why I'm surprised. You could always read me." She crossed her arms, rubbing them in a self-soothing gesture. "I won't lie and say I'm not still... processing what you said the other day. But that's not why I'm upset. Genevieve blocked my access to the servers at work. I'm cut off every bit as effectively as if she'd fired me."

That wasn't what he'd expected. "Why?"

"She says it's for my own good. Because if I have access, I'll use it and then I won't rest." Her self-deprecatory laugh echoed off the shiplap walls. "And obviously she was right, or I wouldn't have discovered she'd done it in the first place."

A workaholic to the core.

"I'm sorry. That's shitty. Maybe kind of genius on her part, but shitty. I know how much your job means to you."

She shrugged. "It just means I have to come up with something else to occupy my brain."

He weighed his options. Would asking for her help set back her recovery? He just needed some information. Surely that wouldn't take too much out of her.

"Maybe I can help with that. Or rather, maybe you could help me."

Her gaze sharpened with interest. "With what?"

"You remember how we were supposed to be starting construction on the new resort this fall?"

"Sure. That was supposed to be formalized sometime soon, right?"

"While I was in California, actually."

The blood drained from her cheeks. "Oh God. You didn't lose the contract because you were with me, did you?"

"No. It was fine. My business partner was here to handle the meeting."

Maggie blinked. "Business partner? Oh, right. Mia. Someone mentioned her the other day. With all the excitement over the baby, I'd forgotten. When exactly did you get a business partner?"

He could hear the *Why didn't you tell me about her?* underneath the question.

"We worked together down in Gatlinburg. She needed a change, and I wanted to start working a bit less. We'd just signed the contracts the day I flew out to California. Anyway, if she hadn't been here to handle the contracts, I would have rescheduled the meeting. But I got back to find out that the funding has fallen through."

"Why?"

"I don't know. Neither does the mayor, apparently. Unless

they find another investor, the project is dead in the water. I didn't know if you maybe had some business contacts who might be interested in the opportunity."

She considered. "It's hard to be able to recommend it, or even know who to recommend it to, without seeing a prospectus."

"I've got a copy of that. Or the original one, at least."

"There's also the wrinkle of the previous investor pulling out. Was that about them or something about the project itself?" As her mind hooked into the problem, Porter could see the awkwardness falling away.

"I don't know. Is there some kind of business sleuthing you can do to get to the bottom of it?"

Her shoulders straightened, her eyes brightening with the fervor of purpose. "Who was the funder?"

"Faber Development. They're out of Nashville."

"I don't know anything about them offhand, but I can certainly do some digging. And maybe it'll help me think of someone who might be a good fit. Send over the prospectus, and I'll take a look."

"Thanks, Maggie."

"Of course. I'm happy to help, and you just might keep me from turning into a lunatic out of sheer boredom while I'm here."

He wanted to ask her if they were okay, but she'd said she was still processing. Even though the past forty-eight hours had felt like an eternity to him, it probably didn't constitute much for her—especially as Pru and Flynn had just come home with Bailey. So he resigned himself to doing what he'd become a champ at—waiting.

Chapter Seven

Maggie took in the sleek design of the waiting room at Faber Development, knowing this trip was *not* what Porter had in mind when he'd asked for her help. But she'd done some research on the company and hadn't found anything hinky. No rumors of buyouts or financial difficulties. By every metric she knew, they were a highly successful firm, which meant the problem wasn't the finances on their side.

Figuring she could get more out of a face-to-face meeting than over the phone or via email, she'd called and made an appointment with the CFO. So what if she'd had to drop Genevieve's name and pretend she was showing up on behalf of Invation? It was a little white lie that opened doors, and she wasn't above using that if it could help Porter out. And, depending on what she found out, she *could* still take it to Genevieve as an investment opportunity.

"Ms. Faber will see you now."

Maggie rose, smoothing a hand over her pencil skirt. She felt more at home in her business attire than the more casual clothes she'd been wearing around the inn. It was a familiar armor that lent her an air of strength and helped cover up the exhaustion she felt from making the four-hour drive to Nashville.

The secretary escorted her into a corner office with wide windows, showing off the AT&T Building and a swatch of other buildings comprising Nashville's skyline.

A thirty-something woman rose from behind the desk. "Ms. Reynolds, so pleased to meet you. I'm Isabelle Faber."

Maggie shook her hand. "Thank you for seeing me on such short notice."

Isabelle gestured to a chair. "Please, sit. Would you like any coffee?"

More than she wanted her next breath, but she'd been trying to cut back on that, too. "Nothing, thank you." With controlled movements she hoped came off as graceful rather than cautious, Maggie sank into one of the plush leather chairs in front of the desk.

Isabelle returned to her own chair. "I must admit, I was surprised to get your call."

"I realize my being here is somewhat unorthodox, but if I could beg your indulgence."

"Of course."

"I'm in Tennessee reviewing a potential investment opportunity, one I believe you are familiar with. The Paradise Mountain Resort in Eden's Ridge?"

Something flickered over the other woman's face. She inclined her head in acknowledgment.

"I've been over the prospectus, and it seems a solid investment. The growth potential in the tourism sector in that area is excellent. Something you already know, or Faber wouldn't have been the original investor on the project." It was true enough. She and Kennedy had researched the hell out of the tourism possibilities before she and her sisters had opened the inn, and though she had some reservations about what a resort the size of Paradise

Mountain might mean for Eden's Ridge as a whole, it made a lot of financial sense on paper.

"All of that's true."

Maggie fixed her with a direct stare. "Then why did you pull out of the deal? I realize this is incredibly forward of me, but I've researched your firm's track record. You wouldn't have pulled the plug without a good reason. From what I've seen, the resort is a good investment, but I cannot in good conscience make the recommendation to Ms. Kessinger that we back the project unless I've laid all doubts to rest."

"That's admirably thorough of you."

"I didn't get where I am by avoiding my homework."

"Fair enough." Isabelle steepled her fingers. "How long have you worked in the corporate world, Ms. Reynolds?"

It wasn't where she'd expected the conversation to go, but she figured the woman had a point. "Maggie, please." She understood how the game was played. Establish rapport, encourage the lowering of defenses. "It's what I've been doing since I finished graduate school."

"And in that time, even working for a company headed up by a woman, I assume you've run into your share of sexism."

"Of course. Invation isn't problematic, but many, many of the companies we do business with are run by men. More than a few of them have made the mistake of telling me to get them some coffee when I walk into a conference room, simply because I'm the one in a skirt. I confess, putting them in their place is one of the great joys of my job."

The CFO's lips twitched. "I'd like to see that."

"That Southern woman skill of cutting people off at the knees with a smile is exceptionally useful in that arena. But what does that have to do with the resort project?"

"Have you met with the local leadership?"

"Not yet. We were only just contacted about the possibility

of investing. Meeting with leadership seemed premature unless we were seriously considering moving forward."

"I actually meant the mayor."

"The mayor?" Feeling foolish, Maggie realized she had no idea who was presently mayor in Stone County. She'd once interned in that office and known everyone in the building, but after everything had gone to hell, she'd put as much mental, emotional, and physical distance between herself and Eden's Ridge as she could. There'd been no reason to keep up with local politics. Even with the legalities of opening the inn and spa, Kennedy had been the one to liaise with city government and the head of the chamber of commerce.

"Ah, I guarantee you haven't had the dubious pleasure or you wouldn't look so confused."

"You had some kind of run-in with the mayor?"

"You could say that." Leaning forward, Isabelle braced her arms on the desk. "My brother is the CEO and has handled most of our dealings with Mayor Danforth."

A chill crawled down Maggie's spine. "Danforth?"

"Bradley Danforth."

The blood drained out of her head. As the room began to spin, Maggie curled her hands around the arms of the chair. "Bradley Danforth is mayor of Eden's Ridge?" Surely she hadn't heard this right. There was some other explanation.

"Yes. You weren't aware?"

"No." Christ. How could that douchecanoe be mayor of her town and she not know? He'd left Eden's Ridge after that summer. His parents had made sure of it. When the hell had he come back? And why?

Isabelle studied her. "You know him." It wasn't a question.

"I—" Maggie cleared her throat, tried again. "Yes, I know him. Knew him. A long time ago." When she'd been young and foolish and naive enough to be seduced by his attention.

"I'm guessing by the look on your face that you've been exposed to his particular brand of...charm."

"You could say that." Because her hands were starting to shake, she linked them together in her lap. "What happened?"

"Well, as I said, my brother handled most of our business with him, but I went to deal with the final contracts. Let's just say he was...highly inappropriate, regardless of the fact that he's married with kids. His overtures would have been highly inappropriate even if he wasn't. I wasn't comfortable continuing the meeting, and when I told my brother, he pulled the plug, as it were. There are other investment opportunities out there, without my having to directly confront sexual harassment."

"Completely understandable," Maggie murmured. She wondered if he'd pulled the same shit with Porter's business partner.

"My advice to you and your company? If you choose to back the resort—which actually is a solid investment—send men to deal with him. Don't inadvertently put a woman in his path."

Maggie shoved to her feet. She needed to get out of here. Needed to get some air. "I thank you for your candor, Isabelle. You've certainly given me a lot to think about."

The other woman gave her hand a firm shake. "Happy to be of assistance. Are you sure you're all right? You still look a little pale."

"I'm fine." *I've just found out my own personal demon is running my hometown.*

"If I may ask, do you know what your recommendation is going to be? I'm curious."

Maggie met the other woman's gaze. "Run. Fast and far."

* * *

Porter was just stepping out of the shower at the end of the workday when his doorbell rang. It was a little late for deliveries, but maybe it was the custom lock set for the front door of the house his crew was finishing up. He'd already missed signing for it once. Whipping a towel around his hips, he bolted down the hall.

But it wasn't the UPS guy on his front porch. It was Maggie.

For a moment, she took his breath away in the slim pencil skirt and blouse that looked more like something she'd wear for work in California than anything appropriate for the inn. Her pale blonde hair had been put up into one of those fancy twists, but over the course of the day, it had loosened a little, until a few wisps fell down to frame her face, softening the whole look. Exactly how he liked it best. How many times had he fantasized about burying his hands in that hair?

She was staring at him, her mouth pursed in an O of surprise. Or more specifically, she was staring at his bare chest, her pupils going wide and dark. As he watched, the tip of her tongue darted out to moisten her lips and his body stirred.

"This is a bad time." Her voice was a little husky.

He took a firmer grip on the towel and braced one arm on the doorframe, noting her eyes followed the bunch and flex of muscle. Because his body liked that way the hell too much, he stepped back. "No, it's fine. Come on in. I'll be out in a minute."

Leaving the door wide open, he headed for his bedroom, mentally reciting the Gettysburg Address in an effort to kill his erection.

This was new. Not his reaction to her—he'd had years of practice taming that—but she'd never looked at him with blatant sexual attraction before. They'd had moments of tension over the years. Plenty of emotional intimacy. But he'd gone out of his way never to push her on the physical front, first because, despite her protestations to the contrary, he wasn't a hundred percent convinced she hadn't been coerced in high school, and then because he hadn't wanted to spook her away from their renewed friendship. Maybe he should've paraded around her in a towel sooner.

Yanking on jeans and a t-shirt, he padded back through the house to find her in the living room, arms crossed in that self-protective stance again. Determined not to make the situation worse, he kept on going. "Want a beer? Wine?"

"You drink wine?"

No, but she did, so he kept a couple of bottles on hand, just in case. "I've got a bottle of cab and a sauv blanc."

"I'd love a glass of white."

Encouraged, he pulled the wine and a beer for himself out of the fridge and dug out the corkscrew.

She'd wandered into the kitchen behind him, drawn to the picture windows. "You have one of the best views on the Ridge."

"I like to think so." Bringing her a glass, he joined her at the window, looking out at the landscape that never failed to make his heart soar. He loved these mountains and had built his house with the idea of bringing them in as much as possible. Every room boasted wide stretches of glass, and the setting itself, nestled high on the ridge, amid the trees, ensured privacy.

He wondered why she'd come but didn't ask. She'd get to it in her own time. Right now, he was just happy she'd come at all. They stood in not quite companionable silence, sipping their drinks and watching the sun sink behind the mountain. With each degree lower, the tension in her shoulders seemed to ease, just a little. Would she balk if he reached up to knead and press the stress away? Probably. Whatever rights he'd once had to casually touch her had been revoked the moment he'd made his real feelings known. Yet even as he ached with the loss of that intimacy, he knew he'd done the right thing.

When his stomach growled, he turned away, back to the fridge. "Want dinner? Or have you eaten?"

"No, I—that wasn't why I came." She took a bracing breath. "I went to Nashville today."

"Why?"

"To meet with the CFO of Faber Development."

Porter searched her face, not liking what he saw there. "Am I gonna need another beer for this story?"

"Possibly." Back to the crossed arms. "The long and the short of it is that there's not a chance in hell of Faber changing their mind about the resort project, not because there was anything problematic about the deal itself or with their company—I did my homework there—but because the mayor made inappropriate sexual advances on Isabelle Faber."

"He sexually harassed the investor," Porter repeated, hand tightening on his longneck. Of course he had. It was a well-known secret that the mayor strayed from his wife. But Porter hadn't thought Danforth would be fool enough to endanger a project this big for the town.

"Is it possible he said or did something inappropriate to Mia?"

"I mean, she said he was a sexist asshole, but I don't think so. Mia's worked in construction for years. She's used to dealing with men and shutting down unwanted advances. I've seen her do it countless times, and she's not shy about it. If that were the issue, I don't think she'd have balked from telling me."

Maggie pressed her lips together. "It happens more than you probably imagine in the business world."

Porter's hands curled to fists. "To you?"

She shrugged. "Sometimes. Though that's less an issue at Invation."

"Before you got there?"

Her gaze flicked up to his. Would she finally tell him after all these years?

"It is a truth, universally acknowledged by women everywhere, that a huge proportion of the male population are assholes."

Porter clamped down on the familiar disappointment. As always, she kept her own council, never bringing anyone into the inner circle. She never even suspected that he knew so much more about what had happened to her in high school than she could imagine. And yet, not enough, not everything. He had no idea why he kept expecting her to open up, why it hurt him that she didn't. Better to focus on the problem at hand. "It's too much to expect that you know of anyone else who might want to invest."

"I might be able to come up with someone, though this isn't my area."

He didn't want her further involved in this problem. If she got involved, it would put her in Brad's path again, and Porter would do almost anything to keep that from happening. "It's fine. You got the why, and a lot faster than I expected. I appreciate your help."

"Of course."

He circled back around the island, noting her posture going stiff as he approached. That, too, hurt, but it was on him. He didn't know when he'd get another chance to address the elephant in the room. "Listen, I'm really sorry I've made you uncomfortable."

Genuine surprise lit her face. "No, it's not that. You've spent years doing everything you could to make me comfortable. To support me. You've been my rock. And I...I haven't treated that with the kind of respect it deserves."

The last thing he wanted was for her to beat herself up over this. "You can't feel what you don't feel." And that was the truth.

If she didn't—couldn't—love him the way he loved her, then he'd have to find a way to live with it. Better to find out for sure.

She lifted emotion-drenched eyes to his and swallowed hard. "It's not that either."

Hope slammed into him like a freight train. Did that mean there was a chance? He wanted this too badly to misunderstand, so he held himself very still, despite the pounding of his heart. "What is it then?"

"You deserve so much more than someone who's broken, Porter."

Her whispered words were full of a conviction that raked over him like claws. "You're not broken. Scarred, maybe. But not broken."

She huffed a bitter laugh. "The end result is the same. Do you realize I haven't had a functional adult relationship...basically ever? I get to a certain point and just...can't. Because my trust issues would fill up the Titanic."

Porter couldn't stand it. This beautiful, brave, brilliant woman truly believed she was irreparably damaged. There were a lot of different ways he could take that, a lot of interpretations about what, exactly, she couldn't do. All of them meant he had to be very, very careful. Setting all of it aside to consider later, he took a step closer, driven to prove her wrong. "Do you trust me?"

It was a loaded question, and they both knew it.

Maggie stared up at him, her breath quickening. Porter felt his own pulse trip into a gallop as he waited for her answer, wondering if, at long last, he'd get the chance to show her what could be.

Her answer was barely more than a breath of sound. "Yes."

Moving slowly, he invaded her personal space, testing. Though she trembled, she didn't bolt. He skimmed a hand over her cheek—Christ her skin was soft—framing the face that had haunted his dreams more than half his life and closing the distance between them until his lips were a breath from hers.

"You're not broken, Maggie."

* * *

This is a terrible idea.

There were dozens of reasons why. Maggie had spent the last four days reviewing all of them on an infinite loop. But standing there, with Porter's big, capable hands framing her face like she was something precious, she couldn't summon up a single one.

He held there, at the cusp of changing everything, waiting for some sign to proceed or back off. But he'd already changed everything, and a part of her had been curious about this for years. So really, could things get any weirder between them?

Maybe he'd kiss her and it would be terrible, and he'd realize she wasn't being dramatic when she said she was broken. She couldn't feel the way she was supposed to. Almost every time, whatever arousal she could muster was so thoroughly drowned in anxiety, she might as well feel nothing at all. Not of the act itself, but of the consequences. She couldn't get out of her own head to properly enjoy any of it. Every guy she'd gone out with had figured that out in short order. So it was better this way. Porter wouldn't understand until he experienced it firsthand. Then he'd realize that he was better off without her. Or at least without thinking of her like this.

The rough pads of his thumbs stroked over the curve of her cheeks, exquisitely gentle. She shivered, swaying toward him just a little until he laid his lips over hers. She waited for the cold, joy-stealing crush of anxiety. For her brain to kick in with consequences and warnings. But her mind simply stopped. His mouth was so soft and sweet, Maggie couldn't help but sigh, bringing her hands up to curve around his forearms, wanting, needing that link, as she kissed him back.

It was a slow, exploratory kiss. Instead of sensation fizzling out, everything in her warmed, unfurling and stretching toward him like a flower toward the sun. As if she were Sleeping Beauty and he was waking her up after years of sleep.

It terrified and thrilled her in equal measure. But this was Porter. Porter wouldn't press, wouldn't take advantage. He wouldn't hurt her—ever. So she gave herself over to his kiss, to him, in a way she hadn't been able to do since her world fell apart. She moved in, wanting to feel the solid wall of his body pressed against hers. He made some noise deep in his throat, his hands sliding into her hair. She was dimly aware of the pins pulling free, of the weight of it falling down her shoulders. Then his tongue traced the seam of her lips, and she opened for him, forgetting everything else but the heady taste of him. One strong arm banded around her back, pulling her closer. She went willingly, angling her head to take the kiss deeper, needing to chase every sensation, lest it disappear in a flash.

When he broke the kiss, she whimpered at the loss.

Breath heaving, he pressed his brow to hers. "See? Not broken."

Breathless herself, she held on. He'd just kissed the hell out of her—and she'd kissed him back. She'd felt—things. Hot, panty-melting things she was already thinking about pursuing again, just to see if the first time was a fluke.

It scared her to death.

For years she'd thought this part of her had simply died off. Some kind of penance or punishment for reckless behavior and foolish choices. Or maybe simply trauma from what had come after those choices.

But it was different with Porter. Because he knew her? Because he'd been around for all the hell she'd been through, so it wasn't some secret lurking in her closet? Because she actually *did* trust him, down to the ground? She had no idea. All she knew for sure was that he'd just upended her world—again.

"That was—" *Unexpected. Life-altering. Wonderful.* "You're really good at that."

He huffed a laugh. "I've given literally years of thought to how I'd kiss you."

"Really?" The idea of it boggled her mind. What if it hadn't lived up to his expectations? What if he'd just rocked her world and she'd been merely okay? It wasn't as if she had that much experience...especially for a woman her age.

"Even better than I imagined."

Not quite sure he was being serious, she pulled back far enough that she could see his face. The heat and affection in his denim blue eyes tangled her up in knots as all her good intentions warred with the undeniable want simmering in her blood.

If she could give him nothing else, she'd give him honesty. "I have literally no idea what to do with this."

He stroked his hand up and down her spine. "Enjoy it. We don't have to have all the answers today."

She hadn't gotten where she was in life by not addressing inconvenient truths. "But there are some pretty big issues here, Porter. Like the fact that my whole life is in California. And—"

Pressing a finger gently to her lips, he shook his head. "I know there are a lot of practical reasons why this isn't a good idea. But none of them matter more than the fact that there's something here. I think we just proved that beyond the shadow of a doubt. And if we don't take some time to explore it, we'll regret it for the rest of our lives."

So much of her life had been spent thinking about "what is" so she could avoid going down the trail of "what if." But these past few days, she'd been unable to stop herself from thinking about what ifs, especially related to him. And now he'd handed her an even bigger one. What if they could really be something together? Not as teenagers thrown together by circumstance and noble intention, but as mature adults. He was right. If she didn't pursue this, she'd always wonder. And if she didn't do it now, while she was home in Eden's Ridge for a few months without the burden of her career to distract her, then when?

Not quite ready to commit, she asked, "What exactly would exploring this look like?"

His smile spread like slow molasses into a Cheshire Cat grin. "I'm gonna court you."

Maggie blinked. "Excuse me?"

"I'm going to court you. We'll spend some quality time together. I'm going old school. I want to take you to dinner and talk about our days and our interests. I want to go for long walks after, holding your hand where everybody can see."

In public. Aboveboard. Because she hadn't had that before, and he knew it. Her entire single relationship had been in secret, made up of sneaking around and subterfuge. It had all been exciting at the time. An illicit thrill. Once she'd gotten pregnant, that same secrecy had made her feel tawdry, and she'd never fully escaped it.

Porter wanted to give her legitimacy and respect. Her throat went thick and she had to swallow against a knot of emotion that he'd think of that, know it would be important to her.

"What else?" Like the physical? Did he have expectations? That had certainly played a major part before. She'd been willingly seduced at seventeen, but looking back, she could see how she'd been manipulated. Porter was nothing like Bradley, but he was an adult male in his prime. He had to have needs.

"You're in the driver's seat here, Mags. I won't push, and I won't rush. I'm fine with taking our time. I'm just happy to have the chance with you."

From any other guy, that might have been a line. Something

to placate her and set her at ease until he could press his case. But Porter meant it. Because he was, apparently, a unicorn among men. She could pursue this with him and he wouldn't make her feel stupid or embarrassed. And she wanted to. Wanted to see what else he could make her feel.

The entire prospect terrified and excited her.

"Okay. Let's give this a try."

He kissed her again, just a quick, sweet peck, and released her. "Good. Let me cook you dinner, and we can talk about what we'll do for our first date."

"You already have a first date in mind?"

"Sure. Has anybody told you about the Artisan Supper?"

Chapter Eight

"Are you just gonna stand out here all night or are you gonna come in?"

At the sound of Ari's voice, Porter froze midway through wiping sweaty palms on his good jeans. Did the nerves show? It was ridiculous, really. In all the years he'd been in love with Maggie, he'd imagined almost everything. What it would be like to kiss her. How he'd make love to her. What it would be like to marry her and raise a child. But somehow, in all of it, he'd never thought about what it would be like to pick her up for their first date. Probably because they'd leapfrogged right past that possibility when he'd proposed.

He'd never imagined climbing the steps to the house that had been his own home for so many years. Never thought he'd hesitate, unsure of whether to just walk on in as normal or ring the bell. What was the protocol here? This was an honest-to-God date with Maggie Reynolds. His dream girl. He wanted—needed—to get this right.

Ari cocked a brow, and Porter realized he still hadn't said

anything. Stepping inside he tried for a casual tone. "I'm a little early. I wasn't sure if Maggie was ready."

Maggie's disembodied voice floated down from the second floor. "I was ready twenty minutes ago, but Ari made me come back up here."

"Because you have to make an entrance," the girl insisted.

Pru came out of the kitchen, Bailey drowsing on her shoulder. "Be glad Ari stopped with this. She wanted to take pictures."

"Because it should be *documented*. Duh."

"It's not like this is prom or something," Maggie argued.

Ari crossed her arms and snorted in disgust. "So not the point."

Flynn swung an arm around his daughter's shoulders. "She's a romantic, our Ari."

Porter's lips twitched. That was putting it mildly. Her matchmaking efforts knew no bounds, and she was more than happy to claim credit for the successful pairings of her mother and her other two aunts.

"Do I have your permission to come down now, oh Grand Poobah of Dates? Or is there some soundtrack you have to cue up first?"

"Oh! I didn't think of that. I could—"

"That was not a suggestion!" The sound of footsteps at the top of the stairs drew Porter's gaze up.

He caught sight of the strappy, heeled sandals first, framing rose-pink toenails and drawing his gaze up slim, shapely calves. The dark-blue patterned sundress was modest, flirting just past her knees. But it nipped in at her narrow waist, seeming to invite his hands to pull her in. The v-neck gave just a hint of cleavage, showcasing the simple pendant necklace she wore. Her hair was loose around her shoulders, as he'd rarely seen it since she was a girl. She looked fresh as a daisy and more rested than she had in days.

"Hi." The hands she flexed in the sweater she carried showed he wasn't the only one feeling a little nervous. Somehow that small sign that he wasn't the only one affected made his own nerves settle.

Relieved he didn't have to hide his feelings anymore, Porter threaded his fingers with hers and lifted one of those hands to his lips, letting her see all his pleasure and anticipation. "You look beautiful."

A blush painted her fair cheeks. "Thanks."

Porter didn't let himself glance down to see if the blush continued down her throat and into that tantalizing cleavage.

From somewhere to the side, a chorus of sniffs and "aww"s sounded. Pru and Ari looked a little watery around the eyes and even Flynn beamed like a proud papa. "That's beautiful, that is."

Maggie rolled her eyes. "Y'all are being ridiculous."

"Oh hush and let the romantics have our moment," Ari insisted. "We've been waiting for this forever."

"Not as long as I have." Porter tucked Maggie's arm through his, reminding himself that this was just a first step, a first date. He couldn't get ahead of himself. "Don't wait up."

They escaped to his truck, trailed by "ooo"s and cheerful farewells.

As he pulled out of the drive, he felt Maggie's eyes on him. "What?"

"I just...I never realized how much you've had to hide from me over the years. I'm sorry for that."

Snagging her hand again, he squeezed. "No more apologies. I don't have to hide now. That's all that matters." Liking the feel of her fingers curved around his, he didn't release her. Her smaller hand fit so well in his, the delicate, feminine shape of it a contrast to his big, work-roughened mitts. He stroked a thumb over her knuckles, pleased at the faint shiver. She didn't mind his hands, so he'd hang on to hers as long as she'd let him.

"What have you been up to today?"

Settling back against the seat, she let out a sigh. "Paperwork."

"Why do you sound relieved when you say that? Are you missing work that much?"

Maggie huffed a laugh. "No. I'm relieved because Mom's estate is officially out of probate, so I've been going over remaining assets. Did you know we own the old saw mill?"

"Really?"

"Yeah. Apparently our great, great, however many greats grandfather Reynolds—the lumber baron that built the house—is also the one who built and ran the mill. Which makes sense. I thought it got sold off years ago. Certainly nobody's used it in ages."

"Not a surprise. The access road was overgrown before we were all born. Not that that stopped Xander and me from exploring out there when we were teenagers."

"I've never been. Mom never talked about it, so I guess I just forgot it was even a thing."

"I remember it being pretty big and a cool space. Lots of wood and stone. It was in surprisingly good shape, considering it was built over a hundred years ago." He'd admired the craftsmanship that had gone into the construction of something that had lasted that long.

"I have no idea what to do with it."

"Do you have to do something with it?"

"Well, we're paying taxes on it, so it seems like it ought to serve some purpose or we should get rid of it. But it's hard to say without seeing it for myself."

"Did you bring any shoes from California that aren't heels?"

"None suitable for tromping through the woods, but I'm sure I could borrow some from Kennedy."

"Do that. I'll take you out there, and we can see what's what."

Conversation came easy on the rest of the drive into town.

When he turned in at the VFW, Maggie went brows up. "We're going here?"

"It's not exactly the picture of refinement, but it's the only building in town big enough to house all the artisans and the tables for the pot luck."

The gravel lot was overflowing, but Porter parked his truck along the side of the drive that circled around the building. When he came around to help Maggie out of the truck, he couldn't help but notice the tension that hadn't been there before. He understood she was leery of going out in public in the Ridge, but the Artisan Supper would be full of a pretty eclectic, bohemian group of folks. The chances of old gossip coming up seemed slim. Giving her a bolstering smile, he pulled her toward the building. "C'mon. I want to get in there before all of Mrs. Lowry's red velvet cake disappears."

The interior was packed. Booths showing off assorted wares from hand-sewn quilts to pottery to bent-wood furniture lined three sides of the perimeter. The fourth side was a long row of tables covered in crock pots and casserole dishes in a massive buffet. In one corner, Ford MacIntosh strummed a mandolin, along with a couple of other faces Porter recognized from the summer Jam Nights at the inn. People were everywhere, browsing the artisan goods or stuffing their faces at the cluster of tables in the middle. Not even five feet into the door, and he saw people noticing Maggie. And why shouldn't they? She naturally commanded any room she walked into.

She edged closer to him. "How exactly does this work?"

Porter paid for their tickets and pressed a hand to the small of her back to steer her toward a display in one corner. "Everybody pays the ticket price. That entitles you to dinner from the buffet over there and puts you in a drawing for tonight's door prize, which is the hand-thrown bowl on the table over there. All this stuff here is available for this month's silent auction. Proceeds from all of it are going into a fund dedicated to building a maker's space."

"A what now?"

"The idea is to have a communal space with communal tools and equipment that members can all use. We've got artisans in the area who want to pass on the knowledge of their craft, and a lot of folks are interested in learning different skills, but the cost of getting into a lot of it is prohibitive. A maker's space would help split the cost and also provide some space for teaching."

"Where are they planning on building?"

"No idea. It's a long way out yet. Originally, these artisan suppers were just meant as a monthly showcase of wares, but the idea kind of evolved from there."

"At ten bucks a head, I imagine it's going to take a while to come to fruition."

"A lot of it will probably get done on a volunteer basis, but you're not wrong. It's a big project. C'mon, let's get some food. I'm starved."

They filled their plates from the home-cooked offerings, and he did manage to snag a piece of cake. By the time they got to the end of the line, he caught sight of Dahlia Atwood waving them over. She'd been one of Maggie's closest friends back in high school, but he wasn't sure how things were between them. Before he could ask, Maggie was making a beeline in her direction.

"You came!" Dahlia squealed.

"I promised I would." Maggie set down her plate and gave Dahlia a tight hug. "It's good to see you again." She shifted her gaze to the broad-shouldered guy seated beside her. "You must be Landon."

He rose from his seat and offered a hand. "Landon Harris. And you're Maggie. I've heard a lot about you."

Maggie grinned. "I haven't heard too much about you yet except that you're wonderful."

Landon cracked a smile. "Well, I'd say the same of her."

Dahlia beamed up at her boyfriend. "Oh, I'll have to tell you the story of how we met while we eat. It's a doozy."

"I look forward to hearing your version of this story," Porter told her. "I'm not sure we quite believe the one he's told us at work. A fake engagement? Really?"

Dahlia pressed a hand to her heart. "Hand to God. Really."

"I can't wait to hear this." Maggie shifted her attention back to Porter. "Landon works with you?"

"Just brought him on about six weeks ago."

"And we can't thank you enough for that," Dahlia gushed. "It's been so wonderful not having to do the long-distance thing between here and Knoxville anymore."

And if that wasn't a fresh reminder that he'd damned well better figure shit out with respect to keeping all his people employed, he didn't know what was. But that was for thinking about tomorrow. "It's working out well for me, too. I'll go get us drinks. Maggie, you want sweet tea?"

"God, yes. I haven't had decent tea in ages."

Leaving them to visit, he wove his way across the room. In line at the drink station, he heard her name.

"Oh yeah. That's Maggie Reynolds. One of Joan's girls. The one that went to them fancy schools up north. Does something out on the West Coast, I think."

"I wonder what she's doing here."

"Visiting her sister, I expect. You know Pru just had her baby."

"No! I hadn't heard. Boy or girl?"

Amused, Porter filled a couple of cups with tea from the giant coolers. As ever, gossip was the town's favorite form of entertainment. On the way back to their table, he heard her name again.

"Oh you remember Maggie Reynolds. It was a whole big

scandal, maybe ten or twelve years ago. She turned up pregnant and wouldn't ever name the daddy."

Porter stopped where he was, hands tightening until the cups began to groan from the pressure.

"Well, that sounds all kinds of shady. Why wouldn't she say unless she was involved with somebody she shouldn't have been?"

He didn't realize he was growling until the speaker—Jana Samson—looked in his direction, eyes going wide. He wanted so badly to go over there and set them straight. It had been more than a decade. This wasn't who Maggie was. But he knew she wouldn't want a scene and that addressing it directly would only add fuel to the fire, so he merely narrowed his eyes before turning away. Maybe Maggie hadn't heard.

The rigid set to her shoulders disabused him of that notion. She'd heard. If not them, then someone else. He recognized that ramrod straight posture, the squared shoulders, head held high, full ice princess routine on display.

Damn it.

Sliding into the seat beside her, he set down the tea and leaned over to wrap an arm around her and murmur in her ear. "We can go."

"I'm fine. Let's just eat before it gets cold, okay?"

He exchanged a look with Dahlia, who looked every bit as incensed as he felt. It was on them to distract Maggie and make her comfortable again. "So you promised to tell the story about how you and Landon met."

Dahlia's outrage melted into a beaming grin. "It all started when I accidentally felt him up on a plane..."

* * *

Deep quiet had settled in by the time they got back to the house. A light still burned on the front porch, but only a few upper windows were still lit. Guests who hadn't yet turned in. No doubt the Bohannon contingent was grabbing sleep as long as they could, before the baby woke them for the next feeding. After the swirl of voices and press of people at the VFW, Maggie and Porter had taken a leisurely stroll downtown, holding hands like a couple of teenagers. But she still wasn't ready to say goodnight.

"Will you come sit with me on the porch?"

Porter took her hand again. "I'd come sit with you anywhere."

His easy words gave her a thrill. They climbed the steps and circled around back to an old-fashioned glider, where they could look out over the moonlit mountains. She settled beside him on the cushion and let herself be lulled by the warm press of his leg against hers and the gentle sway of the glider. Leaning into the curve of his shoulder felt natural as breathing, and as his arm settled around her, she exhaled a slow sigh of contentment.

"I forgot how much I like quiet."

"Not a lot of that in Los Angeles."

"No. I think I made myself forget about a lot of things I love about home so I didn't miss it so much."

"You had plenty of other stuff to drown them out. I'm sorry for the assholes tonight."

Maggie jerked her shoulders in a shrug. "It's nothing new."

"That's exactly it. It's not new. So why the hell are people still talking about it?" The frustrated bafflement in his voice almost made her smile. He really didn't understand because he wasn't the kind of person who'd keep feeding old gossip like some kind of feral cat that only came around once in a while.

"Nothing better to do. It's what people know about me here. It's nothing I didn't expect." Though a part of her had hoped she'd be wrong. That people would have moved on to something new, as he'd said. Having to put that armor back on after years away was like slipping into an itchy, ill-fitting suit. She didn't like it. Didn't like the need for it. Didn't like that she still couldn't just let it roll off her. But she never had.

"Still. I'm sorry they ruined things. I wanted our first date to be perfect."

"They didn't ruin anything."

Porter made some noise like he didn't believe her, so she sat up enough to look at him, though she could barely see his eyes in the dark. "I mean it. I had a good time tonight. It was good food, good company, and I came home with a beautiful hand-thrown bowl."

He skimmed the hair back from her face. Her stomach flipped at the touch, and she was tempted, so tempted, to press into his hand, into him. She'd been so long without any kind of physical touch that she found herself soaking up every drop of contact, wanting so much more.

"That all it takes to make you happy?"

Your hands all over me? Yeah, I'm pretty sure that would make me more than happy. She was dying to know the feel of those callused fingers in far more intimate places. What would he say if she asked? Even as she thought it, she pulled back, heart thumping with nerves.

Porter just squeezed her hand. "Hey, it's okay. Whatever's going through your head, we're not rushing things here."

But she wanted to, and that was absolutely terrifying. He nudged the glider into motion again. Maggie eased back into the curve of his shoulder. The gentle rocking and the slow stroke of his thumb against her arm unwound the knot in her gut until she'd relaxed again, content. Safe.

Because it felt like the moment was past, she jumped back into conversation mode. "I had a brief conversation with Misty. She told me what Tabitha Dutton charges regularly for her work, and it just floored me. This bowl would fetch at least four or five times that in California. And I got the impression from some of the other folks I talked to that pricing like that is the norm. People are consistently undervaluing their work."

"Cost of living isn't the same here as out on the West Coast. Folks around here couldn't afford those prices."

"Yes, but around here shouldn't be the limit of their audience. There are a lot of really talented people in the Ridge. It's a shame they aren't better known."

"Some are better known than others. I know several folks who have quite the following online. Like Hale Copeland, the glass artist. But for every one that's embraced modern technology, there are half a dozen others who rely on word of mouth or the sales they get through Misty's shop."

The unfulfilled potential was an itch in her mind. Not her problem, but part of her was still looking for work to fill up every spare second of the day, and she couldn't seem to help herself. "There's a market for this. Kennedy's done some networking with a few of the local artists. We've got pieces in every room for sale to guests as our own little effort at raising visibility. Quite a few have sold since we opened last year. I wonder if we could talk Celeste, up at the Chamber of Commerce, into helping organize a broader sort of swap for different artisans with other businesses in town?"

"That's a nice thought. I'm sure Misty would be up for helping organize the artists and crafters who would be into something like that."

A phone call was a small and simple thing that wouldn't wear her out. But when had she ever stopped with small and simple?

"What's going on in that head of yours?" She could hear the smile in his voice.

"Nothing, really. I just keep thinking how much more they could accomplish if they all really worked together."

"That's a big part of the impetus behind the maker's space."

It was a cool idea, even if they were a long, long way from bringing it to fruition. "It's too bad they aren't closer to achieving their funding goals. That'd be a good project for you while the search is on for new investors for the resort."

"From your mouth to God's ear."

They hadn't talked about it since she'd brought back her report from Faber Development. "Are you worried?"

"I mean, I'd be foolish not to be. I've got a whole crew depending on me. But it's not dire."

The "yet" hung unspoken between them.

Maybe she should consider calling Genevieve. It wasn't the kind of investment Invation typically made, but she might know someone who'd be interested. The woman had contacts all over the world.

"Why don't you give that busy brain of yours a break? You don't have to figure out the answer to my problem. Just sit for a bit," he suggested. "I figure part of this whole break for you is not just about slowing down but actually stopping once in a while."

The very idea of it instinctively made her tense up. "I don't... know how. I've never been one to just sit."

"You've always had your eye on everywhere but where you were. Always looking to the next thing."

"Distracting myself, you mean."

"Sometimes. And that's totally fair considering a lot of what you've been through. But sometimes it's good to just sit with where you are. Feel whatever it is you feel."

She didn't want to feel what she felt. That was the exact opposite of what she wanted. But she'd try it. For him.

They lapsed into silence, and instantly her mind filled with the overheard gossip from earlier. She'd played it off as no big deal, but it still stung, as it always did. This was who she was here. What she'd always be remembered for. And that just... sucked.

Porter trailed his fingers along the skin just below her sleeve, a slow, soft stroke that gradually soothed the feathers still ruffled by the words of the opinionated and ignorant. As she'd told him, she'd expected something, and in fact, it hadn't been as bad as she'd feared. That was probably because she'd been with him. Did he realize that people who'd speculated he was the baby's father years ago would start right back up again seeing them together now? Probably not. He wasn't a man who lived in the past. But neither did he live perpetually in the future, as she did. Maybe it was time she took a page out of his book and lived in the now.

"You know there aren't many people I can do this with," she murmured.

"Cuddle?"

Huffing a laugh, she snuggled in closer, enjoying the feel of closeness. "That, too. But no, I meant sit in silence, lost in my own thoughts. Usually it makes me want to crawl out of my skin. But it's comfortable with you. It's been so many years, I'd forgotten that was always one of my favorite things about you."

"A lot of people aren't easy being silent. I guess I got used to it when I was younger, working on various projects by myself. First because I wasn't fit for company, and then because it became my time to come to terms with whatever I was wrestling with. That was Joan's doing and probably served me better than any of the therapists."

He was so well-adjusted, it was easy to forget he'd had his own demons to fight when he'd come to Joan. His mother's abandonment. His father's rejection. And yet none of that had stopped him from becoming one of the kindest, most giving, most caring men she knew. She had no idea how he'd made peace with his past. Maybe it was because it hadn't been constantly thrown in his face as hers was.

"She was always good at knowing exactly what all of us

needed. Maybe that's why she didn't say anything about all that time we spent together that last year. She knew I needed you."

His arm tightened around her as he pressed a kiss to her temple.

Throat going thick, she whispered, "I still need you." The idea of it scared her to death. She didn't like needing anyone. Didn't like depending on anybody or anything but herself. But she'd promised herself she'd give him honesty, and this was the absolute truth.

"Maggie." Emotion clogged his voice, and when she straightened to look at him, she could read the longing on his face.

When he didn't move to close the distance between them, she cupped his cheek, testing them both as she tipped his face to hers and took his mouth. On a sound somewhere between a contented sigh and a groan, he pulled her closer, rubbing his lips against hers in another soul-stealing, toe-curling kiss. How had she not known this was here? How had she not realized this solid, steady man could rock her world?

Arousal fizzed in her blood, making her feel just a little drunk on his kisses. And it wasn't terrifying this time because it was Porter. They wouldn't go further than this tonight—not sitting on the porch of her family's inn, when anybody could walk out at any time. But she could just enjoy this, enjoy him, reveling in the fact that she could simply *feel*. She, Maggie Reynolds, was making out like a teenager with Porter Ingram. And it was glorious.

Sometime much, much later, when she finally came up for air, she gasped, "I don't want to go inside."

"I mean, I'll stay out here as long as you like. I'm prepared. I've got Chapstick."

Another laugh burbled out. She hadn't realized how seldom she laughed in her normal life. "You are a sweet, wonderful man, you know that?"

He trailed a hand over her hair and down her back. "Since I'm so sweet and wonderful, why don't you spend tomorrow afternoon with me? We can go check out the mill site."

"Eager to see how well it's held up?"

His lips curved in a wry grin. "More like eager to kiss you without prospective witnesses."

"Hey, it's not my fault you didn't hear me pull up," Athena called from the edge of the porch. "I'm going in now."

Cheeks burning with embarrassment, Maggie pressed her face into Porter's shoulder. "I'll be hearing about that later."

"I'm sure I will, too. You know she tells Logan everything and that he and Xander gossip like little girls."

They totally did. "Then yeah. I say we head out to the mill tomorrow and try to avoid the inquisition."

"It's a date."

Grinning, Maggie thought she could get used to that.

Chapter Nine

Maggie tapped a spoon against the big farmhouse table. "Okay, I'm calling this family meeting to order." As her sisters and Ari quieted down, she continued. "The latest numbers for *The Misfit Kitchen* web series project another fifteen percent jump by the end of this quarter, which gives a nice, extra cushion for the construction project of the new commercial kitchen. Porter's revised estimates put the building finished in time for the New Year, possibly sooner, depending on some scheduling issues." Like whether or not new funding could be found for Paradise Mountain. So far, there'd been nothing.

"Yeah, yeah, we'll get to that." Athena waved a hand, dismissing discussion of her own business. "First, let's talk about how I totally walked up on you making out with Porter on the porch last night."

Not even Maggie's iron will could stop the blush from creeping up her cheeks at the chorus of adolescent "oooooo"s that followed. So she squared her shoulders and lifted her head in defiance, much as she had at the Artisan Supper. "And?"

"I just want to say you go girl and it's about damned time. I didn't think you'd ever wake up to what was right in front of you."

Pru sighed. "They were so frigging cute when he picked her up last night."

"The way he kissed her hand?" Ari lifted a hand to her brow and feigned a swoon.

"So romantic," her mother agreed.

"And he was nervous when he got here. How adorable was that?" Ari insisted.

Maggie eyed them all. "Y'all are really invested in this."

"Well, of course we're invested. We love you and we love him, and he's loved you forever and you're perfect together." Athena said it like the whole thing was a foregone conclusion that everything would work out simply because Maggie was giving this a try. Love had amplified whatever nascent romanticism Athena harbored, and it was just plain weird to see on her cynical sister.

Their enthusiasm worried Maggie. She hadn't made any kind of promises to anybody, least of all Porter. They were still just exploring what was between them. "Don't get ahead of yourselves. We're just taking things one day at a time. None of this is as simple as you're making it."

Kennedy was the only one who hadn't added her two cents to the discussion. "You're right. It's not. I'd be lying if I said I wasn't worried about this."

A little offended, Maggie struggled to keep the ice from her voice. "You think I'm not?"

Kennedy's expression softened. "No, of course not. I know you're not playing with him. I know you wouldn't be pursuing this at all if you didn't have feelings for him. There's just a lot of stuff hanging in the air, and I don't know what it's going to do to him when you go back to California in a couple of weeks."

They didn't know. Of course, they didn't. She'd done everything she could to avoid telling them about her health, not wanting to worry them. Not wanting to ignite false hope about what it could mean in the long term. But they needed to know.

"I'm not going back in a couple of weeks." She took a breath. "I'm on mandatory medical leave until January."

The blood drained out of Pru's face. "Medical leave? Why?"

That instant worry was exactly why she'd kept it to herself. "A couple of weeks ago, I passed out in the middle of a meeting at work. Genevieve dragged me to the hospital and more or less demanded they test me for everything under the sun."

Athena leaned forward, both hands braced on the table as if ready for battle. "What the hell is wrong?"

"Is it cancer?" Ari whispered.

"Something autoimmune?" Kennedy asked.

"No. Nothing like that. They didn't find any kind of disease. I just have a lot of symptoms of chronic stress and overwork. It's the kind of thing that *can* lead to worse things, to permanent things, if left unchecked. And since I'm about as likely to slow down as a stampeding elephant, she took matters into her own hands and forced me on leave for the rest of the year."

Pru laid a hand on Maggie's shoulder. "Honey, why didn't you tell us?"

"Because you were about a million weeks pregnant, and I wasn't going to do a single thing to worry you. Genevieve knew that, so she called Porter to bring me home."

Her sisters exchanged a Look.

"She called Porter," Athena repeated.

"She figured if she called any of you, it would get back to Pru, and then I'd have her head. He was the next logical choice."

"He went to California?" Pru asked.

"He came flying to my rescue. It's kind of his thing."

He'd come running the moment he'd heard "hospital." Because he'd understood what that would do to her. She hadn't let herself fully appreciate that at the time. Hadn't let herself take more than the barest of comfort from him because she'd been afraid of the temptation he presented. Afraid that if she let somebody else shoulder the weight, she'd never be able to pick it up again.

But she took a moment to appreciate it now. He'd come because he loved her. Because he'd wanted to support her. No quid pro quo, no balance sheet. He'd simply come, like her very own white knight. She'd never looked for that in a man. After watching her birth mother try on one after another, Maggie had learned it was best to depend only on herself. But she could depend on Porter, and the knowledge of that warmed something deep inside.

"Before this devolves again into a discussion of how romantic that is," Kennedy interjected, "how are you feeling? Do we need to cut back on what you're doing around the inn and spa?"

It took everything Maggie had not to outright panic at the threat. "Oh God, please don't. I'm fine. Or I'm getting there. Much as I hate to admit it, Genevieve was probably right to force me into this. I needed to slow down. I'm still learning how the hell to do that, but I know it needs to be done. And that's fine. It gives me time to deal with things here. But don't take everything away from me at once. I can't cope with doing nothing. And in that vein, I want to circle this whole thing back to why I actually wanted to talk to y'all."

Maggie waited until she was certain they weren't going to digress again. "As you know, Mom's estate is finally out of probate, and I've been going over what assets we still retain. Among those assets is the old lumber mill. It was built by the same guy who built the house. From what I've been able to dig up, it was a pretty big deal back in the day, one of the busiest mills in the region, at least until TVA got involved."

"TVA?" Ari asked.

"The Tennessee Valley Authority. It was a reform passed in the 1930s to address flooding issues due to massive and rapid deforestation as a result of over-cutting. In their efforts to get the flooding under control, they ended up diverting the river that turned the wheel that powered the place. Without a major overhaul to convert it to more traditional electricity, the whole place was left nonfunctional. Our family timber baron couldn't afford to do that by then because he was more or less land poor because of the Depression. So...the place has been just sitting there, unused all this time. And I think we should explore the possibilities."

"The possibilities for what, exactly?" Kennedy asked.

"I don't know yet. I need to see the place first. See what's left of the building. What the lay of the land is. Which is all easier said than done. The access road was overgrown years ago. Porter's going to take me out there this afternoon to check it out."

Another beat of silence passed as they looked at each other.

Irritation prickled. "What?"

"You're gonna hike?" Pru asked.

"I'm sorry, did y'all all forget that I'm from here?"

Athena looked askance in her direction. "I mean no, but it's not like you've been hiking in anything but high heels in years."

"I am aware, but it's not like I've forgotten how it works."

"Should you be doing that, though?" Kennedy asked. "I mean, aren't you meant to be resting?"

"This isn't a pilgrimage up the Appalachian Trail. It's just a walk. Fresh air and exercise is good for me. And I promise, Porter isn't about to let me overdo either. Genevieve read him the riot act before we came home. I was going to see if I could borrow a pair of hiking boots from Kennedy. We're still the same size, aren't we?"

"We are, and of course you can."

"Excellent. Now that that's settled, let's go over the rest of the details of the estate."

* * *

"Here." Athena plunked a backpack on the kitchen counter, startling Maggie from where she was lacing up her borrowed boots.

"What is this?"

"A thank you."

Surprised, Maggie unzipped the bag to peek inside at the series of neatly stacked plastic containers and a bottle of sparkling lemonade. "For what?"

"For about a million things. For all your help with the business side of *The Misfit Kitchen*. For everything you've taken on since Mom died so the rest of us didn't have to. For being the one who always understood me best. Maybe for that last part most of all. I didn't fully appreciate it, not until I found Logan. I just realized you've always been that for me, and I'm really glad you're here now and that we're getting some time before life changes again, and I wanted to do something for you."

She said the last in a rush of breath, as if she wouldn't be able to finish if she didn't get it all out at once. It was the longest emotional speech Maggie had ever heard from her sister. Athena had always considered *feelings* to be a four letter word, one she avoided at all costs. Logan might have given up therapy for farming, but he was absolutely rubbing off on Athena.

"So you made me a picnic?"

"Well, you couldn't be trusted. You'd have just made a couple of sandwiches and called it done."

As that was exactly what she'd planned to do, Maggie just arched a brow. "What's wrong with sandwiches?"

With an irritated huff, Athena crossed her arms. "There is nothing romantic about sandwiches."

Equal parts moved and amused, she wrapped her sister in a hug. "Being with Logan has changed you." At Athena's indrawn breath—no doubt to protest—Maggie pushed on. "Just a little, in the very best way."

Athena opened her mouth as if to argue, then relaxed. "Yeah, I guess I have. I feel...different with him."

"A little softer?"

"I mean, don't be going crazy now." She shifted, running a kitchen towel through her hands. "He gets me—like, really gets me."

"I know." Knowing Athena was with a guy who saw clear through her prickly exterior was a serious comfort. "He's been good for you."

Athena fixed uncharacteristically serious gray eyes on her. "I want that for you. I want you to be as happy as the rest of us."

The sucker punch of her words left Maggie breathless. What could she say? *I want that, too.* She did. Of course she did. Surrounded on all sides by solid, loving relationships, Maggie couldn't help but look at this thing with Porter and wonder if this could be it for her. No question, he understood her like no one else. And in the stretches when she could stay in the present instead of getting lost in the past or worried about the future, she was happy.

The front door opened. "Maggie?" Porter's voice echoed from the foyer.

"In the kitchen." Giving Athena a grateful squeeze, she stepped back.

"You ready? Oh, hey, Athena."

"Porter."

He eyed the bag. "What's that?"

"Your lunch. You're welcome. Now both of you get out of my kitchen." Athena made shooing motions with her hands.

"Yes, Chef." Laughing, Porter scooped up the bag and grabbed Maggie's hand.

The moment his fingers closed around hers, she felt some of the tension ease. She could enjoy this, enjoy him, without worrying about a five-year plan. So she consciously let go of the rest as they stepped out onto the porch.

Eying the gray sky, scudded with clouds, she hesitated. "Are you sure we should still do this today?" Getting caught in a downpour wasn't high on her list of things to do.

Porter swung an arm around her shoulders, following her gaze. "It'll be fine. At most, it'll be one of those little pop-up showers. And we ought to be well clear of things by then. Besides, it'd be a shame to let this fancy picnic, prepared by our resident chef, go to waste."

"True enough."

He hustled her to his truck, opening her door like the gentleman he was and making her heart skip a beat as he leaned in for a quick kiss under the guise of snapping her seatbelt on.

"Hi." His grin was boyish and carefree, something Maggie realized she hadn't seen on him in years. She wanted to taste that freedom.

Before she could overthink it, she framed his face and took that smiling mouth in a longer, more exploratory kiss. He didn't touch her, but she could feel his body tighten as it leaned into hers. That simmer of heat was still there, still beyond intriguing. Not just a product of a night of quiet confidences. Satisfied with that for now, she eased back.

His eyes were dark, his pupils blown wide. "What was that for?"

"Because I really like seeing you smile."

The corners of that mouth quirked up again. "Plenty of

reason for me to do that when I'm spending the rest of the day with you."

Oh yeah, she could get used to that kind of sweet talking.

He climbed behind the wheel and drove the few miles toward town. "We're gonna take the old access road in. There are other, prettier hikes, but they're more difficult and I'm pretty sure Genevieve would have my balls if I let you overdo it. So the mile-and-a-half trek it is."

Maggie didn't see much reason to argue with that. She wasn't in anything resembling her best shape. A mile and a half sounded like a comfortable distance to tromp in borrowed boots.

At what amounted to the trailhead, Porter shrugged into the pack with the food and held out his hand again. "C'mon. It's all grown up through here, but it's an easy enough shot."

She laced her fingers with his. She didn't think she'd ever get tired of the easy way his big hand wrapped around hers. It was such a simple gesture, and a chaste one at that, but it made her feel safe and cared for. For so long, she'd been the one looking out for everyone else. It was nice having someone look out for her.

They stepped into the trees, which didn't look like any kind of access road she'd ever seen.

"Are you sure this was a road?"

"Yep. You can see the edges of the roadbed just there." He pointed out the rise on either side of where they walked. "Mother nature's had the better part of a century to retake everything. But you can still see there's a sort of natural tunnel the way the older growth trees around it arch over."

They soared high overhead, knitting into a canopy that thrust them into a deep green sort of twilight. But smaller, newer trees had grown up all along the path, spearing up from what had once been hard-packed dirt and gravel. Over the years, weather and decaying vegetation had made a layer of new soil, providing home for the same undergrowth that stretched over the rest of the mountains in the area.

She stepped carefully over a root, her brain already calculating angles and expenses. "For this property to be used for anything at all, someone would have to clear the road out. Or put a new one in for access. Maybe I'm fooling myself. The mill itself can't be in any kind of decent condition, given the shape of the road."

"You might be surprised. A lot of the timber structures of that time period were built of American chestnut, which is amazingly rot resistant. Demand for it is part of what led to the massive over-cutting of the region."

She shot him a glance. "Look at you with the history lesson."

"You aren't the only one who can do homework." His self-satisfied grin was adorable. "What'd your sisters say about the idea of doing something with the mill?"

"Not a whole lot. They were more interested in talking about us."

He chuckled. "Athena didn't waste any time, did she?"

"Not a bit."

I want that for you. I want you to be as happy as the rest of us. Athena's words played through Maggie's mind on repeat. She could be happy with Porter. She *was* happy out here with him, strolling through the woods on a fall afternoon. But nothing was that simple.

"Guess I should have picked you up first thing this morning to save you from the Inquisition."

"It wouldn't have mattered. They'd have just pinned me down when I got back. And anyway, I distracted them well enough when I told them about my adrenal fatigue. After which point it took a lot of talking to convince them all I wasn't about to die."

He winced. "It's better that they know."

"I know. Apart from the fact that they'd start to wonder why I wasn't going back to work, I had to tell them something. The idea that I'd get involved with you and promptly head back to California would've gotten me excommunicated from the family." She shot a wry smile in his direction. "They're very invested in this."

"Are they pressuring you about staying?" There was something in his tone that wasn't quite right.

"No. They assume that I'll be here through the end of the year because of you."

Maggie felt the change in the air, the subtle tension in his hand and turned to catch him blanking his face. He hummed a noncommittal noise and didn't look at her. Surely he didn't think she was leaving. But now that she'd seen behind his mask, she recognized the unnaturally neutral expression. Digging in her heels, she tugged him to a stop. "Porter."

He turned toward her, that awful not-Real-Porter face firmly in place. "Yeah?"

God, it hurt her to see it. To realize he felt like he still had reason to use it with her.

"I know I originally said I'd only make it here for a few weeks. But that was before this." She squeezed his hand, searching his face for some kind of understanding. "I'm not going to run back to California. I wouldn't do that to you."

The mask cracked and he closed his eyes. "Thank God. I didn't want to push you."

"There is a very big difference between letting me set the pace and not having the basic expectations of a relationship. I promised we'd give this a try, and I meant it. I can't do that if I'm not here."

His eyes popped open again. "So we're in a relationship." His tone wasn't quite blasé enough, and it made her smile.

"That is what I was under the impression we were doing, yes.

We're not casual dating sort of people. And even if we were, I think there's too much history here to make that possible."

"Good." Porter pulled her in, resting his brow against hers, and the sick feeling in her stomach waned. "Sometimes it's hard to know what the right thing is. I've been living with these feelings for you for so long, it'd be easy to skip about a hundred steps. But I know you need time to catch up. And I don't say that as some other kind of pressure. I just need to know if I misstep."

"I don't think you've ever made a misstep when it comes to me. Not really." The idea that this man, of all people, would misstep was laughable. He always did things exactly right, just as she needed. How often could someone say that? He saw her, understood her, and she was coming to appreciate what a true gift that was.

He tugged her into motion again. "C'mon. Let's keep walking while you still think I'm perfect."

She laughed, as she knew he wanted. But her thoughts were still on what he'd said. He was being so open and honest about what he felt for her. Didn't he deserve some vulnerability from her in return?

"It seems only fair to mention...I have less catching up to do than you might imagine."

His hand tensed in hers before releasing again. "Yeah?"

Nerves made her own hands shake. But this was Porter. If she couldn't be honest with him, she couldn't be honest with anyone. "I've felt things for you for years. I just...tried to convince myself it was because of circumstance. Because you were so kind and amazing and doing everything as if it was your baby. And then after, I didn't imagine it could be reciprocated. Not really. I thought you'd realize it had just been circumstance too, and that I'd saved you from yourself. So I left."

She stayed quiet as he absorbed that, marveling that even now their silences weren't uncomfortable.

"What would you have done if I'd said something sooner?"

She shrugged. "I don't know. And that's not a healthy game of what if to play. I think maybe I had to be knocked down again before I was in a place to lower my defenses enough to hear you. Anyway, I didn't mean to turn things all serious again. I just wanted to say that I'm not starting from zero here."

He turned to face her, so much hope and joy shining in his eyes, she could physically feel it, like sunshine soaking into cold bones. Everything in her swayed toward him, wanting more. More of his adoration. More of his touch. More of this feeling like everything was possible. Like nothing else mattered but this pull between them. It would be so, so easy to just dive headlong into all of it. But they were neither of them made for no strings attached affairs, and she'd learned long ago never to just leap.

* * *

Slow the hell down, Ingram.

But it was hard, so hard, when the woman he loved had just admitted she had feelings for him. That she had for *years*. Everything in him wanted to take that and run with it, not wasting another second. Because Maggie Reynolds loving him back had been his holy grail, and for the first time, the possibility of a real future with her finally felt like it was within his grasp. He could see the yearning on her face, feel her responding to the pull between them. But he also saw her hesitation. Read that flicker of uncertainty in her eyes as she processed and analyzed and turned over all the angles. She was still learning to trust—herself and what she felt as much as him. Not starting from zero didn't mean she was fully caught up either.

You can be patient a while longer. She's worth it.

He lifted her hand and brushed a kiss across her knuckles. "Good to know." The sky rumbled, somewhat closer than he

119

liked. "We should get moving. Don't want to get caught in the rain."

They lapsed into a weighted but comfortable silence. Porter couldn't help but feel like they'd turned some corner. She wouldn't have made the admission if she didn't feel it, and she wouldn't be worried about it if she wasn't thinking ahead to what it meant, how it could work. That meant the idea of a them beyond this sabbatical was at least on the table. So he held on to that as they hoofed it the rest of the way down the access road.

The forest had encroached on most of the rest of the lumber yard, but the mill itself sat on the rise, a throwback to another time, with its stone and wood construction. Set into the slope, the whole building stood three stories from bottom to top. It made a picture, if a lonely one, with the clouds boiling gray above them. Looked like the rain was gonna hit sooner rather than later.

"It's beautiful. I didn't imagine a mill could be beautiful," Maggie breathed.

"A new one probably wouldn't be. But back then, yeah." The place had been built at a time when craftsmanship still meant something.

"From here, it looks like anybody could just come along and start the whole thing up again."

"Not without that waterwheel." The riverbed had gone dry, but for a small pool just beneath the wheel.

As if his words had tripped a switch, the sky rumbled with thunder and rain began to spit.

"Better run for it!" Before he could argue, Maggie had tugged free and was sprinting across the weedy lawn.

By the time they slipped inside, it had begun to rain in earnest. They narrowly avoided getting completely soaked.

Maggie scooped her wet hair back and looked out at the sheets of driving rain. "Well, I guess we're here for a while. We should look around."

Porter snagged her hand again. "Hold up. We have no idea how stable this floor is. Let me go first." He paused to dig out a flashlight.

They'd entered on the second floor, what had been the main mill space. Most of the equipment had been pulled years ago, probably sold when the mill had been shut down, but he could see where the saw lines had been. Moving slow and careful, he tested the floor, pleased when it barely groaned beneath his weight. Satisfied neither of them was likely to crash through it, he led Maggie through the building. Though there were signs of mice and birds having gotten inside, it didn't seem like weather had made the place too much worse for wear. No signs of major leaks, even as the rain drummed steadily on the tin roof. They made their way downstairs to the basement area that housed the workings of the waterwheel and, it turned out, a collection of old barrels tucked away against the side of the building carved into the mountainside.

"Looks like they had a cooperage down here. Randall Parsons would totally be into that. He makes them the old-fashioned way in his workshop."

"Most of that's probably done by machine these days, I guess," Maggie observed.

They wandered back to the second floor and started to check out the third, but Porter drew the line at either of them climbing the old wooden ladder leading up to it. "We should have our picnic and wait out the storm."

They found a clear spot, where gray light streamed in from the high windows, and he unrolled the tarp and blanket from the pack, glad he'd had them in his truck for extra padding.

Maggie dropped down and immediately pulled off her boots and socks. "Do you suppose they've got a prayer of drying before we leave?"

"As long as they aren't completely soaked and you aren't in a hurry, there's a chance." Porter sat beside her and followed suit, setting his boots and socks to the side.

He expected her to start unpacking the food, but instead she stretched out, propping her head on one hand. "In your estimation, is the structural integrity intact?"

Stretching out himself, he tugged her closer, loving when she tangled her legs with his and snuggled closer. "In that it's not going to crash down on our heads while we're in here, yes."

"For purposes of conversion. Is it a solid enough structure that it could be converted rather than torn down?"

He snaked his hand beneath the hem of her damp shirt, finding a narrow swatch of skin to trace with his fingers. "You've clearly got something in mind. So spill."

Her eyes dropped to half-mast, and she arched into his touch. The low hum of pleasure resonating in her throat had his brain veering off the conversation and on to whether she'd let him warm her up some other way.

"There are a ton of variables that would have to line up, but I think this could be used as the site for the maker's space."

Porter stilled, dragging his brain back to what she was saying. "This is a helluva lot bigger than what they were imagining."

"Well, I'm thinking bigger. Not just a maker's space but a full artisan center. Something with classrooms where people could teach their crafts, booths for a retail space, maybe even a small museum. We could convert this into a facility that really showcases the artisans in the area. A space that houses a formalized artisan guild as an organization."

Tipping his head back, Porter looked around, already considering how it could be done, what the outlay might be. This kind of project, converting something old into something new, was his absolute favorite thing to do. "It's a brilliant concept, and I think it'd be a serious boon to the area if you could pull it off. But why this?"

"It would be a significant tourist draw. One that, I think, might do more for Eden's Ridge than the resort because it's unique. There's nothing like it anywhere in the area, and it does something to preserve our heritage and history. And it fits a demonstrated need, not only for the artists and crafters in the area, but also for you."

"Me?"

"There's no telling whether the mayor will manage to secure new funding for the resort. I *know* I can find funding for this. And there's no one else I'd trust with the renovation. Think about it. It could be an amazing project." Her eyes lit with unbridled enthusiasm. "We'd have so much fun with it."

We.

Porter loved the sound of that. Loved that she wanted to do something like this to give back to the town. He tried to caution himself that this didn't mean she was coming home for good. It didn't mean she'd be here to head up the project from start to finish, even if she did pull off the miracle of funding for an undertaking of this scope. But she was thinking about the immediate future, at least, and in it they were together. That was good enough for him. It would have to be. For now.

"I think if anybody can pull it off, it's you. But—"

Maggie frowned. "I don't like 'but'."

"Does this really fit in with the whole rest and relaxation thing you're supposed to be doing?"

"If all y'all think I'm going to lay around on a beach, drinking something out of a coconut with little umbrellas and doing nothing but binge-watching Netflix all day, then you might as well put me in the nearest loony bin."

Porter fought a smile. "I think you're mixing your metaphors."

"Whatever. The point is, I can't do *nothing*. I *will* go nuts. Planning and organizing stuff is fun for me. And I know it looks a lot like work to everybody else. But believe me, this has been so much slower than my normal life. No more sixteen-hour days. I'm sleeping properly for the first time in I don't know how long. Athena's shoving food at me at every turn, so I'm not missing meals. I promise, I'm behaving. If I don't do this, I'll just come up with something else. I'd rather it be something that matters. And, if I'm really honest, I want to do this for an entirely selfish reason."

"Which is?"

Something vulnerable crept into those big brown eyes. "I want to give this town something else to talk about."

Even if he hadn't been about to say yes, that would have done it. She deserved the chance to rise above the lowest common gossip. And maybe, if he helped her conquer this, she'd finally be able to conquer the demons that had kept her so far from home all these years.

"Okay. If this is what you want to do with the place, I'll do everything I can to help you."

Maggie beamed and cuddled against him. "Thank you."

"But—"

She rocked back, pulling a face. "That word again."

"We do this together. Partners. You're not going to take on All The Things just because you can."

"I can agree to that."

"Good." And he'd just make certain that every step that involved the courthouse or the mayor fell on his to-do list, so she was kept as far from Bradley Danforth as possible. "So what's the first step?"

She arched one delicate brow. "Really?"

"I mean, I figure you'll want to dive right in. That's usually how you operate."

"True, but I got what I wanted out of this trip. I can take my time with this." She pressed a hand to his chest, trailing one finger slowly down between his pecs. "For now, I do believe we've achieved the lack of audience you wanted." Her voice had gone husky and her hand slipped around to mirror his position, her fingers stroking the skin of his back. The simple touch seemed to go straight to his dick.

He wanted to roll her beneath him, settle into the cradle of her hips, and make her cry out his name. But that wasn't why he'd brought her out here. No matter what he felt, he wouldn't do anything to scare her off. So he fought to pull himself back, to keep his tone light and flirty as he leaned forward and brushed his lips to hers.

"I do love the way you think."

Chapter Ten

The moment Maggie stepped through the door of Crystal's Diner, her stomach twisted into a queasy knot. Not from the scents of frying bacon, home fries, and coffee, but from the almost synchronized stares of the breakfast patrons. She'd thought it wouldn't be this bad at nine on a weekday, but evidently she'd underestimated the senior crowd's desire to linger over crossword puzzles and bottomless cups of joe.

I should have asked Dahlia to meet me at the house.

Except she'd wanted to get away from the inn for a bit. Athena had the guests covered this morning, and Kennedy was helping out at the spa. They'd all be on duty to clean and turn rooms once she got back, so this was the time she had.

A quick scan of the tables showed that Dahlia hadn't made it yet. Maggie was a little early. She considered stepping back outside and waiting on one of the benches intermittently placed along Main Street, but that felt too much like retreat. She hadn't been a coward in high school, and she sure as hell wasn't one now. For the next few months, this was home, and she had nothing to be ashamed of. Straightening her shoulders, she headed for an empty booth.

Almost as soon as her butt hit the cracked vinyl seat, Crystal herself materialized with the coffee pot. "Hey there, sugar. What can I get you?"

"Morning, Crystal. Just coffee for now. Black, please."

The older woman flipped one of the cups ready and waiting on the table and poured without looking. "You meeting Porter this morning?"

Maggie had known word would get around about them, especially as he'd been so intent on being so public and visible with their relationship. Certainly, in the past couple of weeks, they'd been out and about together several times. Yet somehow, that casual assumption caught her by surprise.

It seemed as if conversation dropped several more decibels, waiting on her answer. One hand clenched on the purse at her side. "No, he's visiting job-sites today. I'm having breakfast with a friend."

Crystal straightened the coffee pot without spilling a drop. "Good deal. You let me know when you're ready. And let me just say how good it is to see you home and to know you and Porter are getting a second chance. It does my heart good to see it."

Maggie opened her mouth to correct her, but Dahlia slid into the opposite side of the booth. "Morning! Oh coffee, thank God. I'm behind on caffeinating this morning." As Crystal filled her cup, too, Dahlia flashed Maggie an I've-got-you-girl wink. "Crystal, did you hear the latest about Miss Dottie's grandson?"

"No!"

The two of them made idle chitchat, while Maggie tried to kick her brain back in gear.

"I'll just give y'all a minute to look over the menu."

As Crystal walked back toward the kitchen, Dahlia finally focused on Maggie. "You look bumfuzzled."

"I guess I am a little. How many people think that's what this is with Porter? A second chance instead of our first?"

"Dunno. You two were tight back then. Plenty of assumptions were made. Does it bother you?"

"It's not like it's a hardship to have my name linked to his. He's a good man, and everyone knows it. And he's a man, so it's not like they're going to drag *him* through the mud the same way they did me. Either way, it hardly matters. People are going to say what they're going to say, with no particular regard for the truth, and this version is far less horrible than what people usually spout about me. At least Crystal's happy for us."

"Add me to that list, too. Whatever go round this is for you two, you seem happy together, and that's really great to see. Y'all both deserve it."

"Thank you. Things with Porter are good." Better than good. So comfortable, it felt as if they'd been together for years, not weeks. And maybe, in a sense, with their long history, they had. Just...without any of the benefits. And she was really enjoying the benefits.

Nothing about being with him was like any of her failed dating attempts. She was starting to realize that the difference was all about trust. She'd known she trusted him. After half a lifetime of standing by her, how could she not? But trusting him with her body and maybe her heart was a whole different thing. It meant letting down walls and finally, *finally* being in the moment, where she could enjoy being a normal woman in her prime, enjoy having an interesting, attractive, attentive man look at her as if the sun rose and set in her eyes. Enjoy being able to kiss him, touch him, be touched by him, without shutting down. That was getting easier, less scary. It was enough to make her drunk. To make her yearn for more.

Dahlia pursed her lips. "I'm thinking 'good' is an understatement by the look on your face just now."

Heat crept over Maggie's cheeks and her gaze dipped to the menu. "We're taking things slowly," she muttered.

"Nothing wrong with that. And it's not like you don't have plenty of time since you moved home."

"I haven't."

"Wait, what? But I thought..." Dahlia shook her head. "Well, I guess it doesn't matter what I thought. How long are you here for?"

"I'm on an extended sabbatical from work until January."

Maggie could easily read the curiosity about why in her eyes, but that wasn't what Dahlia asked.

"So this thing with Porter?"

"Wasn't planned."

She grinned. "Did he finally just kiss the bejeezus out of you?"

"Oh, please say yes," Crystal breathed, her order pad clutched to her chest.

Maggie just arched a brow and picked up her coffee. "A girl doesn't kiss and tell."

Someone from the other side of the diner whispered, "She certainly never did."

Maggie clenched the mug and indulged in a brief fantasy of hurling it toward the speaker with a shriek. Instead, she set it very carefully back on the table. "Can I get the mushroom omelet with a side of bacon, please?"

With a moue of disappointment, Crystal took their orders and disappeared back into the kitchen.

Dahlia leaned closer, her chin propped in one hand. "You were saying."

Maggie lowered her voice. "There's always been...something...between us. I guess we hit the 'if not now, then when' point. So, we're seeing where it goes."

"Wow. So...what happens if things get serious?"

That was where her brain went off the rails. Because a future with Porter meant giving up the life she'd worked so hard to build, and she wasn't ready to make that kind of decision.

"Honestly, I've been trying not to think about it. It's too much pressure, and our relationship is too new. We'll cross that bridge when and if we get there."

"Fair enough. But you'll forgive me if I totally hope you get there and come home."

"Yeah, I'm getting a lot of that from my sisters, too, especially with my latest project."

Dahlia drummed her fingers together. "Ooo, what kind of project?"

"One that I was hoping you could help me with. That's actually part of why I asked you to breakfast this morning. I want your opinion as an artisan."

"Okay. Lay it on me."

Maggie told her about the mill and what she envisioned for it, gratified as her friend's eyes went wider and wider.

"Wow. That's...ambitious. I mean, you're you, so that's not a shock. But still. Wow. A place like that would be absolutely incredible."

"Do you think other artisans in the area would be into it?"

"Absolutely. Seriously, the concept is genius. And I really think the idea of formalizing an artisan guild is a great idea one way or the other. How can I help?"

"There's no way I can pull this off, and no point in even trying, unless I can get buy-in from most of the crafters and artisans in the area. I was hoping you'd have some suggestions about the best way to approach them. I could get a list of people from Misty and talk to them individually, but that would be inefficient and time consuming. I'm hoping to start moving on this pretty quickly."

"The quickest way would be to speak at the next meeting.

We meet once a month, usually at the Methodist Church fellowship hall, to sort out the details for the Artisan Supper."

"When's the next meeting?"

"In two weeks."

Maggie smiled. "How do you think they'd feel about a change in venue?"

* * *

Porter eyed the barely touched food on Maggie's plate. Over the past twenty minutes, she'd made a good show of pushing it around and rearranging, without actually putting much in her mouth. "Athena's going to be offended."

With an apprehensive look toward the back door, Maggie scraped the food into the trash and slid the plate onto the stack of dirty dishes waiting to be loaded into the dishwasher. "It's not the food. I'm too amped up to eat." She laced her fingers together in an uncharacteristic show of nerves.

Needing to put her more at ease, he pulled her in, lacing his hands at the small of her back. "You ready for this?" She'd been working on it for weeks. He couldn't imagine there was anything she'd left undone.

Maggie leaned into him on a sigh. "I'm prepared. Which isn't the same thing as ready."

"You're not usually anxious about presentations, are you?" He'd never seen her be anything but fearless at public speaking.

"No. But this feels important. Big somehow in a way it usually doesn't. Which is ridiculous. I regularly negotiate multi-million-dollar corporate contracts without a qualm. A few dozen crafters and artisans should be nothing."

The fifty or so people gathered around tables on the back lawn of the inn weren't nothing, and they both knew it.

"It's personal. Not only because this involves your family's property, but because it means facing down the locals."

"Yeah. Yeah, it does." She rose to her toes just enough to press her cheek to his, sliding her arms around his shoulders, and he reveled in the fact that she'd reached a point where she'd do that, just take the comfort she needed without question.

"Look, I know you hate having to deal with them. But why let gossipy assholes impact your life? You're a successful, brilliant, take-no-prisoners woman, who can have whatever she sets her mind to. Don't give them the satisfaction of belittling you."

He felt her spine straighten and when she lifted her chin, her eyes sparked with determination. "You're right. I'm no sniveling coward."

"Damned straight. You're Maggie Reynolds, and you've got this."

Someone knocked on the doorjamb. Porter glanced up to see Mia in the doorway to the kitchen. "Hey! You made it!"

"Sorry I'm late. I needed to shower off several layers of work." She crossed over, eyes fixed on Maggie. "You must be Maggie."

"And you must be Mia. It's so nice to finally meet you. I was beginning to think Porter was making you up."

Mia laughed and took Maggie's offered hand. "No. I've been running a home renovation in the south end of the county for the last month, so I haven't been around too much. But I love your ideas for the mill." She jerked a thumb in Porter's direction. "This one talks about you all the time. It's nice to put a face with the goo-goo eyes."

Offended on behalf of his man card, Porter straightened his shoulders. "I do *not* have goo-goo eyes."

"You totally do. It's adorable," Ari proclaimed as she carried a tray of desserts out the back door.

He scowled. "Brat."

"Try living here. My entire family is watching us like we're their own personal episode of *The Bachelorette*."

"Well, if you'd just give him a rose already," Athena muttered, hefting another tray.

Maggie narrowed her eyes. "You just catered this meeting for me, so I'm not going to dignify that with the response it deserves."

Athena stuck her tongue out as she followed Ari out the door.

Mia snickered. "It must be entertaining to have sisters."

Maggie rolled her eyes. "That's one word for it."

Porter thought back to the regular insanity that had been a part of living among the ragtag and rotating group of misfits collected by Joan Reynolds. "It wasn't dull growing up in this house. Couldn't be with twelve kids under one roof."

"Twelve?" Mia goggled.

"I think that was the peak at any given point during my time here," Porter said.

"We once got up to thirteen, but that didn't last long," Maggie put in.

"It's hard to imagine that many foster kids in one house. The most we had at any of my placements was four. Although I think Brax had one with more. He didn't stay there long."

Mia seldom talked about her past in more than generalities. Porter figured this guy must have been someone important. "Brax?"

Her dark eyes flashed with pain for just a moment before she dug up a wry smile. "Let's just say you aren't the only one who fell for one of your foster siblings."

"Ah. Mr. It's Complicated?"

"Got it in one."

Well that explained a lot.

Before he could pursue it, Kennedy sailed in. "The natives are getting restless. I think it's about time to get this show on the road. The projector is all set up and ready to go when you are."

Maggie sucked in a breath, knotting her hands again.

Porter untangled them, lacing his fingers with hers. "You've got this."

She nodded.

"A kiss for luck?" he asked.

A smile cracked through her anxious expression. "I need my brain for this presentation, thanks."

On a laugh, he kissed her hands. "Knock 'em dead."

They all trailed her outside, where the alfresco meeting of the area artisans had been set up on the back lawn. People had turned out in droves, many out of sheer curiosity, maybe more for Athena's food. It was a smart move on Maggie's part. The food got people's butts in chairs long enough to listen to her pitch. She'd already put in a ton of work on the concept over the past few weeks since they'd visited the mill. There was always the possibility it would be time wasted, if the guild didn't go for the idea. But Porter had faith that she'd sway them. They only had to give her half a chance.

Porter and Mia found seats toward the back as Misty Pennebaker made introductions.

"On behalf of our group, let me just say thank you for offering up this beautiful location and this amazing food for our meeting. Everybody, let's give our hostess a big round of applause."

Maggie offered up a gracious smile and nod, waiting for the noise to die away. "Thank you all for coming. I'm no artistan or crafter, so I'm sure you're all wondering why I offered to host tonight's meeting. The fact is, I met quite a few of you at last month's Artisan Supper, and y'all told me about the maker's space y'all want to put together. It's an admirable goal, but I think that if we all work together, we can accomplish something a lot bigger. Something that has the potential to impact each and every one of you, along with future generations."

She flipped on her powerpoint and began. As she warmed up to her spiel, Porter couldn't help but think how sexy she was, exuding all that confidence. She was a natural-born leader. He'd always seen that, been drawn to it. But everything she'd been through her senior year had dimmed that light, encasing it in a lacquered shell. It was a helluva thing to see her come alive again, secure in the knowledge that she was offering something of worth.

Mia nudged him with her elbow and smirked. "You are a hundred percent gone on this woman."

"I have absolutely no shame about that," he whispered.

"I admire the hell out of that. And her. You've got excellent taste, my friend. She's amazing."

"Yes, she is."

They weren't the only ones to think so. All around them, guild members were nodding, getting fired up by the idea. They lobbed questions in her direction, and Maggie fielded them like the pro she was, with a lot more information than they'd been expecting because his girl was prepared.

"Well, hold on now." Willard Samson spoke up. "We've been hearing all kinds of promises about jobs and tourism related to the Paradise Mountain Resort and it's been damned near two years with nothin'. Why should we get excited about this or think it's any more likely to happen? I mean, why exactly, should we trust *your* judgment? You don't exactly have the best track record."

Maggie stiffened. "Excuse me?"

He crossed his arms. "I'm just sayin', you don't have the reputation for making the smartest decisions."

In a flash, Porter was eighteen again, hustling Maggie out of the grocery store because this asshole and his wife had actively tugged their little girl away to another aisle, like even being in Maggie's presence was going to taint her. She'd been devastated by their cruelty, barely containing her tears until they'd made it to his truck.

One glance at Maggie at the front of the crowd made it clear she remembered, too and recognized Willard's bullshit for the insult it was. Her face was pale but for the two bright splotches of color burning high in her cheeks and her hands were shaking. This was exactly what she'd been afraid of in coming home. Having her mistake thrown back in her face.

Vibrating with fury, Porter's own hands curled to fists, and he'd already taken two steps toward Willard before Maggie lifted a hand in his direction, a clear order for him to stop. He recognized the war she fought within herself over what to say. Recognized, too, that no matter how much he wanted to act, she needed to fight this battle for herself.

She met his gaze, and Porter poured every ounce of strength and support he could into the contact.

You've got this, he mouthed.

One corner of her mouth quirked as she looked around the assembly. "How many people here have any idea what I do for a living? Raise your hands."

No one did.

"Let me give you a little background on my qualifications. I'm a corporate attorney and senior advisor for Invation." As a murmur of recognition went through the crowd, she nodded. "Yeah, that Invation. I have a bachelor's degree in business from Brown University, where I graduated second in my class after only three years. I have a law degree from Yale, where I also graduated in the top one percent of my class. I've spent the past five years negotiating multi-million- and multi-billion-dollar deals. I know business, and I have contacts with investors all over the country. Can I promise you everything will work out exactly as I've laid out here? No. But I can promise to leverage all of my expertise and connections in the name of trying, because I am lightyears away from being that high school girl you're so fond of remembering, so perhaps you could do me the courtesy of having a little faith."

Nobody said a word as Willard's face reddened under her stare. Porter had never been more proud of her.

Satisfied she'd made her point, Maggie's gaze came back to his. "Now I'd like to give the floor to Porter Ingram to show you some mockups of how the mill could be renovated."

He straightened and strode up to the front, accepting the clicker for the projector. Before she turned away, Maggie caught his hand, something more than gratitude in her eyes. A beat passed. Two. His heart gave a hard kick in his chest for reasons he couldn't quite name as she looked into his eyes and smiled. When she squeezed his hand and stepped away, it took him a few more seconds to pull his wits together to speak.

"Right, so I've got a few ideas for how the space could be converted."

He took them through it, keeping his eye on Maggie at the edge of the crowd, answering questions, making a few notes based on suggestions from various craftsmen. At one point she slipped away, and he stumbled a bit, wondering if someone else had said something. But she was back by the time he'd finished, no sign of upset on her face or in her posture as she re-joined him, taking over the presentation as if they'd planned it this way.

"If you're interested in seeing this project become a reality, please sign the petition being circulated by my sisters before you leave. There's also a second sign-up sheet for those of you interested in formalizing into a recognized artisan guild, which I can certainly help you do, either way. Any other questions, jot them down, and we'll get back to you as soon as we have some kind of an answer. Thank you for coming out tonight!"

Surprised at her abrupt wrap-up, Porter didn't hesitate to follow when she jerked her head toward the kitchen.

As soon as they were inside, he reached for her hand again. "What's going on?"

In answer, she tugged him into the foyer. A single rose sat on the entryway table. He recognized it as one of the climbers Joan had coaxed up a trellis on the side of the house.

Maggie picked it up and turned toward him. "For you."

He took it automatically, his pulse tripping into a gallop as he remembered Athena's flip comment earlier in the evening. "I don't want to misinterpret this."

"I'm not a romantic, so I'll just be direct." Crouching, she scooped up a small bag from beneath the table. "I want to go home with you. And if we want to make it out of here without hearing from the peanut gallery, we need to escape now."

Sending up prayers of thanks, Porter yanked open the front door. "I'm driving."

Chapter Eleven

Maggie couldn't quite breathe on the drive to Porter's house. But it wasn't anxiety snapping in her blood—it was anticipation. Her body fairly sang with it, wanting to touch and be touched and get lost in the kind of heat she'd stopped imagining years ago.

She kept waiting for her phone to blow up in response to the quickly fired off text to Athena.

*Home tomorrow. *rose emoji**

Porter glanced at her from the driver's seat "You okay? We can turn around if you've changed your mind."

"If you turn around, I might have to kill you." She didn't want to turn around. She didn't want to slow down. She didn't want the chance to get lost in her head and think about all the what ifs and whys and hows. She just wanted to be with him.

His low laugh seemed to stroke over her skin like a touch. "Understood. And can I just say, 'Thank God.' But I meant what I said before. You're in control here. If you need me to back off, I will."

Sweet, frustratingly patient man.

"Porter, I love this honorable streak of yours, but what I need is to be naked and sweaty in the next fifteen minutes. Bonus points if it's against the inside of your front door." God, just the idea of that had heat pooling low in her belly.

"Fuck me," he groaned.

"That is the general idea."

The truck leapt forward as he hit the gas.

She wanted to trail her hand up his thigh and find out if he was as aroused as she was. But there were too many switchbacks between here and his house, and she didn't dare risk distracting him any more from driving.

"At the risk of blowing the mood, why tonight?"

Why indeed? "Because you reminded me that I won't break. That I can face down all my demons and their bullshit and come out whole on the other side. Because I did exactly that with Willard Samson, and it felt freaking amazing. It's the first time since I came home that I've really felt like *me*...grown-up, in-control, adult me. And I was able to do that because of you. Because you believe in me." It was an incredible high, one that overrode her natural caution and gave her the courage to ask for what she wanted. "It seemed like something worth celebrating."

"For the record, I don't think I've ever been prouder of you than I was watching you put Willard in his place."

"It was one of the most satisfying things I've ever done." She shot him a saucy grin. "Although I'm hoping to outdo that a few times over before tomorrow."

"God, I love a challenge."

A tiny voice in the back of her mind tried to whisper doubt. She was talking big talk, but she hadn't actually managed to get this far since high school.

Squeezing her eyes shut, she struck back at the anxiety. *Shut up.*

She wouldn't think about the past now. Not with Porter. She

wanted him more than she'd thought possible. He'd proved to her over and over that she wasn't broken. Given her the space to explore and test herself and what she felt for him. At every step, she'd expected fear and there'd been none—because it was Porter. Because she trusted him. And that trust made her brave.

His big, broad palm settled on her leg. Her mind zeroed in on the warm weight of his hand, so close and yet so far from where she wanted it. The twinge of anxiety faded as she absorbed the sensation, imagined him stroking beneath her skirt, higher and higher until he covered the heat between her thighs. The idea of it had her pulse picking up speed. Curling her hand over his, she dragged it a little bit higher.

His fingers flexed hard. "I've never had cause to regret building my place so high up on the ridge." Now he sounded as breathless as she felt.

"We'll appreciate the privacy once we get there."

"Damned straight." The hand on her thigh squeezed again as they leaned hard into the last curve before his driveway and her nipples went hard.

"Porter?"

"Yeah?"

"Have you spent as much time thinking about this as you did about kissing me?"

She felt his eyes on her again. "More. You've been the center of my fantasies for years."

Maggie met his eyes in the darkness of the cab. "I want all of them."

He nearly overshot the driveway, yanking the wheel hard at the last second so the tires screeched. Something thumped.

"Did you just take out your mailbox?"

"Don't know. Don't care." He didn't even try to get into the garage, instead slamming to a stop in the driveway and throwing the truck into park.

He grabbed her bag and they both stumbled out of the truck, meeting on the front walkway and sprinting for the front door. Her blood pounded a frantic rhythm. *Hurry. Hurry. Hurry.* He stabbed a code into the keypad on the lock and it disengaged. Then the door was open and he was yanking her inside, slamming it shut and dropping the bag he carried before backing her against the wood, his hips pressing into hers and leaving no doubt that he was every bit as turned on as she.

"Maggie." His voice shook, and she loved hearing him at the edge of control.

"Naked and sweaty, remember? I won't break." It was as much a reminder to herself as to him.

They dove at each other, stealing frantic, greedy kisses as their hands made quick work of clothes. He got her entirely naked before she managed more than his shirt, mostly because she'd paused to admire that expanse of bare chest and all the rippling muscle built by his work. When his gaze raked over her, fevered and hungry, a fresh bolt of lust shot through her.

"Christ, you're beautiful. I need to touch you."

"Then do. Everywhere."

Running both hands down her arms, he lifted them, braceleting her wrists and pinning them to the door above her head. "This okay?"

It felt delicious and decadent, as if she were on display only for him. Maggie loved it. "More than. Touch me, Porter."

His hands lit her up, sparking nerve endings as he explored and kneaded and possessed her. When his lips closed around her nipple and sucked, her legs trembled and she gasped out his name, dropping her arms to his magnificent shoulders and threading her fingers in his hair as much to brace herself as hold him closer.

"More. More." It became a chant that ended on a moan as he

finally, *finally* covered her mound and stroked his fingers through her folds.

"Christ, Maggie, you're so wet."

She tensed at the intimate touch, every muscle quivering. But it wasn't anxiety taking over, it was need. Deep, desperate need for more. For him. She dropped her head back against the door. "Please." If he didn't fill this aching inside her, she might die.

He didn't make her ask again. One thick finger slid into her and they both groaned.

"Okay?" he ground out.

"More." As the second finger filled her, she hissed out a, "Yes," and began to move. She rode his fingers with the same reckless speed he'd driven up the mountain, and when he shifted his thumb to rub at her clit, she shot straight over the peak and shattered.

If not for the press of his body against hers, she'd have slid right down the door to the floor.

"We need a bed." Porter slid his hands over her ass and under her legs to lift her.

"No."

He froze.

Maggie struggled to get her brain cells to fire, to reassure him. If he got her to a bed, he'd take his time with her, and she'd have too much chance to think and might freeze up. She didn't want to freeze. She wanted him inside her. With trembling hands, she reached for his belt. "Here."

His brow furrowed. "I don't think I can be gentle here."

"I don't want gentle right now. I just want you." When he didn't move, she lifted her hand to cup his cheek. "You've been waiting for this for twelve years. So have I."

"Maggie." His voice held a ragged edge that told her his control was fraying.

"We have all night to take our time. Right now, I want to

know you feel as desperate as I do. So stop holding back and give us what we both want." *Don't let me stop to overthink.*

Turning his head, he pressed a kiss to her palm. "I'll give you anything you want."

She knew he would, and that was a dangerously addictive power. "Then take me. Right here. Right now."

He'd stripped out of his jeans and boxers and snagged the condom from his wallet almost before she could blink. When he'd rolled it on, he caged her in against the door, close enough that his erection nudged her belly.

"Be sure," he growled.

Her body went molten again at the gravel in his voice.

"I am." Threading her fingers in the hair at his nape, she kissed him, pouring out everything she wasn't yet ready to say.

He lifted her, wrapping her legs around his waist and pressing her back against the door. The blunt head of him nudged her entrance, parting her, stretching her one slow inch at a time. Even after the first, screaming orgasm, she was tight, so tight, and he was almost too much. She had the fleeting, foolish thought that it had been so long, maybe things had grown back. Then he snapped his hips forward, and she lost her breath at the feel of him spreading her wide, filling her up. A completion, not an invasion.

"Christ, Maggie, you feel perfect."

As he began to move, she felt...whole for the first time in years, pinned against a door with him driving deep. Because this time, with this man, it was absolutely right. Something inside her broke free, a long-buried truth she'd tried too hard to deny. She loved him. Maybe she always had.

Pressing her face to his throat, she let go, crying out his name as she came hard around him, pulling him over the edge behind her. Wave after wave of pleasure crashed over them. By the end they were both sagging against the door, barely able to stay upright.

"Now we absolutely need a bed," he gasped.

"Okay."

When she thought he'd let her down, he simply turned and staggered down the hall toward his bedroom.

"I can walk. Probably," Maggie protested. But it was pretty amazing to be carted around as if she weighed nothing.

"You got your fantasy. Now I'm getting mine."

He dropped her on the bed with a bounce that had her giggling. "Did your fantasy have something to do with a trampoline?"

"Hold whatcha got. I'll be right back." He disappeared into the bathroom to take care of necessities. When he came back a minute later, glass of water in hand, she was still sprawled where she'd landed. "Hydration is important."

Maggie sat up and gulped down half. "Thanks."

Porter sank down beside her, hand settling on her bare thigh. "You okay? I tried hard not to be too rough, but you were awfully tight."

Some of the afterglow dimmed. She sipped at the water and didn't look at him. "That's to be expected after a twelve-year dry spell."

"Maggie," he breathed.

"Don't get weird about it. I told you before, I haven't ever had a functional relationship. Not until you. I couldn't, after what happened. I didn't trust anyone else."

"But you trusted me."

Every step of the way. He made it easy, being exactly what she needed, what she wanted. "Always."

He took her hand, drawing it to his heart. "Look at me."

Afraid of what she'd see in his face, she gripped the glass tight and lifted her gaze. The tenderness in his eyes all but undid her.

"I love you. And I'm humbled that you trust me enough for this."

Tell him. The words trembled on her tongue. But she swallowed them back. She couldn't tell him. Not yet. Saying it back would mean things to him. Commitments and a permanency she wasn't ready for. She couldn't say it until she had everything else figured out. Until or unless she knew she could stay.

But she could show him.

Setting the glass aside she framed his face, drawing his lips to hers in a long, lingering kiss. "Make love with me the rest of the night, Porter."

His arms came around her, pulling her close. "Anything you want."

* * *

Porter woke wrapped around a warm woman. The only thing that told him it wasn't a dream was the faint scent of jasmine in her hair and the rather insistent erection pressed up against her bare backside. For a moment, he instinctively tightened his hold, gently rocking his hips to test his chances of starting his day making love to her again. But Maggie didn't arch back against him. She didn't stir at all. And no wonder. It was only seven. They'd barely been asleep for two hours.

He'd spent the entire night making every inch of her thoroughly his, fulfilling as many of her fantasies and his own as he could manage. Between the two them, they had a lot. She'd exceeded all of his, and he hoped like hell that he'd been able to wipe out whatever memories she'd been carting around about her previous experience. Jesus. Twelve years. He didn't know how to feel about the fact that he was her first since then. It was a big fucking deal that she'd trusted him with her body. How long would it take her to trust him with her heart? And her secrets?

One step at a time.

Knowing she needed the sleep and that he didn't have a chance in hell of dozing off again himself, Porter carefully extricated himself and headed for the shower. He'd clean up, get dressed, and see what the damage was to his truck and mailbox.

By the time he'd finished in the shower, she hadn't stirred more than to roll over into the spot he'd vacated, one slender hand on his pillow, the faintest of smiles curving her lips. His heart turned over in his chest. He wanted her right here, in his bed, in his life, for the rest of forever.

All his patience had evaporated overnight. He wanted answers. Promises. Commitments. The same things he'd always wanted from her, but they were finally, actually within reach. And she wasn't there yet. So he left her sleeping, tangled in his sheets, and quietly shut the door to the bedroom.

Their clothes lay in a scatter beside the door, a mute testament to their night of pleasure. Damn. Would he ever be able to even look at this door again without getting hard? Adjusting his jeans, he scooped their clothes into a pile beside her overnight bag and retrieved his keys and to go see about his truck.

When he saw how he'd left it, he decided he was damned lucky if the mailbox was the only thing he'd taken out. His rear taillight was cracked, and there was a dent in the back panel. "Well shit."

As he ran his fingers over the depression in the metal, his gaze tracked back to his front door, his brain helpfully reminding him of exactly what they'd done against it last night. Seeing Maggie come apart for him right there, not wanting to wait...yeah that had been worth a helluva lot more than a taillight. And this was a work truck, so it wasn't like this was the first dent it had collected.

He was halfway down the driveway when the police cruiser pulled in. *Just fucking perfect.*

Xander stepped out. "Got a call from one of your neighbors.

Did you know you've got a vandalized mailbox?" His attention flicked to the truck, still parked catywampus by the front walk, one tire in the flower bed. "Hell, did somebody steal your truck and take it for a joyride?"

"Nobody stole my truck. I parked it there myself. Clipped the mailbox, too."

Xander's tongue slid into his cheek. "That so?"

"Cut the crap. I have no doubt your wife told you already that Maggie came home with me last night."

"She might have mentioned it."

Porter strode past him, intent on getting his first look at what was left of his mailbox. "Then what the hell are you doing here?"

"Maybe a better question is what you're doing out here instead of in there?"

"She's sleeping. And I'm too conditioned to waking up early." He'd be paying for that lack of sleep later, but he wouldn't change a thing.

Xander joined him, studying the remains. The post had snapped clean in two and the side of the box itself was caved in. The whole thing had fallen partway into a juniper shrub.

"No salvaging that."

"Nope," Porter agreed. "Easy enough to replace. I'll get to it after I take Maggie home." He was aware of Xander's attention as he bent to haul up the box and post. "Spit it out."

"I'm happy for you, man. I know how long you've wanted this." But there was no grin, no backslapping enthusiasm.

"You don't look happy. You look like you're about to deliver a death notice."

"I'm just concerned, is all. You're in deep with her. Have y'all talked about what comes next?"

"That's between me and Maggie." Never mind that he'd put off the discussion more than once because he was afraid of what the answer would be.

"Which means you haven't."

"I'm not gonna pressure her. Things are good with us. She's getting invested more and more in the Ridge, beyond me, beyond family. She's getting healthier by the day. And she hasn't been talking about California."

"Doesn't mean it's not still there."

Because he'd had a hard enough time shutting down those thoughts himself, Porter scowled. "Look, what do you want from me?"

Xander hooked his thumbs in his duty belt and rocked back on his heels. "Nothing. I just don't want to see you get hurt."

Porter stared at his oldest friend, seeing the truth he didn't want to voice. "You don't think she's going to stay."

"I don't know what she's gonna do. She hasn't told her sisters either way. I just know her coming back here would be a big, damned deal, and nobody would blame her if it was too much. Or if she didn't want to give up that career she's worked so hard for."

Yeah, he'd thought of that. With a shrug, he hefted the mailbox post over his shoulder. "If she has to go, she has to go."

Xander frowned. "And you're okay with that?"

"Fuck no. If she goes, I'm going with her." He'd barely admitted it to himself, but there it was.

"You'd leave home, leave the business you've poured your blood, sweat, and tears into?"

"You can't tell me you wouldn't have followed if Kennedy had needed to leave again. Not after you finally got her back."

"No. I can't tell you that. But I didn't have to make that choice."

"This isn't a choice. I love her. I always have. I can build stuff anywhere, but there's only one Maggie Reynolds, and I'm not letting something as simple as geography get in our way. Not now that she's finally mine."

"Shit, dude. I don't wanna see you leave."

"I've been gone before. In the Army. On the job."

"I was gone to college most of your Army years, and you weren't in Gatlinburg that long. And, for the record, I hated it. Look, I'm not saying don't do it if that's what you need to do. I want you both to be happy. But I'm allowed to cross my fingers that it'll be here, where you'll still be a regular part of my life."

That made two of them.

"Fair enough. Are we gonna braid our hair now?"

"Asshole," Xander grinned.

"Get out of here, you sap. I've got better things to do this morning than stand around talking to you."

Xander opened the door to the cruiser. "Tell Maggie I said hi."

"Or, you know, not. I'd just as soon she not know you've been checking up on us."

He made an eyes-on-you gesture with his hands. "Watch it. That's my sister-in-law you're sleeping with."

Turning his back on Xander, Porter shot up his middle finger, then marched up the driveway, his buddy's laughter in his wake.

Chapter Twelve

It was nearly two in the afternoon by the time Maggie got back to the inn.

Porter glanced up at the house. "I'd offer to pull around by the old bodock tree, but I'm not sure you can shimmy up it in those shoes."

She hadn't thought to pack others when she'd shoved clothes into a bag, so she was still wearing last night's heels. "Sneaking inside in broad daylight seems like a pointless endeavor anyway. Nobody's under any delusion about where I've been."

He rolled to a stop in front of the house and parked. "Regrets?"

"Never." Hooking a hand behind his neck, she drew his mouth to hers for one last kiss and hummed with pleasure as his tongue snaked out to tease hers. When she found herself sinking into a fresh haze of lust, she pulled back. "Okay, this time it's really goodbye. We can't get derailed like we did before we left the house." There'd been two failed attempts that had ended with them both sweaty and naked. If she could even walk tomorrow, it would be a miracle.

His face screwed up in something far too manly to be called a pout. "I hate goodbye."

Knowing if she gave him more than half a chance, he could seduce her again, she unbuckled her seatbelt and cracked the door. "We'll see each other soon, but we have *work*."

"Overrated."

When he made to reach for her again, she shoved him back with a laugh. "Necessary."

Huffing a sigh, he unbuckled himself. "Fine. I'll walk you to the door."

"No." She pointed, as if that would make him stay in his seat. "You are going to keep your hands off me."

His wicked grin made her heart trip. "You like my hands."

"I love your hands. Which is exactly why you're staying in this truck and driving away."

"Spoilsport." But he dutifully wrapped his hands around the steering wheel. "Are you sure you want to go in there alone?"

Maggie shouldered her bag, grateful she'd thought to pack it so she at least didn't *look* like she was doing the walk of shame. Because she wasn't ashamed of what they'd shared. She wasn't ashamed of giving herself to this extraordinary, loving man, and she really didn't care if her entire family knew it. "I'll be fine. Talk to you tonight."

"Tonight. I'll be counting the minutes."

As she blew him a kiss and shut the door, she thought he'd probably call the moment the sun went down, arguing that counted as night. Something buoyant filled her chest almost to bursting. The sensation was so alien, it took her a moment to recognize it as joy. She was happy. Down-to-the-marrow happy, for the first time in years.

What a miracle that was.

She held it close to her heart as she slipped into the house and quietly shut the front door.

"Well, I'd say that right there is the face of a well-satisfied woman." Kennedy smiled from the doorway to the kitchen.

"It's certainly the walk of one," Athena smirked.

"I can't even be annoyed with you. It's the truth." Now that Porter was out of sight, Maggie didn't bother trying to hide the hobble as she crossed the foyer. "Christ, I need a long soak."

"Come have some tea first," Pru called from the kitchen.

Maggie reversed directions, feeling oddly pulled by the lure of girl time with her sisters. "Are we having a powwow?"

"We're plying you with cookies so you give us all the details," Pru declared, shifting Bailey to her shoulder and patting her back.

"Why? I'm pretty sure all of you have perfectly satisfying love lives."

"Well, they do. I'm still on hiatus." Pru kissed the baby's downy head. "Six weeks is a *long time*."

Maggie couldn't help it. She snorted. "Six weeks is nothing. Come talk to me when you've hit twelve years."

"You haven't had sex in *twelve years*?" Kennedy goggled and dropped onto the bench at the table.

"That's like...long enough to be considered revirginated," Athena declared.

Because that snark struck far too close to the truth, Maggie shrugged with more nonchalance than she actually felt. "I had a bit of a complex. Every time I got anywhere close to being intimate with a guy, I'd look at him and wonder, 'Could I raise a child with him?' The answer was always no."

"I mean...birth control?" Pru suggested.

"I was on birth control before. It didn't help. The only guaranteed way to avoid pregnancy was to avoid sex."

"Shit. Have a cookie." Athena shoved the platter in front of her.

Maggie grabbed a snickerdoodle and jerked her shoulders

again. "My first experience in that department wasn't sufficiently good as to be worth repeating, so it didn't seem like that big a loss." She sucked in a breath and released it long and slow. "Boy was I wrong."

Athena hooted with laughter. "You go, sis. Did you really give him a rose? Ari said she saw you cutting one off the trellis."

"It was your idea." Though he'd put it to more erotic use sometime in the middle of the night. At the memory, she shivered.

Kennedy's brow creased. "So it was good? You're okay? I mean, that's a long hiatus."

"I have no doubt I'll be feeling muscles I forgot existed for a good long while, but I really stopped caring after the sixth orgasm."

"Oh, well now you're just bragging," Pru accused, beaming. "Brag more."

"Hand over the baby. I haven't gotten my snuggle quotient." Maggie made grabby hands, accepting the warm bundle of her niece and cuddling her close. Pitching her voice higher, she answered the question. "He's had twelve years to think about what he wanted to do with me. He put all those years to very, very good use. Yes he did."

Bailey burbled. Delighted, Maggie rubbed her little nose with Eskimo kisses.

"So hold up." Kennedy snagged a cookie for herself. "If your yardstick about making this decision is whether you could raise a child together...what does that mean for you and Porter?"

"It means that, if it happened, I know he'd do right by me. It means I know I can trust him. It does not mean he's clearing out space in his closet or registering for china patterns. We're still new in so many ways, and we're taking our time."

But it didn't stop her brain from running with an image of the future. One where the baby in her arms had blonde hair instead of dark, and she lived her life for something more than work. It was a potential future she'd given up on years ago, a dream she thought she'd buried. As she held her niece in the big, sprawling kitchen, surrounded by her sisters, that future took root and bloomed, filling her mind with Technicolor possibilities that all had Porter at their center. And for the first time she considered not going back to Los Angeles.

"It's not an easy choice. Being back here is...complicated. But it's not as bad as I thought it'd be. I've realized how much I've missed home, missed family, missed Tennessee. And things with Porter are better than I could have dreamed. But I love my job. I've poured all of my blood, sweat, and tears into getting where I am. I can't just walk away from that. I know I have a lot of serious thinking to do. Decisions will have to be made. But I'm just not there yet."

Pru laid a hand on her shoulder. "And that's okay. You don't have to have all the answers right now. It's just good knowing you're thinking about it."

Maggie had a feeling that, over the coming weeks, she'd be thinking of little else. Because she wasn't ready to face that, she zeroed in on the one thing likely to occupy her mind. "On an entirely separate note, who has the petition from the artisan guild?"

"I've got all of it in the office, along with a list of crafters who've expressed interest in renting booth space and those who want to teach, when and if it happens. And there's overwhelming support for formalizing an artisan guild. Everybody loves the concept. You're hitting it out of the park with this one," Kennedy told her.

"It's not a home run until the investors are on board."

Pru sighed. "I hate that that part takes so long."

"It doesn't take a long time if you know your audience and

present the right project to the right person at the right time." Rising, Maggie handed Bailey back to her mother.

"And you've got that perfect combo in mind?" Athena asked.

"Only one way to find out." Digging out her phone, she found the phone number she'd gotten a few weeks before and dialed.

"Hello?"

God bless Genevieve for giving her his direct line. "Mr. Lewis?"

"Yes?"

"This is Margaret Reynolds from Invation. You may not remember me—"

"Of course I remember you! It isn't every day I get to play the hero and catch a lovely young woman in a swoon. How are you feeling?"

"Much better. Thank you for asking. And thank you for catching me."

"Of course, of course. To what do I owe the pleasure of your call?"

"I've been thinking about what you said at the merger meeting that day. About how your passion is in the development of new businesses, getting to see innovation at the ground level and bringing it into reality."

"You've a good memory."

"No head injury, thanks to you. Are you still looking for something new and different to invest in?"

"A good businessman is always looking for something new and different to invest in. What have you got for me? A new project with Invation"

"No. I'm not actually in L.A. right now. This particular opportunity is considerably further afield and outside Genevieve's wheelhouse. But I think it's going to tick all of your boxes, and she's given me her blessing to pitch it to you."

She could practically hear his interest pique. "I'm listening."

"Let me send you the proposal. Look it over, and if you're still intrigued, we'll talk about when you can come out to Tennessee."

"I'll send you my email address."

* * *

"Roman, it was great to meet you." Porter shook the older man's hand.

"Likewise, son. It's a helluva project, and I'm thrilled to be on board."

Maggie beamed. "I just knew this would be a good fit. I hate to see you go so soon."

"Whirlwind trip."

He wasn't kidding. Only a week after Maggie had called him, Roman Lewis had flown in for an in-person meeting. In twenty-four hours he'd attended the Artisan Supper, gone over the more detailed elevations and floor plans Porter had worked up in Auto-CAD, been out to visit the mill itself, and hashed out preliminary contracts with Maggie. The man didn't waste time.

"I'll stay longer next time and bring my wife. She's gonna love your family's inn and spa."

"We'll be sure to give you both the star treatment."

"Looking forward to it, Maggie." Roman clasped her hand and smiled. "It suits you. Maggie instead of Margaret."

"It's who I am here."

"I think Tennessee suits you, too. Or maybe it's just besotted contractors."

As color bloomed across her cheeks, Porter decided he liked the guy even more.

Roman slid his carry-on suitcase into the trunk of the rental car. "So what's the next step?"

"We'll need to meet with local government to get approval on the project." Porter had done that often enough over the years. He could probably sweet-talk his way onto the next meeting's agenda, even though the deadline was past.

"How long will that take?"

"As it happens we're already on their next agenda." Maggie's smile was smug.

"How?" Porter demanded. "He literally just agreed an hour ago!"

One brow lifted as his too-sharp tone. "I submitted it last week."

Roman laughed. "Cocky?"

"Confident," she corrected.

Getting on the agenda meant she had to go by the courthouse to fill out the paperwork. Through this whole project, he'd done everything he could to keep her the hell away from there, away from Brad. She'd gone up there without telling him?

Oblivious to his concern, Maggie and Roman continued to chat.

"Anyway, the meeting is at the end of next week, so we should have something to report pretty quickly."

"Excellent. It's a killer concept you've developed. I can't wait to bring it to fruition."

"May this be the beginning of a beautiful partnership."

Roman shook their hands one more time. "I'd best get going. Don't want to miss the red-eye back to California."

Porter managed to pull his attention back to the present. "Have a good trip."

Then he was gone and Maggie was doing a pirouette on the front lawn. "We *did it!*"

"You went up to the courthouse without me?"

She paused in her happy dance. "What?"

"I thought we agreed I'd handle all the city government stuff."

"The permits and things, absolutely. But this was nothing. Just filling out a form." She grabbed his hands and tried to tug him into a spin. "Porter, focus. We just landed funding for the project. This is going to happen!"

"Don't count your chickens. We've still got to get approval from the board of commissioners."

Some of her excitement dimmed. "What is with this sudden Eeyore routine? You've been right there with me on this whole thing. We're going to get approval. I'm handing them a virtual guaranteed success with an investor already signed on the dotted line. They'd be insane to say no."

Remember who we're dealing with. Porter wanted to say it. Because it might have been the board of commissioners they had to deal with, but there wasn't a chance in hell the mayor wouldn't get himself involved. The idea of him being anywhere near Maggie made Porter's blood boil. But he couldn't admit that without admitting that he knew her secret or how.

"Maybe I should do the pitch." As soon as the words left his mouth, he knew how stupid they were. This was absolutely Maggie's forte. She was fucking amazing at it, so why wouldn't she do it? He cast around for some way to salvage his idiocy. "They all know me and are used to working with me."

The last flush of delight faded from her cheeks and she stepped back, dropping his hands. "So I'm a liability. All of my hard work is worthless because they aren't going to see past my old reputation to actually listen to what I'm presenting. Is that what you're saying?"

"No! Jesus God. I am not saying that at all." *Fuck.* He called himself ten kinds of ass for flubbing this whole thing.

He just wanted to protect her. To keep her out of the crosshairs of Bradley Danforth, as he hadn't managed all those years ago. He'd made countless mistakes when it came to Maggie. Mistakes that had permanently impacted her life. He didn't want to make more. But Porter couldn't say that. Because Maggie had no idea that, at the end of the day, all of the hell she'd been through was his fault. And he didn't know how she'd take it if she found out.

Things were too uncertain between them. She'd let him in, deeper, closer than anyone else before. But it wasn't enough. He didn't know, not for sure, what this was for her. He didn't know what her plans were for the long term. She hadn't told him, and he was too much a chicken shit to ask because he was afraid of the answer. Afraid he'd have her, only to lose her in the end.

She was still staring at him, her expression caught somewhere between betrayal and ice queen.

He fought to find a way to salvage this. "I'm just realizing that you've done almost *all* the work. It hardly seems fair for me not to pull my share of the load." *There. That sounded reasonable. Right?*

Apparently he hit the right note because her face lightened with wry amusement. "The load? Porter, you do realize that this is all *fun* for me, right? This isn't some odious task I'm having to slog through. Besides, it's not like I don't know my way all the way around our city government. I can't imagine it's changed all that much since I interned there back in high school."

He was overreacting. If she wasn't rattled about the prospect of being in the same room with Danforth after all these years, maybe he shouldn't be either. It wasn't as if the douchecanoe was gonna come out and make a public announcement about their former involvement. It wouldn't be in his own self-interest, and that was the only thing guys like him cared about. As long as Porter was there, by her side, Brad couldn't and wouldn't do anything to her. Everything would be fine.

Porter forced a smile, putting on the mask he'd worn for so many years to hide the turbulent emotions roiling inside. "You're right. You've definitely got more experience presenting things than I do. I have absolutely no doubt, you'll knock their socks off."

"Damned straight." She nodded for emphasis and stepped into him, sliding her arms around his shoulders with a feline smile. "In the meantime, I think this is cause for celebration. Have any ideas on that front?"

"As a matter of fact, I do." He began backing her toward his truck.

"Oh, do tell?"

"They involve me peeling you out of this little outfit and worshipping every inch of your body." He'd basically been thinking about it from the moment he laid eyes on the charcoal gray pencil skirt and heels.

"That seems rather one-sided. What if I want to do the same to you?"

His dick jumped at the mental image of her exploring his body with her tongue. "I'm certainly amenable. As long as we get a solid jump on making up for all those years of missing orgasms." He opened the truck door and nudged her inside.

She laughed. "Is that what we're doing?"

"I'm making it my personal mission in life."

Color streaked across her cheeks and her voice went a little breathless. "Let it be known that I fully support this plan."

"Then buckle up, darlin'. We're going for a ride."

Chapter Thirteen

"The Artisan Guild project would be good for not only the town, but for all of Stone County and the surrounding region. With the Memorandum of Understanding and preliminary contracts with our investor, we only need your blessing to get started. Thank you for your time."

Maggie sat down to a small round of applause from the group of artisans who'd shown up for tonight's county commissioners meeting at the courthouse. She held up both hands with her fingers crossed in their direction, then settled back in her chair beside Porter. His fingers laced with hers as the board members huddled up to discuss in low voices.

"You did great," he murmured.

"We'll see." On paper the whole thing should have been a slam dunk. But there had been a weird tension in the room all during her presentation, and she couldn't put her finger on what the problem was. Maybe it was simply the difference in presenting to high-powered players of the business world versus people who'd been around to witness her greatest humiliation.

She couldn't quite shake the feeling that at least some of the people who'd come were waiting for her to fall on her face.

Or maybe that was just Bradley Danforth.

Really, it was a minor miracle she'd managed to avoid him this long in a town the size of Eden's Ridge. But they hardly ran in the same circles. They hadn't run in the same circles twelve years ago either, and she should've seen that for the sign it was. But she'd been flattered by his attention, seduced by his charm, so desperate to believe that someone like the prince of Stone County could be interested in *her* that she hadn't looked past the silver tongue to see the fair-faced devil beneath. No, she hadn't seen his true face until she'd confronted him with her pregnancy.

He'd tossed money in her face. *"So get an abortion. Or not. Either way, you're not my problem. I'm meant for better things than being stuck in this backwater town. I'm not gonna be trapped by the daughter of the town slut."*

He hadn't counted on her having a brain or a spine. Even so, she hadn't seen him since the paperwork was signed all those years ago. Paperwork that was supposed to protect their child. Not until today. She couldn't, for the life of her, figure out why the hell he'd run for mayor. He hadn't wanted to stay here. Maybe it was meant to be a stepping stone for bigger political aspirations. Trading on his family name to gain some kind of credibility before moving on to State Senate or Congress. That seemed more like him.

She kept her eyes forward, determined not to look to the far corner of the front row, where he'd taken up residence. There were plenty of others to see. She'd wager this was the best-attended commissioners meeting in years. Apart from the artisans who'd come to support her, quite a few others had turned out in response to the gossip that she'd be presenting an alternative to the resort. It wasn't accurate. The mill project was entirely sepa-rate, but it didn't hurt to have the powers that be realize that there was community support for the endeavor beyond the crafters themselves. There was even someone from the high school taking notes at the far end of the dais. The girl was easily the youngest person here, but she was well put together, obviously mature for her age. Once upon a time, that had been Maggie. Idealistic and full of dreams for how she'd change the world. Or at least this little piece of it. She'd thought that internship would change her life. And it had. Just not in any of the ways she'd expected.

One of the commissioners called the room back to order. "We are ready to take a vote on this proposal."

Maggie squeezed Porter's hand. There were seven commissioners in all, so they needed four votes in favor to proceed.

"All those in favor."

A small chorus of "aye"s rang out and hands lifted. Maggie scanned. *One. Two. Three.* Hands were going down before she could finish.

"All those against."

"Nay." Frantic, she looked at each hand, counting. *One. Two. Three...Four.*

"No. That can't be right," she muttered, but the sound got lost in a fresh uproar from the assembly.

Someone banged a gavel and hollered for "Order!"

Too many people were talking, out of their seats, demanding answers. Maggie's head was reeling.

"Porter, can you believe this shit?"

He released her as Landon came over, thunder in his eyes, as the commissioners tried to get things under control again.

They'd been outvoted. How? What possible objections could they have to the project?

Desperate for answers, Maggie looked at each face up on the dais, as if that was going to explain anything. The girl at the end caught her eye, making a sympathetic face. And then she did the oddest thing. She pointed. Maggie followed the direction of her finger to see Bradley beating a swift retreat out a side door. It was exactly his style and all the admission of guilt she needed. Fueled by temper, she slipped through the crowd to go after him for the first time since she was seventeen.

She caught up at the end of the hall outside the courtroom. "This is your doing, isn't it?"

For a moment, Maggie thought he would keep going, but he paused and turned to face her, that fake smile he'd probably plastered all over his campaign posters firmly in place. How had she not seen this for the mask it was? He'd been nineteen that last time she saw him. But there was no sign of that sullen, petulant heir who'd been forced to accept his father's edict. This was a man grown, fully confident in his power and position.

Well, she was confident in who she'd become, too.

"Maggie. How good to see you."

They both knew that for the lie it was.

She didn't beat around the bush. "You did something to skew the vote."

He feigned surprise and insult. "As county mayor, I have no voting rights and no control over the county commissioners."

"Seriously? You're going to stick to that line? Do you really hate me so much that you'd put your personal vendetta against me ahead of something that would benefit the entire county?"

"It was their decision. Although I support it. All our focus needs to be on finding new investors for the resort project."

"Right. Because you were so responsible in your dealings with the last ones."

Those golden boy brows drew together. "What is that supposed to mean?"

"Just that you haven't changed your stripes in the least. You still lead with your dick instead of your brain. I really thought you'd paid enough for those habits, but evidently some lessons are harder to learn than others." It hadn't been enough. It would never be enough. But she'd been working with limited options.

Rage flared in those pale blue eyes. He stepped into her, curling a hand around her arm and leaning close enough she could feel the heat of his breath. "Watch yourself, Maggie. All these years, you've been a good little girl, keeping your mouth shut. Don't go and ruin that perfect record. You know the consequences if you don't."

She fought back a snarl. She'd never said a word to anyone. She knew the terms she'd agreed to, no matter how bad it had looked for her. That this sleazeball would call her integrity into question...

"Take your hands off her before I take them off at the wrists."

Bradley lifted his hands before Maggie had even registered that the low, furious voice belonged to Porter. He closed the short distance, grabbing her hand and tugging her behind him, as if Bradley were a thug in an alley instead of a well-dressed man in a suit.

What the hell?

Bradley's expression turned amused. "Still the pitbull, I see. You can stand down. Maggie and I were just talking."

Porter made a sound suspiciously like a growl.

"Look, Ingram, I have no beef with you. And you obviously got what you wanted." Bradley offered a condescending pat on the shoulder. "Good for you. Better late than never."

Porter's hands curled to fists. "You bast—"

"Ah, ah, remember who you're talking about."

Porter's jaw clenched so hard, Maggie swore she heard his teeth grind. But he lapsed into silence, glaring at the other man as if he could peel the skin from his bones by will alone.

"That's what I thought. Have a good night." Without another word, Bradley spun on his heel and walked out the door.

Porter's shoulders rose and fell, his breath hissing in and out like an enraged bull about to charge. Maggie circled around, laying a hand on his arm. It felt like iron, every vein standing out in sharp relief.

"Porter, w—"

"We need to talk." He turned and stalked in the opposite direction.

She hated being dictated to, but she'd never seen him like this, so she fell into step beside him, not speaking again until he'd found an open office and dragged her inside. By then an ugly suspicion had begun to form in the back of her mind.

"What was that about?"

He paced a furious lap around the office, not saying a word.

"Porter, what did he mean about you still playing the pitbull?"

Shoving a hand through his hair, he turned a baleful glance her way. "I know." He bit the words out like gravel.

Maggie felt the blood drain from her face. "You know what?"

"That Danforth was Jessica's father."

* * *

Maggie's face went chalk white. Her expression of stunned pain was all Porter could stand to see. He turned away, needing to move, needing to scream, needing to hit something. His control was in absolute tatters.

The fucker had put his hands on her.

Porter had vowed he'd protect her. That he wouldn't let Danforth anywhere near her. And the moment he'd turned around, she'd disappeared. The son of a bitch had threatened her. Porter had no idea what had been said, but menace had been written all over Danforth's face. What would he have done if Porter hadn't shown up? Hadn't intervened?

"Wh...what?"

He wondered if it was shock or fear making her stammer. He hoped it was the former because it wasn't in him to pack his rage away right now. It was a live thing, rampaging free of the cage he'd locked it in for years. Some small, exhausted part of him felt relief at no longer having to be on guard, no longer having to battle back the beast.

"I know. I've always known."

"How?" Her voice was barely above a whisper.

He paced to a window, curling his hands around the sill until his knuckles turned white, wishing it was Danforth's neck. "The piece of shit told me himself."

Porter would never forget being cornered and taunted. Would never forget the vicious, demeaning things the asshole had said about Maggie. That mocking voice had stayed with him all these years. *"Cheer up, Ingram. I'm just breaking her in for you, good and proper."*

"Why would he do that?"

"Because he hates me. He wanted to rub it in my face that he'd been with you."

"I don't understand. Y'all didn't even know each other. Why would Bradley even care what you think?"

"You've made my life hell, so I only thought it fair to return the favor."

The wood groaned beneath Porter's hands as he tried to force Brad's voice from his mind. "Because that dickwad is my brother."

"He's *what?*"

Not daring to look at Maggie, he stayed at the window, staring out and seeing nothing, knowing he had to give some kind of explanation. "You remember my parents split when I was thirteen."

"Your mom had had an affair."

"It was with Howard Danforth, and it was long standing.

When my dad found out, he became convinced I wasn't his son, and he kicked us both out. Mom up and left, and I came to Joan."

"A suspicion isn't proof—"

"I got proof. When I was eighteen, I managed to have a paternity test done. Because I needed to know for myself, one way or the other. Howard Danforth is my father."

The words settled over them like a lead blanket. Shame burned in his gut. He'd never told another soul. He hadn't wanted anyone to know he shared a connection to that family. Not because he was a bastard son but because he hated everything they stood for.

"Howard knows?"

"Oh yeah. I went to confront him about it. He offered me money to keep quiet, because that's his thing. I turned him down cold. I didn't want a goddamned thing to do with that family. Not their money. Not their legacy. Not their name. Apparently, Howard was fascinated by that. That I'd choose to work for something instead of having it handed to me. So he got it into his head that it was high time Brad actually had to work for something, especially since he was home on academic probation his second semester of college. That's how he landed the gig up at the courthouse. He hated me for that. For his father taking away even one iota of his cushy, privileged life, and he wanted to get back at me however he could. And there you were, right under his nose."

"I don't...what did I have to do with anything?"

"He knew I loved you. Everyone knew I loved you." The words felt like razor blades in his throat. His love had painted a target on her back. It was his fault she'd been in his brother's sights at all. If he'd spoken up, if he hadn't buried the secret so fucking deep, maybe she'd have been wary and not so vulnerable to whatever charm Brad had used.

Miserable, defeated, Porter hung his head. "I didn't know he was working at the courthouse when you were. He's such a spoiled pansy-ass, the idea of him working at all hadn't occurred to me. I didn't know about the edict handed down from his father. I didn't know a goddamned thing until he came to brag to me about it."

"She's a sweet little lay. So enthusiastic. Got a real future there, just like her mama."

Porter swallowed back the roar and fought to keep his voice level. "I didn't believe him. You were too smart to get lured in by the likes of him. So I brushed it off, at least until I got home a few weeks later and you came stumbling out of that bathroom. Even then, I tried to find some other explanation. Not pressing you about it right then was one of the hardest things I've ever done. But I thought you'd tell me."

"I couldn't. Not before I'd told him."

No matter how much he'd hated it, Porter understood that, for Maggie, that was the proper way to handle things. She'd been very black and white about right and wrong well before she went to law school. "Yeah. I figured as much, so I tailed you when you went to tell him about the baby."

"You followed me?" Ice was starting to edge out the shock in her tone, but he wouldn't apologize for this part.

"I needed to know. It seemed the most expedient way to find out, without putting any more pressure on you. And I didn't want you to confront him alone."

"So you eavesdropped on our private conversation—"

"No. I wasn't close enough for that." Not for lack of trying. But he'd been close enough to see the asswipe toss cash at her, as if she were some kind of cheap hooker. Close enough to see her walk away from Danforth and his money, tears streaming down her face. "It was obvious it didn't go well. So after you left, I confronted him. I don't know what I thought I was going to accomplish. I don't think I thought much at all past defending your honor and demanding he treat you better. I won't repeat what he said."

"She's carrying your child, you asshole."

"What do I care? I'm headed back to college and my girlfriend. It's not my problem. I got what I wanted from her. The perfect way to fuck you over, little brother. Because no matter whether you manage to hit that or not, I'll always have gotten there first."

Maggie said nothing. Porter couldn't look. Couldn't stand whatever he might see in her face. Not when part of him was so much back in that alley.

"I wanted to kill him. I wanted to break him in half for ever laying a hand on you. I probably would've tried, but Crystal came out the back door of the diner." It had been enough to snap him back to rational thought. If he went to jail for assault, there'd be no one to take care of Maggie and the baby. No one to support her, to shield her. The whole fucking mess was his fault. He had to be around to help make it whatever kind of right could be managed.

"All these years you knew and you said nothing. Why?"

"I know something about shame. After the public way my parents split, everyone talking about it, after my dad kicked me out and I was brought to Joan with my trash bag of stuff, I'd learned what it is to walk around day after day with it eating you from the inside out. Yours wasn't mine to share with anyone. You had to be ready, be willing, to share it yourself, and I've been waiting for fucking *years* for you to tell me. To trust me enough. But, of course, you didn't. Because you're Maggie Reynolds. An island unto herself." The words tasted like ash on his tongue, and he could hear the bitterness painting his tone, but he couldn't pull it back.

"I couldn't tell you. Can't."

How could she sound so calm and in control when he was breaking apart? He'd thought they were making progress.

Thought she trusted him, and yet here they were, back to square one. His temper snapped. "What the fuck more do you want from me? Everything I've done, I've done for you. For *years*. I just bared my soul, told you something *no one* else knows. What more do I have to do for you to trust me?"

"It's not about trust." More with the calm, the rational. The ice queen. This wasn't his Maggie. Maybe she'd never been his at all.

"Yes it is. At the end of the day, yes it damned well is." All these weeks, he'd believed they were building something solid, something lasting. But if she still didn't trust him, then this wasn't as real as he'd thought. He'd been existing in some kind of dream world and now he was waking up to reality. "We're fooling ourselves."

"What are you saying?" The first hint of panic threaded into her words, and a small, vicious part of him took satisfaction that he'd finally cracked that ice, gotten a reaction. But it was too little, too late.

"I'm done." He couldn't do this anymore. Couldn't shove all the shit down and away just because it was easier for her. He couldn't keep waiting for her to love him the way he loved her. He'd laid himself bare, and she was just going to leave in the end. Tear his heart out and take it with her.

"Porter—"

Needing to get away from her before his resolve crumbled and he got sucked back into the same, toxic dance they'd been doing for years, he crossed to the door and yanked it open.

"It's not what you think—"

"I don't care. Not anymore. I'm done with this." *With this conversation. With this situation. With you.*

Chapter Fourteen

"I don't care. Not anymore. I'm done with this."

The shock of his words had Maggie flinching back, as if he'd struck her. Because she heard what he wasn't saying. *I'm done with you.*

She stumbled, grabbing for a chair. But he didn't turn back. Didn't even glance her way as he walked out the door and, quite possibly, out of her life.

Porter Ingram, the man who'd been there for her through the worst stretch of her life—Her friend. Her confidant. Her lover—had finally had enough and left her.

Maggie wanted to go after him, wanted to beg him to listen. But to what? She was still bound to silence, as she'd always been. And it was more than obvious he was too angry to listen to her reasons. Him knowing about Bradley was only part of the whole.

Bradley Danforth. His half-brother.

Maggie just sank into the chair as the reality of that crashed over her. Bradley's seduction was never about her. Never about attraction. Never even about wanting some form of entertainment while away from his girlfriend for months. She'd been nothing more than a pawn for him. A tool for revenge. That made the whole unbearable situation so much worse. She'd been a fool, and the agreement she'd signed at seventeen to guarantee her future might just have cost her the man she loved.

The truth of it slid between her ribs like a knife, piercing the armor she so prized. She doubled over, wrapping both arms around herself, as if she could physically hold herself together. She needed to get out of here. The idea of going home, of having to face Pru and Ari, even Athena, without being able to explain what went wrong, made her physically ill. She was so tired of holding back. Of walking the lonely line of secrets. Fumbling for her phone, she dialed the one person who might understand.

"Hey! How did the commissioner's vote go?"

"Kennedy." Maggie could barely get out her name.

"Honey? What's wrong?" Her tone went from concerned to ready for battle in a nanosecond.

"I...I need you to come get me."

"Where are you?"

"The c...courthouse."

"I'm on my way." No questions. Because unlike the rest of her sisters, Kennedy wouldn't need the why. Not yet, anyway.

Maggie was grateful for the relative cover of darkness as she made her way out the back of the building. Few people were still around, most having left after the vote. Only a couple of cars remained in the parking lot. Porter's truck wasn't among them. That was another blow. He'd well and truly left her here, not just walked out to get some space and calm down.

Kennedy made it in less than ten minutes, rolling up and leaping out of the driver's seat before Maggie had even stepped out of the shadows. The moment her sister's arms closed around her, Maggie lost whatever tenuous control she'd managed to cobble together. On a gasping sob, she buried her face against Kennedy's shoulder.

"Okay, okay." Kennedy held tighter, stroking her hair. "Is anybody dead?"

Maggie managed to shake her head.

"Does anybody need to be?"

Well, that was debatable. Maggie sure as hell wouldn't mourn if Bradley Danforth got hit by a bus, but he wasn't worth committing murder over.

"You probably shouldn't answer that," Kennedy continued. "Plausible deniability. Come on. Get in the car."

She bundled Maggie into the front passenger seat and hustled around to the other side. "Do you want everybody?"

Mute, Maggie could only shake her head again.

"Okay. We'll go to my house."

Maggie shot out a hand to grip Kennedy's arm. "Is Xander home?"

"No. He's on duty tonight."

She sank back in the seat. "Okay."

With another look of concern, Kennedy curled her fingers around Maggie's and drove. Maggie wept the whole way. Out of town. Into the house. Until Kennedy shoved a mug of tea into her hands and simply sat on the coffeetable across from the sofa.

"I could probably do with something stronger."

"It's got a stiff shot of whisky added to cover all bases."

It smelled kind of terrible, but Maggie drank it anyway, hoping the combination of tea and alcohol would warm the core of her.

"Can you tell me what happened?"

She stared down at the tea, as if it would tell her where to begin. "I have to preface all of this with a warning that there's a whole lot I can't tell you."

"Understood."

Maggie sipped and winced as the bitter drink slid down her

ravaged throat. "Porter and I had a fight, and I think he broke up with me."

"What? Why?"

"He knows who Jessica's father is."

Kennedy stared. "He broke up with you over *that?*"

"No. Apparently he's always known. But he thinks I don't trust him because I never told him."

"Wait, he's mad because you didn't tell him a thing it turns out he already knows?"

"He doesn't know everything. And I still can't tell him."

"Why the hell not? He already knows, doesn't he?"

"He's known who the father was. But not why I kept his name out of it—why I never told Porter or anyone else. I signed a non-disclosure agreement."

"So?"

"I'm legally bound to silence. It's why I've never told any of you."

"What do they have on you? How did they force you into that?"

Of course Kennedy would see it as blackmail. She *had* been blackmailed by Xander's father to leave town, leave him, all those years ago. For ten years none of them had known. Not until their mother died and Kennedy finally came home. A part of Maggie had hated Kennedy for abandoning them, abandoning her. But finding out the why had changed everything and enabled them to start rebuilding their relationship. It was why Maggie knew Kennedy would understand the pain of keeping a secret. The pain of hurting others by keeping it.

"I wasn't forced. I negotiated for it myself."

Kennedy frowned. "At seventeen?"

Maggie flashed a humorless smile. "I was always preco-cious. I knew he wasn't going to stand by me, and I knew I didn't stand a chance of saving myself and the future of my child without help. So I agreed to silence in exchange for security."

"What kind of security?" Kennedy asked gently.

Maggie hesitated. This was treading a line. And beyond the legal implications, she was ashamed of what she'd accepted for her silence. "Financial support."

"Child support."

Maggie pressed her lips together. "It was a lot more than child support."

Kennedy arched a brow. "And that still holds, even though you lost the baby? Even after all this time?"

"Even so. I'm an expert in contract law. Believe me, I've been over that agreement with a fine-toothed comb. If I violate the NDA, I'll have a lawsuit on my hands. I could pay back the money now, but I could be disbarred. And they wouldn't be satisfied with just taking back what they gave me. They'd come after me, and through me, prospectively the inn and spa. It would depend on the judge and jury as to what kind of damages are demanded, but I'm not willing to take the chance." The Danforths had too many connections.

"Damn, who *are* these people." Kennedy waved a hand. "You can't tell me that. That's the whole point. But Maggie, it's Porter."

"I don't have a *choice!*" Did no one understand that?

"Look, I of all people understand the weight of carrying a secret like that for years. I kept quiet when I came home because I was trying to protect Xander and his relationship with his dad. But your situation is different. You're not talking about some kind of wide disclosure. You're talking about Porter. He already knows the who. Whatever details you give him, he'll take to the grave. The man's a fucking vault, especially where you're concerned. He's proven that. He loves you."

Maggie hadn't trusted in his feelings back then. And maybe they had been part nobility, part guilt. Or maybe his wanting to marry her, to give a name to that child was as much about being the man Bobby Ingram hadn't been able to be. The man neither of his fathers were. Porter had kept her secret all these years, never breathing a word. Every day he'd made this gesture, this silent declaration of commitment. Because he loved her.

And she'd never expressly told him how she felt. Because she hadn't been able to reconcile a life with him with the parts of her life she didn't want to give up. And now...she might very well have lost her chance. The idea of it cracked her heart in two.

"I don't think he'll listen," she whispered. "I've never seen him like this before. Ever. He's so incredibly angry. I think I've finally pushed him past his breaking point."

"You have to talk to him. No matter how angry he is, he'll listen if you really talk. And if we have to get Xander to handcuff him to a chair, we will."

Maybe it wasn't too late. Maybe she could fix this. She had to try.

Maggie shoved up from her seat. "I'm going to wash my face. Then can you help me find him?"

"Of course."

From the depths of her purse, her phone began to ring. Maggie pounced on it, answering with a breathless, "Hello?" without even checking the display.

"Hey sweetie. I know you're tied up with stuff tonight, but there's someone here at the house to see you about the board of commissioners meeting."

Not Porter. Pru.

Pinching the bridge of her nose, Maggie began to pace. "It's really not a good time. Just take a message and send them on home."

Pru hesitated. "It's Claudia Samson. She says she's interning at the courthouse and that you're going to want to talk to her."

Maggie thought of the girl who'd pointed her at Bradley. She obviously knew something. It was definitely worth finding out what.

"I'll be there as soon as I can."

* * *

Porter felt like a walking wound, every atom saturated with hurt and anger and shame. He wanted nothing more than to stop the raw agony. Fat chance of that. Was this what his dad had felt like? Out of control with grief and betrayal? The temptation to find a bottle and fall into it was a siren song, but he'd never turned to alcohol to dull his pain. He'd made it a lifelong policy not to, even though he didn't technically share Bobby Ingram's genes.

So he didn't go home, where he knew there was a fifth of bourbon. He didn't go to the tavern. The last thing he needed was crowds. He simply drove on autopilot, with no destination in mind, until he found himself on Mia's doorstep. The porch light was off, but a dim glow showed she was still up. He pounded on the door, not really knowing what he was doing here or what he'd say. Inside, the dog began barking like a maniac.

The porch light flickered on and the door opened. Leno's intruder alert turned to joyful yips, and Mia pivoted to keep him from wriggling out the door. She stood in flannel pants and a sweatshirt so old, the design had faded beyond recognition, her hair bundled up into a messy knot, her features set in lines of sympathy. "Hey. I heard about the vote."

"Fuck the vote." He couldn't even think about *that* right now. Not when everything that mattered in his life was falling apart.

She squinted, looking closer. "I'd ask if you're okay, but you're clearly not."

"I'm losing my shit." He might as well continue his streak of total honesty.

"Come in." She hauled the wagging pit bull back from the door.

Porter stepped inside. The dog immediately butted his over-sized head against Porter's knees with a whine, effectively herding him over to the sofa and nudging him down. Then he leapt up and sprawled all seventy plus pounds of his bulk across Porter's lap, presenting his belly for scratches.

"Leno clearly thinks you need canine therapy. What's going on, Porter?"

Not meeting Mia's gaze, he began to rub at the dog. "Maggie."

"You had a fight?"

"Something like that. I don't think we'll survive it." He couldn't imagine coming back from this. They were diametrically opposed, and he didn't see that changing.

"Jesus. I'm sorry. What happened?"

He wished he could just spill everything out in a torrent. But Maggie's secret was still not his to tell, and holding that close to the vest wasn't something he was going to change, even now. He'd have to tread carefully. "What do you know about Maggie's past?"

"I try not to pay attention, but I've heard she got pregnant at seventeen and never named the father—even after she lost the baby. Some people in this town..." Mia shook her head in disgust. "It seems like that's the reason they can't let it go. Because they still want to know who the father was. Like they have a right to know, and they're pissed she never told."

Like they have a right to know. Porter flinched.

Mia dropped into a chair. "Is that it? You found out who it was?"

"I've always known who it was. And I've kept that secret. I even kept it from her that I knew. I always thought someday, when she trusted me enough, she'd tell me."

"But she hasn't yet."

"She never will! I thought we were building something. I thought..." This trod so close to all the things he couldn't say. Lifting his head to meet her gaze, he drilled down to the only essential point he could share. "Something happened tonight. Yet another opportunity for her to open up to me. To show she finally trusts me—that what we have is real—and she didn't. She doesn't. It's not."

Mia just stared at him, her expression a mix of exasperation and disbelief. "Porter."

"I'm just a part of her R&R. I fucking love her, and I'm nothing more than a vacation fling to her."

"Do you hear yourself being a drama queen? That's not true."

Her instant dismissal had him scowling. "You don't know that."

"Neither do you." She leaned forward, bracing her forearms on her knees. "Is this really the hill you want to die on?"

"Excuse me?"

"Are you really gonna throw away what you've found with her after *all this time* over the fact that she won't give you the details?"

"If she's not going to trust me, that's hardly grounds for a lasting relationship."

"Oh bullshit. Leaving aside the fact that you probably blindsided her by revealing that you already know the secret she's kept from everybody all these years, her withholding that information isn't about trust. Did you ever consider that she really *couldn't* tell you?"

Porter bristled. "Of course she can tell me. She can tell me anything."

"No, I mean legally couldn't tell you."

"What do you mean?"

"Sometimes there are reasons—good ones—you can't tell

something to the person you care most about in the world." Mia crossed both arms around her middle and paced to the fireplace. "I lost my husband because of reasons like that."

Hed' wondered, because of the rings she wore around her neck, if she'd been widowed, but it was still a shock to hear. "You were married?" On his lap, Leno wiggled and whined, bumping Porter's shoulder to remind him not to stop with his petting. He resumed the belly rubs.

"Am. We've never gotten divorced. But we've been estranged for years. There were things I couldn't tell him, and in the absence of any explanation, he made assumptions. I know his history, know what he thought and why. I've never gotten the chance to tell him he was wrong."

It was the most she'd ever said about that part of her past, and it inspired a whole host of questions Porter knew she wouldn't answer. Not yet anyway. But he couldn't help asking one. "Why not track him down now?"

"Because even if I was free to explain—and I'm not—he has no reason to believe me after all this time. I've lived with the regret of that for the better part of a decade. My point, though, is that if Maggie says she can't tell you, she has a reason. And that reason's got nothing to do with you. I'd lay money on her having signed some kind of nondisclosure agreement."

"What makes you say that?"

"You said she went Ivy League for college and grad school. How the hell did she pay for that and didn't come out under crippling debt?"

"She had scholarships."

"Did she?"

He didn't actually know that for sure. After the miscarriage, she'd gotten into Brown and he'd left for basic training and the Army. She'd said she had scholarships, and he'd never questioned it. God knew she'd been smart enough to earn boatloads of them.

But what if Mia was right? The Danforth family's answer to everything was to throw money at it, like Howard had done with him. Had they paid for Maggie's education in exchange for her silence?

"Yeah, I can see you thinking about it now. It makes sense—especially if her baby daddy is who I suspect it is."

Porter's head whipped up. He hadn't meant to say anything that would reveal the truth.

Mia held up a hand. "Not my business and not a thing I'll share with anybody. Anyway, Maggie's a woman who minds her Ps and Qs. Rules matter to her. I could tell that from one conversation, even if I didn't know she was an attorney. If she's held on to the secret for this long, she has a damned good reason. And I think you owe it to her to let go of this little tantrum you've got going on and give her the chance to explain what that reason is."

"It's not what you think." That's what Maggie had said.

But he'd been so caught up in his rage at Brad, his own impotence at keeping the bastard out of her life, and his fear about what her continuing to withhold from him meant about them, he hadn't been willing to listen to excuses. In his mind, there wasn't a good reason for still holding back. But Maggie did care about rules, and she wasn't a woman who shied away from doing the hard stuff. So maybe it wasn't too late. Assuming she didn't hate him for the role he'd played in her pregnancy. He hadn't stuck around long enough to find out her reaction to *that*. There'd been no damage control for the dropping of that bomb. He'd thrown his involvement in her face and just left her with it. Literally left her with no ride.

Shit. Shit. Oh fuck.

He started to shove the dog over, but there was no way Maggie would still be there. She'd have called Dahlia or one of her sisters to come get her. And after everything he'd said, would she even want to talk to him again? What if she'd finally been ready to tell him and he'd shut her down?

Porter did shove Leno off his lap then. "I fucked up."

"Yup," Mia agreed. "And before you go racing off again, let me offer you some advice. Don't go storming over there, while emotions are high. That's when people say things they don't mean."

Yeah he'd been a textbook example of that already tonight. Shit, what had he done?

"Maybe just go home. Try to sleep on it."

"There's not a chance in hell I'm going to be able to sleep."

"Then that'll give you plenty of time to think about how to make this right."

Chapter Fifteen

The porch light cast a welcoming glow over the inn's front door. Somehow it did nothing to thaw the cold knot that had set up in Maggie's gut. What exactly was she about to get into with Claudia Samson?

"Do you want me to come in with you?" Kennedy asked.

"No. I don't know what this is about, but I doubt I'll get a chance to talk to Porter before tomorrow. He probably needs the time to cool down anyway." Maggie hoped by then she'd have figured out what to say.

"I'm done with this."

What if he meant it?

Kennedy reached across the console to squeeze her hand. "You two are going to get through this. I have faith."

"I've never been great with faith."

"You can borrow some of mine. I love you, sis."

"I love you, too. Thanks for coming for me." Maggie leaned over to wrap her in a hug.

"I'm really glad I could be here for you this time."

Maggie's throat went thick. This was the sister she'd lost all those years ago. The sister she hadn't let all the way back in until tonight. She squeezed Kennedy just a little bit tighter. "Me, too. I've missed you."

"Check in tomorrow?"

"Yeah." She straightened, running a hand over her hair. "How do I look?"

Kennedy studied her with a critical eye. "I mean, not your best, but not like you've gone ten rounds with Mike Tyson."

"Like I've been crying my eyes out?"

"Eh..." She wiggled her hand.

Maggie sighed. "Best I can do. I'll talk to you tomorrow."

She let herself into the house, following the sound of voices back to the family parlor. Claudia perched on the edge of a chair, a glass of sweet tea in her hands.

Pru rose from her spot on the sofa, tipping Bailey to her shoulder. "Good timing. This one's about ready to go down for the night."

Maggie automatically crossed to her, pressing a kiss to the baby's downy head. "Sweet dreams, pumpkin."

Pru watched her with worried eyes that told her whatever efforts she'd made at Kennedy's to clean herself up weren't enough to hide the crying. Later. She'd deal with that later.

"I'll just leave you two to chat. Claudia, it was nice to meet you."

"And you. Thank you for the tea."

Maggie shut the door behind her and strode over, offering a hand. "Well, we've not been formally introduced. I'm Maggie Reynolds."

The girl shook it. "Claudia Samson."

Maggie took the seat Pru had vacated. "My sister said you were an intern at the courthouse."

Claudia nodded.

"I did that myself when I was your age." It felt weird to make casual conversation, when this visit felt anything but casual.

"I know. That's part of why I wanted to talk to you."

"Okay." She settled back against the cushions. "I'm listening."

The girl tucked a lock of dark hair behind one ear, and Maggie noted the faint tremble in her hand. "I have some more information about the vote tonight that you might find useful."

"You sent me after the mayor tonight." Might as well put it out there.

Claudia nodded, her shoulders squaring, as if she were more comfortable with plain speaking. "Yes. He influenced the vote."

"I suspected as much. How?"

"He put pressure on the four commissioners to vote against the project."

"That's a lot of political capital to expend just to stop this project from moving forward."

"It wasn't that kind of pressure. He threatened the leases on their businesses, which are part of his family's holdings."

"That's a serious accusation. How do you know this?"

She jerked her shoulders. "I'm an intern. Nobody pays much attention to me. You can overhear a lot when you're filing."

She wasn't wrong. During the year Maggie had worked at the courthouse, she'd overheard all kinds of things she probably shouldn't have. "Okay...so why would the mayor do that? What's in it for him? The artisan guild wouldn't impact his resort plans and would be good for the town's economy."

"I eavesdropped on some conversations with Bradley and his dad about the resort."

The familiar use of his name struck Maggie as odd, but before she could comment, Claudia continued.

"To boil it down, daddy isn't pleased with him for having lost the investors, and he's putting a bunch of pressure on Bradley to sort it out because the family is counting on this resort to pay back the insane amount they spent to get him elected in the first place."

Maggie hadn't realized the Danforths had a financial stake in the resort, but she wasn't surprised. They had their fingers in all kinds of pies around Stone County and beyond. This explained a lot. Not that she was entirely certain what she'd do with the information.

"I appreciate you letting me know, but why bring this to me?"

"My parents are artisans."

Maggie angled her head, thinking. "Jana and Willard?"

"Yes. The mill project would be really good for their business. I want to see it happen, and I figured if anybody could manage to overturn the ruling, it would be you."

Oh, wouldn't they just love knowing their daughter had been talking to her. The two of them had been perpetuating plenty of gossip since Maggie got home. She worked up a smile. "Thanks for the vote of confidence."

"You've earned it. I listened to what you said at the meeting tonight. You're really a lot more impressive than people give you credit for."

Maggie felt her smile turn wry. "Thanks?"

Claudia linked her hands and leaned forward. "How did you do it?"

"Do what?"

"Handle all the whispers and the gossip and the judgment. How did you get through all that to become what you are today?"

The question set Maggie back. She didn't want to talk about this with anyone, least of all the child of a couple of gossipmongers. But she could tell it wasn't idle curiosity. Sweat beaded along the girl's brow, and the hands she'd linked twisted in her lap.

"It wasn't easy. I was lucky enough to have the support of some really great people." An image of Porter flashed through her mind, but she shut it down in a hurry. She couldn't think about him right now. "Why are you asking?"

Claudia bit her lip and looked toward the door, as if checking to make sure they were still alone. She dropped her voice to barely above a whisper. "I heard Bradley threatening you tonight. That's what that was about, wasn't it? He was the father."

Maggie felt the blood drain from her face. All these years she'd managed to keep the secret and now she was being confronted with it twice in one night? Whatever was going on with this girl, Maggie didn't owe her this. "I'm sorry, I'm not discussing this with you."

She stood up, intending to put an end to the conversation, but Claudia's hand shot out to grab Maggie's. "Please. I need to know."

"No, you don't. And you need to go now." Her reaction had probably already confirmed the truth, but damned if she was going to say anything more.

"Please, Maggie." Claudia's tone was desperate. "I need to talk to someone who's been there."

"I don't understand what you're talking about."

"He did the same thing to me." The words seemed to burst out of her like a pressurized cork.

Maggie froze, turning to stare down at the girl with a dawning horror. "What?"

Claudia swallowed, tears spilling over. "I'm pregnant."

* * *

Maggie parked in front of the eighties-era ranch house and let out a long, slow breath. She didn't want to be here. She'd have preferred scrubbing toilets at the inn or studying for the bar exam or being stuck on a transatlantic flight with the seat in front of her jammed against her knees. But she'd never been one to take the easy way out. They'd discussed the details and the options at length last night, and Claudia had made a decision. Now Maggie was here, in part, to lend her support. When she was in Claudia's place, she'd had people—Porter, Joan, her sisters. It was time to pay that forward.

Bracing herself for a shitshow, she headed up the front walk. The concrete was cracked in multiple places, but the foundation plantings along the side were neat and weeded. The house itself was comfortably dated on the outside, well-worn but not shabby. The home of solid, middle class people. It seemed like a palace compared to the string of dingy apartments Maggie had lived in with her mother in the years before she came to Joan.

The front door opened, and Claudia slipped out. "Oh thank God, you're here."

"I said I would be."

The girl twisted her hands. "I feel sick."

"That's not surprising." Reaching out, she squeezed Claudia's shoulder. "This is the right thing to do."

Pressing her lips together, Claudia nodded and jerked her head back toward the house.

Maggie followed her inside and down a hall lined with a gallery of younger Claudias. As their only child, it was obvious she was the apple of her parents' eyes. Would that change once they knew?

Jana Samson stood at the kitchen sink, doing breakfast dishes. "Are you still here? You're going to be late for school."

"I'm not going to school today, Mom."

Her mother turned with a frown. "What? Are you sick?" She caught sight of Maggie, confusion flickering over her features. "What are you doing here?"

"Claudia asked me."

That obviously just confused Jana more. "I don't understand. How do you know my daughter?"

"Where's Dad? I need to talk to both of you."

"Claudia Marie, what is going on?"

"I'm going to tell you, but I'm doing it all at once. Where's Dad?"

"In his workshop."

"Okay. Get Maggie a cup of coffee or something, while I go get him." She slipped out the back door, leaving Maggie and her mother staring at each other.

"Coffee's not necessary," Maggie assured her. Not that Jana had made a move in that direction.

Willard came tromping in the back door a minute later. "You'd better have a good explanation for this, young lady. You're supposed to be in school." He pulled up short as he realized Maggie was there. "Why are you here?"

"She's here as my legal counsel," Claudia said.

"Informal," Maggie hurriedly added. "I'm not licensed to practice law in the state of Tennessee."

"Is that supposed to be comforting?" Willard demanded.

"Let's all just go sit in the family room." With admirable calm, and the kind of precocious maturity that reminded Maggie of herself at that age, Claudia herded them out of the kitchen. "Mom, Dad, sit down."

Dread curdled in Maggie's gut at what was coming. Some version of it scrolled across Jana and Willard's faces as they sank onto the sofa, linking hands.

"Honey, why would you need legal counsel? Are you in some kind of trouble?" Jana's voice shot up half an octave.

Claudia bit her lip, her already pale cheeks going paler as she nodded.

"Whatever it is, we'll get through it," Willard assured her.

Tears glimmered in Claudia's eyes, and Maggie tensed as she opened her mouth.

"I'm pregnant."

What? No. This wasn't what they'd discussed last night. She was supposed to lead with the who, not the pregnancy. Put the blame squarely where it belonged—on Bradley Danforth's head.

"What?" Willard thundered, all traces of support gone from his face.

"You've been sleeping with some boy? How could you? I thought you were better than that," Jana said.

"How could you be so careless? So foolish?" Willard demanded.

The questions and accusations kept coming and every one was a lash, opening Maggie's own wounds as she listened. Joan hadn't done any of this, but plenty of other people had, and the shame of it was still there, ready to bleed out at the hateful, hurtful words.

She shot up from her chair. "Enough!" Her shout interrupted their tirade, so she took advantage. "For the love of all that is holy, this is exactly why she came to me first. Now, both of you keep your mouths shut and listen to your daughter. She is not to blame in this."

Jana's cheeks went ashen. "Oh my God. Were you...were you..." She couldn't even get the words out.

Claudia was staring hard at the floor, tears streaming down her face.

"Claudia," Maggie murmured.

"I wasn't forcibly raped. But I was...coerced."

"Who?" Willard's voice trembled with rage.

The girl sucked in a breath and lifted her head. "Bradley Danforth."

Her parents stared in bafflement, their brains clearly trying to work around to some other explanation but the truth.

"The *mayor?*" Jana hissed.

Claudia could only nod.

"But he's...he's..." Willard stammered.

"Thirty-one," Maggie supplied. "Which makes this statutory rape."

Jana bolted off the sofa. "I'll kill him! I'll kill the bastard for touching her."

Willard's face flushed an alarming shade of eggplant.

"Daddy, breathe!"

Maggie waded into the chaos, intercepting Jana before she could pull a rifle from the gun case in another room and determining that Willard was not, in fact, having a heart attack. They were no longer looking at her as an intruder but as someone who had some kind of answers.

"What do we do?" Willard asked.

"Claudia is prepared to report it and press charges."

"Good," Jana snarled. "Wait...if she presses charges, that means everyone will know. Everyone will be talking about her."

Maggie stared her down. "Everyone will be talking about her, regardless of the circumstances, for years to come. That's how it works."

She and Willard both had the good grace to redden with embarrassment over their own behavior in that arena.

"However, every effort will be made to keep her name out of the media and out of the publicly available records related to the charges. The Sheriff is my brother-in-law. He can give you a better idea of exactly how this will be handled here in Tennessee. Talking to him is the next step."

"But won't people talk if they see a police vehicle at our house?"

"Not if he comes in plainclothes and in his personal vehicle. He'll do that if I ask."

"You'd do that for us?" Jana asked.

"I'll do it for Claudia because I know better than any of you what she's prospectively facing, and I wouldn't wish it on anyone. Excuse me."

She went into the kitchen, taking a moment to brace her shaking hands on the counter. God. This was brutal. And there'd only be more to come because Maggie didn't trust Jana or Willard not to turn the same bullshit they'd shoveled on her onto their daughter. She'd stay as a buffer as long as Claudia wanted her.

Sucking in a calming breath, she made the call.

"Hey Maggie. What's up?"

"I need you to come out to Willard and Jana Samson's place in street clothes and your Bronco. If you can borrow someone else's car, even better."

The easy, relaxed tone vanished. "What?"

"We'll explain when you get here. Just, please, come as low profile as you can and be prepared to take statements."

"I'll be there in fifteen."

Claudia was in the middle of a sandwich hug from her parents when Maggie came back. She hesitated in the doorway. It was more than she'd expected of them, and Maggie hoped it meant that the girl stood a chance of getting through this less scarred than she had been.

"He's on his way. I suggest that you consider retaining formal legal counsel moving forward. I can make some recommendations on that front, if you like."

"That would be amazing. Thank you," Willard said.

"You'll stay while I talk to Sheriff Kincaid?" Claudia looked up at Maggie, panic in her eyes.

"Of course." Later she'd slip away, do something to put this and all the memories it evoked out of her mind. For now she'd do what needed to be done.

Jana and Willard exchanged a look before Jana rose. "We wanted to apologize to you for any role we played in making things harder for you. It wasn't fair of us. I guess nobody ever thinks about that kind of thing until they're in that position. But we won't forget your kindness to our daughter and to us."

It was the first time anyone had ever apologized for gossiping about her. And instead of feeling relief or vindication, she felt rage. Didn't they understand that it was too little, too late? That kicking someone while they were down was damned near unforgivable? Over and over, they'd passed judgment without knowing the facts of the case—the worst kind of injustice.

She wanted to rail at them that their gossip had been a poison in her veins, making her feel dirty, like she could never be good enough ever again. And then she wanted to twist the knife and let them know that was what their daughter was in for, and that maybe, just maybe, she was a victim of their shitty karma.

"I should put on a fresh pot of coffee," Jana said softly, and as she walked by, Jana squeezed Maggie's shoulder. In that moment of connection, the older woman's wet eyes were full of so many things. A thousand apologies, gratitude and wonder, and even a hint of admiration that made Maggie stand just a little bit straighter. There was a new warmth in the exchange, and maybe part of that was the beginning of forgiveness.

As Jana moved away toward the kitchen, Maggie thought that if she could find it in her heart to forgive these people who'd hurt her, maybe she could find a way to begin forgiving herself. Maybe it was finally time she stopped punishing herself for a mistake she'd made when she'd been barely more than a child.

The doorbell rang.

Maggie let Xander in herself. He'd changed out of his Sheriff's Department uniform as she'd asked, but there was no missing the cop in his expression as he stepped inside.

"What the hell is going on, Maggie?"

"Come on." She led him back to the living room and made introductions.

"All right. Now why am I here?"

Because the Samsons seemed to have defaulted to her, Maggie gave him the rundown.

"That's...a hell of an accusation. I have to ask...do you have any corroborating evidence?"

"A paternity test should be clear enough," Jana said.

"True enough, but that'd be a while before we could have one safely done. I don't ask this because I don't believe you, but because part of my job is to gather sufficient evidence to support the charges."

"I have a recording of him admitting it."

Maggie whipped in her direction. "You what?"

"When I went to tell him, I turned on the recorder on my phone and stuck it in my pocket, just in case."

Oh, this kid was smart.

"It's not an outright admission, but the implication is pretty strong."

"Can I hear it?" Xander asked.

Reluctantly, she pulled out her phone, tapping at the screen until a recording began to play. There were muffled sounds of movement, then a door closing and something that might've been a lock.

"I appreciate your enthusiasm, but not today, Firecracker." Bradley's smooth, flirty tone made Maggie's skin crawl. How had this once worked on her?

"I need to talk to you."

"What is it? Conscience getting to you?" He said it like the very idea of a conscience was amusing.

"I'm pregnant."

"Are you lying to me?" Every trace of flirtation had been replaced with steel.

"N..no. Why would I do that?"

"Shit. Fuck. Damn. I'm not dealing with this again. You're getting an abortion. I'll pay for it."

Not dealing with this again.

Maggie must've made some sound because Xander's gaze

shot to her. She could see the moment he put two and two together, and his expression went even darker. But he said nothing as they listened to the rest of the recording.

"That son of a bitch," Willard growled.

"Well, that certainly constitutes solid proof. I'm going to need some information to file the charges, so let's sit down and start at the beginning."

Chapter Sixteen

Porter didn't hear from Maggie by morning. He stared at the blank screen of his phone. No notifications. No voicemail. No texts. No email. Nothing to indicate she hadn't taken him exactly at his word last night. He'd said he was done, that he didn't care what she had to say. He didn't have a right to be disappointed that she hadn't made the next move, that she hadn't pushed him to hear her out. Maybe he should've gone over to the inn last night. But it had been late when he'd left Mia's, and part of him was still fucking terrified that she'd hate him as much as he hated himself for putting her in Brad's crosshairs.

All the site visits he'd put off while prepping for last night's commissioner meeting now demanded his immediate attention and kept him from tracking her down first thing. But it was hard to focus on the progress of the jobs, the next steps, the foreman's reports, as he thought constantly about calling or texting—something to make first contact and gauge her level of pissed off. But a proper grovel wasn't done any way but face to face, and she'd have her own work to do. He'd expected to be able to peel off

sometime mid-morning, but a busted pipe in a second-floor bathroom renovation had him and his entire crew scrambling. The
last thing the company needed was to have to eat the cost of flood
repairs because of a careless mistake. The ensuing chaos was the
only reason he could've missed the text until they finally got a
moment to breathe sometime mid-afternoon.

Maggie: **Insider info suggests Bradley or his
family threatened the leases of the commissioners
who voted down the mill project. I'm dealing with
something else urgent right now. Can you follow up
and talk to any of the commissioners you think
might be willing to admit coercion?**

What the hell?

The text had come in sometime around lunch. There'd been
no follow up, no reference to their fight. What the hell else was
she dealing with that was urgent? Were her sisters okay? The
baby? Surely, even under the circumstances, if something were
wrong on that front, she'd have said so. Unless she'd been deliberately vague because she didn't want his support?

"I think we're gonna be okay." Mia wiped her brow. "We'll
lose a few days to drying out, but the subfloor doesn't need
replacing and we managed to stop it from destroying the wall
underneath. The pipe itself is repaired. We just have to replace
that one section of sheetrock on the ceiling downstairs. All in all,
dodged a bullet, I think."

Porter grunted, only half listening as he reread the text. Of
course Brad was behind the vote. The why of it didn't matter
much. He was a cretin who only gave a damn about his own
interests. If they could prove his interference, they could get the
vote overturned. Maggie obviously expected the usual legal chan-
nels to work in their favor on that front. But if the commissioners
were already being strong-armed, would they go on record
about it?

"What's wrong?"

"Bullshit as usual. Listen, have you got this? There's something I need to do."

"Does that include fixing shit with Maggie?"

"Hopefully a step in that direction."

"Then yeah, sure. I think we're good here."

He left the crew in his partner's capable hands and drove across the valley, up to the highest point of the ridge. It wasn't what Maggie had asked of him, and if he was wrong, they could fall back on the standard legal methods. But Porter suspected he'd get further faster by going straight to the source, as it were.

Even as his gut roiled at the idea of facing down Howard Danforth for the first time since he was eighteen, he couldn't help the spurt of professional appreciation as he reached the top of the winding drive and took in the house for the first time. Over five thousand square feet of wood and glass that took maximum advantage of the mountain views, it had been featured in *Architectural Digest* a few years back. He'd been impressed by the spread, but that was nothing to seeing the place in person. It was palatial by Stone County standards, the terraced lawn giving way to a waterfall of changing foliage.

Get your head in gear. You're not here to talk about the damned view.

Parking in the circular drive, he got out of his truck belatedly realizing he'd come straight from the job site. His pants—paint-stained—were still damp from the flood, and his boots were caked with mud from a site visit earlier in the day. There was a rip at the hem of his t-shirt, and he didn't even know what those stains were on his hands. He'd dressed for hard work, not meetings.

Hearing Joan's voice in his head—*That's no excuse for not making an effort*—he dug wet-wipes out of the center console. He cleaned his hands and face, then, out of long-ingrained manners, he buttoned his chambray work shirt to cover the t-shirt, and tucked them both in. A quick swipe of his boots on the grass dislodged the worst of the mud. It wasn't great, but he wasn't here to win in any beauty contests.

Pamela Danforth answered the door. He'd never met her before, but he recognized Brad in the shape of her eyes and nose. An attractive, older woman, she had the kind of smooth-skinned face that made him wonder if she'd had cosmetic surgery. That seemed like the kind of bullshit this family would be into. Her expression twisted into one of faint distaste as she looked him over from head to toe.

"Can I...help you?"

"Yes, ma'am. I'm here to see Howard."

For a moment, Porter thought she'd refuse and send him on his way. But she stepped back, letting him inside. "He's back this way."

She didn't ask who he was. Maybe she knew. It was a small town, and the name of his company was painted right on the door of his truck. He had no idea if she was aware of his connection to her husband. With Howard's reputation, surely she knew about his extra-marital activities. Then again, knowing your husband was unfaithful and coming face to face with the product of one of those affairs were two very different things.

Pamela opened the door of the study without knocking. "Howard, you have a visitor."

Porter trailed her into the room, and there was his father. The blond hair was shot through with silver, and he'd grown a beard since the last time Porter had seen him. Porter was surprised to see similarities in the older face staring back at him. He didn't want to think about the fact that they shared anything.

"Porter. Well, this is certainly a surprise. Thank you, Pamela."

Porter blinked at the curt dismissal of his wife, as if she were his secretary. The condescension rankled. As she started out of the room, he called after her, "Thank you, Mrs. Danforth. You have a lovely home."

There was a faint hitch in her step before she nodded in acknowledgment and shut the door.

"Such good manners. You definitely didn't get those from Bobby Ingram."

Porter took a firm grip on the leash of his temper. "I got them from Joan Reynolds."

"Good woman, Joan," Howard conceded. "She absolutely did right by you. By all those kids. So sad about her passing."

"I'm not here to talk about Joan."

He circled around behind the big mahogany desk. "Why are you here?"

"We've got business to discuss."

Howard brightened at that, his expression caught somewhere between pleasure and triumph. "I was wondering when you'd come around to wanting to work with me. It's a helluva business you've built. I'm proud of what you've made of yourself."

Was he seriously under some delusion they were having a father-son moment?

"I don't want your approbation. I just want some answers. What do you know about the mill project?"

"Not a lot. I knew there was a proposal on the table. It's an intriguing concept. Are you looking for investors?"

"We have investors. What we don't have is approval from the board of commissioners."

Surprise flickered over his face, but Porter didn't trust the man further than he could throw him. "And you think I can help you get it?"

"I think your family owns the properties housing the businesses of four of the standing commissioners—Nate Calloway, Janice Wooten, Raina Fairfield, and Chuck Lawrence."

"Yes. They've been long-term tenants, most of them. And good ones. What are you getting at?"

"We have reason to believe that Brad's strong-arming the four of them to vote against the project by threatening their leases."

Howard's brows drew down. "That's a hell of an accusation."

"Yep. And somehow it doesn't seem so far-fetched. You and I both know when he doesn't get his way, he'll exact petty revenge against whoever wronged him." Porter watched his father's face, wondering if he knew about Maggie.

The other man's expression went grim. "It is one of his failings."

"One of many. Listen, I get he wants his resort. But putting a stop to this project isn't going to change the fact that he fucked up with the investors."

"What are you talking about?"

"Your precious boy sexually harassed the CFO of Faber Development. That's why they pulled out of the deal."

Legitimate shock rippled over his features.

"Didn't know about that, did you?"

"That oversexed imbecile. He blew a multi-million-dollar deal..." Howard pinched the bridge of his nose and swore under his breath. "Even if he did fuck up with Faber, Bradley doesn't have the power to make decisions about leases. He isn't involved in that part of the business."

"But the commissioners don't know that, do they? How hard would it be for him to put a word in and imply he could make life difficult if they didn't vote the way he wanted? He doesn't think a thing about manipulating people for his own ends. I mean, why should he? He grew up entitled to every damned thing."

"Is that a touch of jealousy I hear?"

"That—*Dad*—is the tone of me thanking God every day I walked away. I'm a better man for it. Now, I'd appreciate it if you'd yank on Brad's leash to remind him who's boss. He's getting too big for his britches."

Howard studied him for a long moment, something like regret and respect flashing in his eyes. "I'll handle him, and I'll speak to the commissioners and clean up his mess."

"Thank you."

The phone on the desk began to ring. Howard glanced at the display. "Speak of the devil." He picked up the receiver and began without preamble. "Son, we need to talk."

Porter couldn't understand the reply, but the burst of rapid, irate speech was clear enough, as was Howard's thundering exclamation. "You're being charged for *what?*"

* * *

Maggie dragged herself through the front door of the inn, every step like moving through quicksand. For the first time in months, she felt as exhausted as she had back in California, and she just wanted to fall face-first into bed for about fourteen hours. It was a good reminder that she was a long way from truly healed, but she figured she got a pass after the day she'd endured.

By the time the interview was finished, Xander had had enough evidence to charge Bradley with statutory rape by an authority figure. Maggie hadn't revealed her own connection to him, and Xander hadn't asked, though it was obvious he'd figured it out. It didn't matter. The son of a bitch would finally get what he deserved. Maggie just hated that it would be at the expense of another innocent teenage girl.

Her hand was already on the newel post at the bottom of the stairs when she heard the excited squealing from the kitchen. For a few seconds she considered going on up, not letting anyone know she was home. But the joy of the sound pulled at her. She could use some kind of good news today. Switching directions, she pulled on the last of her energy reserves to look something other than completely fried as she walked into the chaos of what seemed like almost every member of her family, minus Xander.

"What's going on?"

"Ohmygod!" Ari shrieked, bouncing. "Look. *Look!*"

Athena turned, holding out her left hand. The sight of the ring there left Maggie momentarily speechless.

"You're engaged?" She looked to Logan, whose grin was bright enough to light up all of Stone County.

Her last sister was engaged and her own love life was a complete dumpster fire. Maggie gave herself three seconds to absorb the gut punch of that before yanking hard at her control. This wasn't about her. "You're engaged!" She repeated it with more enthusiasm this time as she got in on the hug-fest, hoping Athena thought the initial lack of it was simply shock. "I'm so happy for you."

"I'm happy for me, too," Athena beamed. "And I have something to ask you."

"Anything."

"Don't kill me, but we want to get married next month."

Maggie's mouth dropped open. "Next *month?*"

"I know it's short notice, and I know you said never again after Kennedy's wedding, but we need to do it during the slower season on the farm if Logan's going to be able to get free for a honeymoon. If it's not now, then it'll be next year, and we don't want to wait that long. Plus, I want to do it before you go back to California."

Back to California. When had Maggie stopped thinking about that? It was coming up, and she'd made no decisions. At this stage, Porter might have made them for her. The idea of that was another stab to the heart. But she smiled through the pain. "Of course. You'd better call Cayla Black. We certainly can't do it without her." The event planner had been just starting out when they'd hired her for Kennedy's wedding, and she'd been a lifesaver.

"We need to throw a party to celebrate," Flynn announced.

Kennedy shot a meaningful glance in Maggie's direction. "Maybe we should move this to the tavern. Drinks and pizza?"

"I can get behind that," Logan agreed.

God love the woman for giving her an out. "I'll stay on call for the guests," Maggie announced. They probably wouldn't need anything and she could get a little rest.

After exacting a promise for them to bring home pizza, Maggie watched them all pile into vehicles for the drive into town. If her sisters shot her worried looks, they let her stay without questions. Those would come later. But by then she'd have had the space she needed to find her bearings again.

No longer ready to go straight up to bed, she followed the path behind the inn, wandering over to the work site of The Misfit Kitchen. The massive commercial kitchen would double as a set for Athena's show and as a small-scale cooking school in conjunction with the inn. The waiting list for those classes was already full of enough people to book Athena up for six months. Another reason for them to get married sooner rather than later. She'd be busy as hell once construction finished.

The work day was well over, but Maggie stepped inside the building anyway. She switched on one of the big work lights and scanned the space. It was really coming together. No appliances yet, but there were walls and windows and all the wiring and plumbing was done. She could see the reality of the plans Porter had drawn coming to life. It would be beautiful and perfect, as everything he built inevitably was.

She still hadn't talked to him. Hadn't, in fact, heard a word in response to the text she sent earlier in the day, which meant he was probably still furious. For all she knew, he'd deleted the text without even reading it. Which meant that she'd have to fight to talk to him, and she didn't have any fight left in her tonight.

The sound of footsteps on concrete slab had her turning, her heart leaping. "Porter?"

"Hello, Maggie." Bradley flashed that politician's smile, looking like the Joker in the harsh glare of the work lights.

For a long moment, Maggie simply froze.

"Surprised to see me?"

Arrested. You were arrested. Her brain kept repeating it over and over as he stalked around the sawhorses and snaking power cables.

"What are you doing here?" If her voice was just a little too high and strident to come off as true non-concern, it couldn't be helped.

"Meaning why am I not in a cell right now? Well, in the name of not causing a scene, I was informed of the charges filed against me and asked to turn myself in. I decided I needed a little detour first." He stalked closer and Maggie edged away, recognizing his precarious mood.

He'd lose everything because of this. His job, his reputation, probably his wife and family. Bradley Danforth was a desperate man. And he was here. Why?

Where the hell was Xander?

"You just couldn't leave well enough alone, could you? Couldn't stay away. No, you had to come back and fuck with my life all over again."

"Excuse me? Are you under some delusion that my coming back here had anything at all to do with you? I didn't even know you were mayor."

"I know it was you." His voice held the edge of a growl. "I know you were the one who put Claudia up to it."

"Up to what?" Maggie pasted on her best poker face, the one

she wore into negotiations for billion dollar deals, but Bradley wasn't buying it.

He stepped into her personal space until she backed up, into a wall. "Don't play stupid! You talked her into pressing charges as payback for high school. For the fact that I didn't want to give up my life for a kid and you refused to get rid of the problem."

Temper had her lashing out, shoving back at him. "My daughter wasn't a problem, you pompous, entitled asshat."

Bradley absorbed the blow and grinned, a savage, crazy baring of teeth, like that guy from *The Shining*. "Oh ho, the kitten has claws. Does that mean you've become a more interesting fuck over the years? Maybe I should ask my little brother, since you're warming his bed these days." He pressed back, caging her in against the wall, laughing and pivoting his hips when she tried to knee him in the balls. "Or maybe I'll just find out for myself. One last hurrah before the circus begins."

Maggie sucked in a breath to scream, only to find her air cut off as Bradley pressed his forearm across her throat. He reached for the hem of her skirt.

She tried to lash out but her body was simply too worn out. Each movement was sluggish and weak, no more effective than a child slapping at a wall. He was so much bigger, so much stronger. Her mind screamed as she felt his hand streaking up her thigh.

No. No no no no no.

And suddenly the pressure against her throat was gone. Maggie sagged against the wall, wheezing in breath as Bradley stumbled back.

What?

She looked up in time to see Porter's fist plowing into Bradley's face. A sickening crunch had her wincing, even as blood sprayed.

Someone swore. Then Xander was racing across the room.

"Lay off, man." When he tried to pull Porter back, Porter only shook him off, continuing to beat Bradley with steady, bruising efficiency, until he was the one sagging back against a wall.

"I can't arrest his ass if you kill him, and I don't want to arrest you. Stand the fuck down."

Bradley slid down the wall, his head lolling to one side. Both eyes were already swelling shut and his nose was unquestionably broken. Blood streaked down his face, staining the front of his suit. "Fucking maniac attacked me." At least, that's what Maggie thought he said. It was hard to tell.

"He was assaulting Maggie." Porter's voice trembled with rage.

"I'll press charges," Maggie croaked. She tried to struggle to her feet and wobbled.

Then Porter was there, his strong hands holding her up, pulling her close, and she burrowed in, too relieved to think about anything beyond the fact that he was here, that he'd saved her.

From somewhere behind him, Xander hauled Bradley to his feet. "I'm taking this son of a bitch down to the station to book him for assault on top of the other charges, then I'll be back for your statement about the attack, and for the full story about whatever the fuck this prick did to you in high school."

Maggie hesitated, pulling back to meet Porter's gaze before nodding. "Can it wait until tomorrow?"

"Won't hurt a damn thing for the fucker to cool his heels in jail. You let me know when you're ready."

"Thank you. And Xander?"

"Yeah?"

"Don't tell Kennedy. Not yet. Everybody's out celebrating Athena and Logan's engagement. I don't want to ruin that." And she didn't want her well-intentioned family interrupting what had to come next.

Xander's expression lightened a fraction. "They got engaged?

'Bout damned time. Logan's been carrying that ring around since she decided to stay. Anyway, sure, I'll sit on this for the night."

"Thank you."

Then she and Porter were alone, staring at each other in the unforgiving work lights. The weight of their fight settled over them.

"I'm sorry."

"I'm sorry."

They both said it, each stumbling over the other. She wanted to cuddle back against him, feel his strong arms around her and pretend the last twenty-four hours hadn't happened. But they had happened, and she still had to deal with the fallout.

"I need to talk to you. There are things I need to tell you."

Porter shook his head. "You don't. I was out of line. I—"

"No you weren't. Not entirely. I'll have to tell this story to Xander tomorrow, and I need you to hear it first."

After a long moment, he nodded. "Let's go inside."

* * *

Maggie didn't lead him into the family room but instead up the stairs. "I want to change."

Her hand shook on the banister and Porter was painfully aware of how much effort it took her to make the two flights. The aftermath of the adrenaline dump from the attack? Or a regression with her adrenal fatigue? What was the something she'd been dealing with today? In twenty-four hours, her eyes had gone back to bruised, and lines fanned out from her mouth and eyes as they had when he'd first seen her in California. He cursed himself for his own role in setting her back.

In her room, she sank immediately onto the bed, as if her legs wouldn't hold her anymore. "Sit with me, please." She held out a hand.

Porter started to take it, then saw the blood on his knuckles. "Just give me a second." He slipped into the bathroom to wash his hands, wincing at the sting of the soapy water.

She was still waiting when he came back, her hand outstretched for his. He curled his fingers around hers, too grateful she wasn't shying away from him to hold on to any of last night's anger.

"Did you get my text this morning?"

He blinked. That wasn't where he'd expected her to start. "Yeah. I skipped talking to the commissioners and went to talk to Howard instead."

"You what? Why?"

"I figured if anybody could yank on Brad's leash to get him back in line, it would be him. Which he planned to do but got somewhat sidetracked when Brad called to say he was being charged with statutory rape. He didn't have any more information than that, and by the time I tracked down Xander to ask, he was on his way over here to find you for reasons he wouldn't tell me."

Maggie winced. "Probably to warn me of exactly what happened."

"I don't understand what you have to do with any of this."

"The victim overheard enough to figure out what I hadn't been saying, and came to me for advice. She's pregnant."

"Oh my God."

"Yeah. I went with her to talk to her parents this morning, and stayed while Xander did the whole interview. They've got him more or less dead to rights. He's going away for what he's done, but I thought it best, for the sake of trying to keep the victim's name under wraps as long as possible, that Xander do everything as quietly and low-key as he could. I never dreamed Bradley would come after me." She rubbed a hand over her throat, as if she could still feel the pressure against it.

Porter's hands tightened on her. "I should have gotten here sooner."

"You didn't know. You didn't know, and that's on me."

"Maggie—"

"No, listen." With her free hand, she reached out to cup his face, stroking a thumb along his cheek. "Let me make one thing one hundred percent clear to you—I have not been sitting on this secret for years because I didn't trust you. This was not a thing you could earn. If it was, you'd have earned the right to know a thousand times over by now. I've been legally bound to silence from everyone since I was seventeen because I signed a non-disclosure agreement."

So Mia had been right. Something else loosened in him at that. "Why?"

Her face twisted. "When I told Bradley about the pregnancy, his immediate answer was abortion. That was never on the table for me. I couldn't...it wasn't something I was willing to do. It was abundantly clear that I'd made an egregious mistake getting involved with him and that he'd never stand by me. All I could think about was my mother. Do you know how many times she told me I was a mistake? That she had to give up her whole future because of me?"

"You weren't a mistake. And if she gave up her future, that was her decision."

"You're right. It was her decision. She went from one guy to another looking for some kind of stability. I wasn't going to do that. I wasn't going to give up my dreams, and I wasn't ever going to make my child feel like she wasn't wanted. But to do that, I needed help. So I took matters into my own hands and went to see his parents."

"You what?" The idea of her facing down Howard and Pamela on her own, pregnant and terrified, made Porter's gut twist.

"The one thing Bradley and I had in common was ambition. The difference is, I understood that I'd have to work for it. He thought it should be handed over. But I knew a baby—particularly a baby out of wedlock to a teenaged mother—would screw things up for him. He hadn't seen that far yet because he didn't think I had any power. But his parents understood that I could make life extremely difficult for him, if I chose. Particularly as he was over eighteen and I wasn't. There's no Romeo and Juliet clause in Tennessee. That made our involvement statutory rape, even though I consented. Being labeled a sex offender wasn't going to do anything for his future, so I used that to negotiate." She dropped her gaze for a moment, the hand in his flexing.

Porter squeezed it, hoping the connection would be the encouragement she needed.

"My mother ended up where she did—dependent on men and without any skills to speak of—because it was always easier for her to rely on others and blame the past for where she was than to find options and work to build a real future. Because she had nothing and no one to help her when she made a mistake. Multiple mistakes that ultimately led to her losing custody and me going into the system. I didn't want that for me or for my baby. So I got them to agree to set up a trust for the child, pay for my education through graduate school, and have Bradley sign over all parental rights. In exchange, I'd keep my mouth shut in perpetuity and never ask them for another thing."

She'd asked them for a helluva lot, and she'd gotten it. "That's—"

"Deplorable?" she whispered, still not looking at him.

It struck him then that she was ashamed to tell him. Ashamed of what she'd had to do to survive. Porter tipped her face back up to his. "Gutsy as fuck. Why the hell would I judge you for that?"

"You walked away from them."

Oh Christ. Had his own admission made her feel even worse

about what she'd had to do? "It wasn't the same. Not at all. You did what you needed to do to provide for your child. For yourself."

"I hated it. I hated needing anything from them. Bradley was furious. He accused me of getting pregnant on purpose to bilk his family for tuition money."

Porter's hands fisted and he wished he could beat the asshole all over again.

"Even if I hadn't signed the NDA, I'd never have told a soul after that for fear other people would think the same. Especially after I lost the baby."

"What did happen after that?"

"The trust went away, but they still paid for my education. But if I broke my silence, they could've come after me for the entire cost of that—which was not an insignificant sum for Brown and Yale. Beyond a forced payback of that, they could have gotten me disbarred, and sued for damages. Since I'm part owner of the inn and spa, they could have come after them as assets. That's my family's livelihood now. I just...I got so accustomed to protecting the secret, for myself and my family—it was like that NDA became a part of who I was. It was as natural to reach for secrecy as it was to reach for my next cup of coffee."

All these years she'd had to carry this burden alone. And he'd made it about him. Throat going thick, he ducked his head. "I'm sorry I didn't give you a chance to say that last night."

She stroked his cheek again. "He baited you. I just didn't understand how much."

"I'm sorry. I'm so fucking sorry for what he did to you. The whole goddamned thing was my fault."

"Bullshit." The snap of her voice had him looking up, into furious eyes. "You didn't have any control over anyone's actions but your own. You've blamed yourself all this time, but Bradley didn't seduce me because of you. He did it because he could.

Because manipulating women is what he does. Isabelle Faber had nothing to do with you. This teenage girl he's going to go to jail over had nothing to do with you. And I guarantee you there are countless others who haven't come forward over the years that he did the same damned thing to. Did he use me to hurt you? Absolutely. But that was just a bonus for him. He would have targeted me no matter what because I was who was in front of him at the time, and I was stupid enough to believe his lies. But that wasn't on you. That's never been on you."

Maggie didn't blame him. Even after everything, she didn't blame him. Maybe she was right. Brad was a user. He was a sexist, predatory asshole. Porter had spent so many years focused on what Brad had done to Maggie, he hadn't given any thought at all to the other women who might've been affected. He wasn't responsible for them.

"I am not my brother's keeper," he murmured.

"No, you're not. And I will say this as many times as it takes for it to sink into that thick skull of yours. You have nothing to be ashamed of. You are a better man than either of the ones you came from. You've made a deliberate choice to be that every day I've known you, and I love who you are. I love your big, generous heart and your faithfulness and your steadiness. I love that you've seen the worst of me, and you love me anyway. And I love that you've held on all these years to give me time to catch up. I love you, Porter. I love you, and I'm sorry it's taken me so long to say it."

He squeezed his eyes shut as her words washed over him, healing some long, raw wound. "Say it again, Maggie."

She brushed a kiss to one cheek. "I love you." She shifted to kiss the other. "I love you."

He shuddered as she brushed her lips over his and pressed a hand to his heart. Could she feel it thundering beneath her palm?

"I love you, Porter."

Even as the relief took hold and began to spread through him, Porter realized she was still blaming herself, still holding herself accountable for her own victimization. He wasn't the only one who needed to let something go.

"Maybe you need to love yourself."

Maggie pulled back, brows knit. "What?"

He covered her hand with his, holding it to his chest. "Let me ask you something. This girl who's pressing charges—is she stupid?"

"No. She's remarkably mature for her age. Very bright."

"Does that make her responsible for what happened to her? Because she should've known better than to get involved with a guy nearly twice her age?"

Her expression turned mutinous. "Of course not. She got into this situation because she was manipulated by someone without conscience, who's really good at it."

"Then why can't you give yourself a break? You were manipulated by that same guy. And at an age where it would've been a lot easier to believe whatever was between you was real. I've never once blamed you for that. He took advantage of you and exploited your vulnerabilities. None of that makes you stupid. It makes you human. So maybe you can stop blaming yourself for what happened."

She opened her mouth as if to protest, then shut it again. "That's really hard to argue with. I guess, I always felt like I should have known better. Should have seen him for what he was."

"Hindsight is twenty-twenty." Porter brushed a kiss over her knuckles. "We're not kids anymore. Maybe it's time we both stopped taking responsibility for the actions of that asshole. It sounds like he's finally going to be forced to take responsibility for himself."

"That certainly feels like something to celebrate."

When her hand moved lower, to tug at his shirt, he stilled and framed her face. "You're exhausted. And you were almost—" He cut himself off, not allowing himself to think about what might have happened if he'd been any later.

"I wasn't." Her voice was firm. "Thanks to you, I wasn't. But I need you, Porter. I need to feel your hands on me. Be with me."

As if he could refuse her anything. His eyes searched hers for a long moment before he brought his hands to the hem of her silk shell, sliding it up and off. He ran his knuckles down her arms in a barely there caress that had gooseflesh erupting in its wake. "I love you."

Maggie reached for him, tunneling her hands beneath his shirt to trace the smooth muscles of his back, as if wanting to claim every inch of him for herself. He wanted the same in return. With each layer, each kiss and touch, they bared more than simply their bodies. They stripped away the last of the secrets, the last of the barriers between them. And as he slipped inside her, she wrapped around him, holding him close, as if she'd never let go, he knew that he'd do whatever, go wherever he had to because she was home.

Chapter Seventeen

Maggie couldn't put off the call any longer. Of everything she'd dealt with since the assault, she'd dreaded this the most. Shutting herself into her room, she sank into a chair and dialed.

"Well, if it isn't my favorite Southern belle. I guess you finally took that edict to check out seriously. It's been ages!"

"Hey, Genevieve."

"God, I've missed you. Tell me you're feeling like a functional human again."

"I am. You may officially leverage the 'I told you so' I rightfully deserve."

"Not even necessary. I'm just glad you're feeling better. How is everything?"

"Good. Crazy. My sister's getting married next week."

"Wait, which one?"

"Athena. The chef."

"Did I even know she was engaged?"

"That only happened three weeks ago." It felt like three months.

Bradley hadn't been released on bail, and with the evidence of his involvement with Claudia, along with the additional assault charges, he hadn't been able to wiggle out of anything. His attorney had recommended he take the offered plea deal. He'd gone to prison, and rumor had it, his wife had already started divorce proceedings.

"You planned *another* wedding in a month? Well, that's sign enough that you're cured. And thank God for it. We've got so much to catch up on when you get back. I know it won't be until after the holidays, but do you have your flight settled yet?"

Maggie winced. "About that."

There was a beat of weighed silence.

Genevieve lost the cheerful buoyancy in her tone. "You're not coming back, are you?"

Maybe if she said it fast like ripping off a Band-aid. "I'm not coming back."

"Well shit. At least tell me it's because of the delicious Porter Ingram."

"He's the biggest part of it."

"You owe me some serious dish on that front."

Maggie huffed a laugh. "Noted. It boils down to the fact that I love him. I always have. Being here these past months finally gave us the chance we never had before. But beyond that, I want to come home, not just for a visit or an extended stay, but for good."

Genevieve sighed. "That it's for love makes it a little bit easier to swallow. You deserve that, you know. But damn it, I don't know how I'm going to do without you."

"What have you been doing the last few months?"

"Let's just say that I've been doing a damned fine impression of everything that put you in the hospital in the first place. Much longer, and I'm gonna have to take a page out of your book and finally step off the merry-go-round."

"There's something to be said for it. Not that our version of that looks like most people's."

"Speaking of, what will you be doing out there?"

"For the immediate future, I'm going into partnership with Roman Lewis to open an artisan guild and education center to preserve the crafting traditions in the area. After that, I don't know."

In the wake of Bradley's arrest, the board of commissioners had reversed their decision. There was a growing contingent trying to talk her into running for mayor in the upcoming emergency election. Maggie didn't want to touch that job with a ten-foot pole, but it was nice to feel valued by the town that had finally seen her as something other than "that girl who got knocked up in high school."

"I hope to God you'll still consult for me."

"Of course. I have no problem whatsoever keeping a couple of toes in." And it would make her feel a little less guilty about bailing.

"I recently heard that another contact of mine—Tess Peyton, brilliant woman—started a small business incubator in the small town where she settled. I loved the concept, but I haven't had the time to really look into it. She's down in Mississippi, so a lot closer to your neck of the woods than mine. Maybe you should check it out."

"I could probably be game for a field trip after Christmas. And you should find some downtime yourself. Come for a visit. Enjoy our spa. By the time you manage to schedule it, we'll probably have The Misfit Kitchen open for classes."

"You're tempting me. I'll find the time. Meanwhile, I've got to figure out how the hell I'm going to continue to do without you. Thanks for that."

"I *am* sorry." Not sorry enough to give up what she'd found here, but she understood the position she was putting Genevieve in.

"Are you happy?"

Maggie wrapped her arms around herself, as if she could hug in all the joy. "Yeah. Yeah, I am."

"At the end of the day, that's all that matters to me. I love you, girl."

"Back atcha. Talk soon. And I'll do whatever I can to smooth the transition."

"I'm holding you to that. Bye."

Maggie said goodbye and hung up. Well, it was done.

No takesies backsies.

Now to tell everyone else.

From the sound of the raised voices carrying up the stairs, Athena was in the midst of her latest panic attack. Who knew the sister who ran a commercial kitchen with the efficiency of a five-star general would lose her mind over a wedding? Maggie hurried downstairs, intending to head to the family room, where everyone was gathered in an assembly line putting favors together, but at the base of the stairs she paused, hearing singing from Pru's room.

She'd been wanting a moment alone with her eldest sister for a while now and hadn't yet found the time. Changing directions, she went down the hall and knocked on the door. "It's me."

"Come in." Pru sat in the glider chair by the window, the baby at her breast. She smiled as Maggie came into the room. "I think she's getting ready for a growth spurt. She's been starving lately."

"I can't believe how big she's getting."

"Growing like a weed. I think she's going to end up tall, like Flynn. Aren't you, my little string bean?" She stroked a finger over Bailey's downy black hair.

Maggie sank down onto the edge of the bed. "I wanted to talk to you for a bit."

Pru automatically reached to stroke Bailey's back in comfort. "Okay."

Maggie hated that her sister's immediate thought was that it was something bad. But hopefully she could rectify that. "I wanted to thank you."

"For what?"

Taking a breath she considered her words. "All of us left. In a way, we all kind of ran away from something. But you stayed here. You made sure we all had a home to come back to, not just a house. I don't know if you really understand how much that meant to us. To me."

Pru shifted the baby to her shoulder and began to gently pat her back. "That makes it sound like I knew what I was doing and it was all on purpose. I fell into it as much as anything."

"Don't diminish what you've done. Mom would've been the first to say that tending is one of the most important jobs."

There was less grief now in Pru's nostalgic smile. "No one did it like her."

"True enough. But you stepped in when she died. With Ari and everything else."

She was already shaking her head. "Which I could do because you took on all the hard stuff with the estate and dealing with the lawyer and everything I was too overwhelmed to do."

Impatient with her sister's continued dismissal of her contributions, Maggie huffed. "Woman, I am trying to compliment you here!"

"And I appreciate that, but don't make me out to be a saint for staying, Maggie. I definitely had my jealous moments that you all were out there seeing the big, wide world."

"I was jealous that you could stay. That you didn't have any demons here."

The words hit her soft-hearted sister like a blow. Pru's face twisted in distress as she struggled to find some way to comfort—because that was her way. "Maggie—"

"But I don't feel that way anymore. It's been...so freeing to finally face everything I left behind. I've been able to really be *home*. To be embraced as part of the community instead of being forever an outcast. After all this time, I feel like I can finally leave behind all the shame I've been carting around for years. And I wouldn't have been able to do that, if you hadn't stayed. If you hadn't picked up Mom's mantle to be the glue for this family."

Clearly stunned, Pru froze, her deep brown eyes welling with tears. "I don't...no one can fill Mom's shoes."

"No one can replace her, but you've been filling those shoes for more than a year now. And that makes it easier to do this."

"Do what?"

"Come home. For good."

The tears spilled over. "Oh, Maggie!"

Pru rose from the chair, pulling her close. Bailey made her objections to being the filling in their hug sandwich known with a burp and an immediate wail.

Laughing, Maggie pressed a kiss to the squirming baby's head and stepped back. "I'm gonna go save Athena from her latest freak out."

"Right behind you. I'll put this one down in the Cadillac stroller in the family room."

"I told you it would be useful."

Pru just shook her head and smiled. "So you did. Welcome home, Maggie."

Athena was pacing like a madwoman when they walked in. "What the hell was I thinking planning a wedding in a month? I'm marrying a *trust fund baby*. His parents have *standards*. And oh my God, his mother is terrifying."

"Take a breath," Maggie advised. "First off, Logan is as far from a trust fund baby as you can get. He left that whole lifestyle behind when he decided to become a farmer, otherwise you wouldn't be in love with him. Second, you're not marrying his parents. It's your and Logan's wedding. If you want small and simple, his parents' opinions don't matter. Third—"

"There's a third?"

"Shush. I'm on a roll. Third, as your husband-to-be is so fond of reminding you, you are a badass chef, and you shall take no shit. Not even from his mother. You wouldn't take insubordination in your kitchen."

"I can't *fire* my mother-in-law."

Ari's lips twitched. "I mean...you could always throw a knife at her. It worked on Jayson."

"Athena is not going to throw cutlery at her mother-in-law. Honestly, she's going to love you," Pru insisted, bending to settle Bailey into the stroller turned bassinet.

"Easy for you to say. You won the mother-in-law lottery with Maura," Athena groused.

"I did. But the grandchildren didn't hurt."

"Grandchildren?" Athena squeaked, her cheeks going pale.

Maggie pushed her down into a chair. "Head between your knees before you keel over. Nobody's saying you and Logan have to have kids right off to appease your in-laws. Nobody's saying you have to have them at all."

"I mean...we want them. Eventually. But, like, later. After we figure this marriage thing out."

"Take your time," Kennedy said. "Practice on the other tiny humans before you decide to have your own."

"Hey! I resent that. I'm not a tiny human," Ari protested. "I'm in high school now."

"No, but there'll be another one to go with Bailey in about eight months."

Everyone stopped and stared.

"You're pregnant?" Pru gasped.

With a sheepish grin, Kennedy nodded. "Only about six weeks, so we're keeping it on the down low, but I wanted y'all to know."

Ari whooped, and Athena jumped up from her seat.

Maggie's heart swelled and her eyes teared up as she crossed the room to pull Kennedy into a tight hug. "I'm going to apologize in advance."

Kennedy pulled back, worry in her green eyes. "I know this might be hard on you."

"No." Maggie gripped her by the shoulders and beamed. "Because I'm going to be here to annoy you every step of the way. I'm not going back to California."

Kennedy grabbed her arms. "You're not? Truly?"

"I'm in love with Porter, and I miss family."

"Oh, thank God." She pulled Maggie into a fierce hug.

"Group hug!" Ari threw her arms around the pair of them, and Athena and Pru piled on, until Maggie lost track of which arm belonged to whom and they were a big, squeezing mass of happy family.

Kennedy tipped her head to Maggie's shoulder. "Welcome home, sis."

* * *

"I can't believe how fast they got the road cleared."

Porter glanced over at Maggie in the passenger seat, leaning forward to take in all the changes. Her cheeks were flushed with healthy color and she looked happier and healthier than she had in a long time. "Beats having to hike in, that's for sure."

She flashed a sassy smile. "Oh, I don't know. I had a really good time the day we did that."

His body stirred. "I mean, it's just us out here today, before construction starts. I'm completely amenable to revisiting that scenario."

"Good to know since I packed a bag accordingly." She jerked her head toward the backpack in the backseat.

"Little cold for that, isn't it?"

"You did say the foreman's office fireplace still worked. I tossed some firewood in the back of the truck."

His grin spread wide. His girl was always prepared. "I do love the way you think. Did Athena send another picnic?"

"Athena's working hard on not letting her head explode over this wedding, so our snack fare is more what I was able to scrounge up in the inn's kitchen. But we won't starve."

"Still freaking out, huh?"

"So much. But Kennedy dropped a bomb this morning that should distract her a bit. She and Xander are pregnant."

"No shit?" Porter grinned. "Xander hasn't said a word."

"She's only six weeks, so mum's the word for now." She slipped out of the truck.

A little worried, Porter followed, circling around to where she was pulling her bag out of the back. "Hey, how are you doing with all this? I know you've made your peace with Bailey, but are you gonna be okay going through this again with another sister?"

"That's actually something I wanted to talk to you about. Come on. Let's get inside and set up. Grab the firewood."

Dread set up like Quikrete in his gut. They were together now. She wasn't about to dump him, but they hadn't talked about what came next. There hadn't been time with all the changes the past few weeks. December was just around the corner and so was the end of her sabbatical. That meant it was time for some tough choices. He'd already been working on contingency plans. He'd just been hoping he wouldn't have to use them.

Maybe if I say it fast, it won't hurt so much.

"I've spoken to Mia."

"About what?"

Because he needed to keep himself busy, he worked on laying in the fire while she unpacked some blankets and an informal picnic.

"About taking over Mountainview and a plan to buy me out over the long-term." The idea of giving up his business, starting over...or worse, working for someone else again, made him feel a little sick. But he'd do it. He'd do anything for her.

"What? Why would you do that?"

That wasn't obvious? He wiped sweaty palms on his jeans. "It'll free me up to come back to California with you. It's not a done deal. We still have to hammer out some stuff." Like all of it. He'd broached the topic with his partner and she'd humored him without actually committing. But he'd bring her around. Mia loved it in Eden's Ridge.

"You're willing to sell your business and follow me to California?"

At the disbelief in her tone, he finally turned around. She knelt on the blanket, a forgotten bottle of wine in her hand as she stared at him with brimming eyes.

"I mean, yeah. That's not even a question. I love you."

Maggie shook her head. "But you put in all this work to build Mountainview."

He shrugged and turned back to light the fire."I'm not afraid of hard work. I built a company here. I can build one there. Or work for somebody else, if I have to. I'll figure it out. It'll take time, but it'll be fine." Maybe if he kept repeating it, he'd start to really believe it.

"Porter, I called Genevieve today."

The match in Porter's hand shook as he carefully lit the kindling. Well, didn't that just make shit get real? "How long do we have? I'll need a little time to turn over the reins to Mia, help get them over the hump."

"Porter—"

"We might have to do long distance for a couple months—"

"Porter!"

"Yeah?"

"I told her I'm not coming back."

Everything stopped. The panicked planning. The desperate determination that he could give up everything but her and be fine. It would be fine because she wasn't going back.

Closing his eyes, he released a silent breath. *Thank God. Thank God.* "Oh. And how did she take that news?"

"Better when I told her it was because of you."

Porter watched the small flame spread, feeling relief and gratitude moving through him at the same pace. She wasn't going back.

Satisfied the fire had caught and that he had his emotions under control, he moved over to settle on the blanket beside her. "Are you really okay with that? With saying goodbye to California?" She'd worked so hard to get where she was with Invation. No matter how much he didn't want to leave Tennessee, he didn't want to see her give up something else she loved because of him.

"I miss Genevieve, but now that I've finally slowed down—"

Porter couldn't help snorting. "I'm sorry, you call this slowed down?"

Laughing, she shoved at his shoulder. "Now that I've finally slowed down, I can appreciate living at a pace where there's time to have a life. Where I actually *have* a life. Where I have you."

She'd picked him. Not because she'd been given a devil's choice, but because she wanted him. Wanted what they had together. All the years of patience, of waiting, had finally paid off. Life couldn't get any better than this.

Leaning in, she took his face in her hands. "It took us so long to finally get here, and I don't want to waste another minute. I love you, Porter. And that brings me to what I wanted to talk to you about."

No longer worried, he slid his hands around her waist and tugged her closer. "Okay."

"You asked me a question twelve years ago."

Porter froze, his heart kicking into a timpani beat in his chest as she smiled at him. Was she really...?

"I've got an answer now." She brushed a tender kiss over his lips. "Yes. I want to marry you. I want to make a family with you. If the offer's still on the table."

Oh God, he'd been wrong. Life could absolutely get better. Proposing again hadn't even been on his radar for at least another few months. He'd thought she'd need more time to adjust and figure out...everything. And here she'd turned the tables. Throat thick, he could barely get out her name as he pressed his brow to hers and closed his eyes to savor this moment when she handed him everything he'd always wanted. "I can wait. We don't have to rush into anything."

"I don't need to wait. I'm where I'm supposed to be. Where I was always supposed to be."

His heart was going to explode. Or he was going to unman himself completely and cry. She was making his dreams come true. Every single one.

"In that case." He shifted to tug his wallet out.

Maggie laughed. "Getting to the celebrating already?"

"Not yet." He fished out the thing that had worn a groove in the leather he'd been carrying it for so long. "I figure we need to do this part first." He held up the ring, gratified when her mouth fell open.

"Seriously?"

"Seriously."

"Porter! How long have you had this?"

"Years. It's just been waiting for the right time."

She held out a trembling hand and he slid the simple diamond solitaire onto her ring finger. He felt the weight of the moment settle over them as they both stared at the symbol of his devotion. It looked right there, as he'd always imagined it would, and he couldn't help but wonder how long it would be before they could do this again, with an audience of all their friends and family.

"Perfect fit," she whispered.

"Just like us."

A joyful laugh burbled out of her as she launched herself at him, peppering his face with kisses. "I love you. God, how I love you."

He'd never get tired of hearing it. Never get tired of reminding her, every single day, for the rest of forever. "I love you, too, Margaret Anne."

Cuddling close, she held out her hand so the ring glinted in the firelight. "We should keep this quiet until after Athena and Logan's wedding. Let them have their day. It's only a week or so."

Porter wanted to shout the news to the world. Maggie Reynolds was going to be his wife. But he could agree to this. "Fair enough."

Suddenly shy, she dropped her gaze as she trailed one hand through the hair at his nape. "But maybe we could get started on the other part."

"Which other part?"

Her eyes came back to his, dark and burning. "The family. I want a baby with you Porter."

Stunned, he stared at her. This, for her, was the ultimate trust, the ultimate sign of love. And she wanted it with him. More, she wanted it now. No more waiting, no more hoping. It humbled him. In this moment, she was his deepest dream come to life.

Uncertainty flickered over her face as the silence spun out.

"We haven't even talked about that. I should've led with a discussion—"

"Yes. Hell yes." The idea of her growing round and ripe with his child had him going hard as iron in an instant. He was absolutely on board with starting their forever right here, right now.

"You'd be okay with fast everything? Wedding, kids?"

"Yes to all that. But maybe not fast everything."

Grinning and overflowing with joy, he pressed her back against the blankets, where they took their slow, sweet time.

Epilogue

Nearly fourteen months after Maggie first laid eyes on the mill, it rose before her, all decked out for the holidays and looking like a Christmas postcard. She leaned forward in her seat, trying to see if there was space left in the parking lot, and feeling a punch of pride as she took in the finished Stone County Artisan's Guild and Education Center. "Looks like a good turnout for the open house."

"I'm still not sure you two should be out among all those people. That's a lot of germs. And you know there's already been flu going around."

Maggie laid a hand on her husband's arm. "Porter, honey, I gave birth. I don't have a compromised immune system. Besides, I had my flu shot."

"But Faith—"

"The baby will be fine. Your wife will not be if she doesn't get to leave the house."

Having been ordered to bed rest the last two months of her pregnancy, she'd accepted Porter's overprotective streak. But she'd fully expected him to dial it back once their healthy baby girl had arrived. Instead, he'd been the proudest, most overprotective papa in the state of Tennessee, practically demanding background checks and full physicals before letting anybody who wasn't family near their daughter.

Porter opened his mouth, as if to argue, then closed it again when Maggie arched a brow.

"I've indulged your crazy long enough. It's time to get out and about as a family. Besides, my sisters are all already here with the rest of the family."

"Okay. But if you start to feel tired, we're going home."

"I won't overdo, Papa Bear." Maggie sealed the promise with a kiss. "Come on. Let's get inside."

Maggie cuddled baby Faith, safely swaddled against the winter chill, and Porter's arm wrapped tight around them both as they walked the neat path to the garland-festooned double doors of the second-floor entrance. Once again, Maggie marveled at Porter's workmanship, how much of the original structure he'd managed to save, and how he'd successfully restored the whole to better-than-new. A pair of twisted, ornamental evergreens occupied pots flanking the doors. Twinkle lights and ribbon were threaded through the branches, and one of the guild members, dressed as an elf, was passing out vendor maps.

"Well, hey you two! Oh, and is this the new addition?" Tabitha Dutton peered at the sleepy bundle in a sling. "Hey cutie pie. Look at that sweet face. Looks just like her mama."

Maggie pressed a kiss to the white-blonde fuzz on her daughter's head. "She's got her daddy's eyes and ears."

"Should we maybe get out of the cold?" Porter asked.

"Of course! Of course. Y'all enjoy yourselves." Tabitha waved them inside.

Past the vestibule, the second floor opened into an enormous, high-ceilinged room that comprised the maker's space. Tools, equipment, and workstations ringed the edges, but the center had been entirely taken over with a massive Christmas tree that soared almost twenty feet. It was covered in lights and ribbon and a whole host of hand-crafted ornaments. Vendor booths had been set up in aisles around it, and the whole place was full of people. Maggie's heart squeezed at the exceptional turnout.

The din of conversation echoed off the walls, mixing with the music coming from the small stage set up to one side of the tree. Recognizing Flynn's fiddle, she reached for Porter's hand and tugged him in that direction. They were stopped countless times for people to coo and fuss over the baby, and Maggie couldn't help but reflect how different everything felt now. She no longer dreaded being in public. No one talked about the past. Now she got asked about her husband, her daughter, and what she and her sisters were going to get up to next.

"Maggie!" Roman Lewis waved and hustled over, his wife Deborah in tow. "You made it."

"Everybody outdid themselves. This turned out so beautifully."

"Couldn't have done it without your planning expertise."

Maggie beamed. "Deborah, how are you enjoying your first Tennessee Christmas season?"

She and Roman had moved to Eden's Ridge back in the summer as the mill project neared completion.

"It's just lovely. The cold makes it feel so much more like Christmas than in California. I'm hoping for a White Christmas."

"It's not a guarantee, but it could happen," Porter conceded.

"There's someone I want you to meet." Roman motioned over another couple. "This is my daughter, Chelsea, her husband, Nick Goodwin, and their son, Grady. And this is Maggie Reynolds Ingram and her husband Porter."

Chelsea's face lit up. She handed the baby off to Nick and

stepped forward to wrap Maggie in a careful hug. "Thank you so much. We wouldn't have him without you."

Maggie felt her throat close up with emotion. During their months working on the mill project, Roman had confided in her about his daughter's struggles with fertility. Maggie had been able to connect them with Claudia, who'd been thrilled knowing her son would be adopted by good people.

She swallowed against the knot. "You're most welcome."

Needing to get back on steadier ground, she turned her attention to Roman. "Are you about ready to start reviewing applications for the small business incubator?"

"Any time. But I figure the new year is soon enough for all of us to hit the ground running."

"Then I'll see you in January."

As they walked away, Porter slipped an arm around her. "They're a good fit."

"Yeah, they are. Let's go find my sisters."

The entire family was clustered not far from the stage, listening to Flynn and some of the other local musicians light up the room with Christmas carols. Xander swayed from side to side, fingers curled into handles for their daughter, Caroline, who was strapped to his front in a baby carrier. Logan hugged Athena from behind, resting his chin on her shoulder as he whispered something into her ear that had Athena's mouth curving into a secret smile. Pru and Ari were in animated conversation about something as Maggie and Porter stepped up.

"Hey y'all."

"Hey! You made it!" Pru immediately slipped in for a side hug.

"Flynn's sounding stellar as usual."

"It never gets old," her sister said. "He's nearly done with his set."

Porter dropped the diaper bag at his feet. "Where's Bailey?"

"She's right—" Ari turned a fast circle. "Crap! Where did she go?"

Maggie spotted her toddling as fast as her little legs would carry her down the aisle between vendor tables. "We've got a runner."

Even as they watched, Bailey ran straight into a pair of long, denim-clad legs. She stumbled and landed flat on her diaper-padded butt, tipping her head back to look up at the guy who owned them. In his black t-shirt and battered leather jacket, he looked like he was auditioning for The Outsiders. He seemed as surprised by the toddler as she was by him.

"Bailey!" Ari wailed, but in a whisper far too soft for her baby sister to hear.

"Who's that?" Pru asked.

"That's Cullen Walker. He's the new guy at school."

Noting the uncharacteristic fluster, Maggie exchanged a look with Pru. "He's cute."

"He's broody," Athena noted.

"He's looking this way, " Kennedy added.

"Oh God." Ari's cheeks flushed and she couldn't seem to make herself move.

Cullen looked back down at Bailey, who held her arms toward him in the universal "Up!" signal.

"Maybe you should go rescue him," Maggie suggested.

Ari whipped around in horror. "I can't talk to him!"

Across the room, Cullen bent and plucked Bailey up, tucking her on his hip with an ease that said she wasn't the first toddler he'd been exposed to.

Interesting. "He's coming this way."

"Oh God." Straight-up panic twisted Ari's features. Maggie was certain she'd start wringing her hands at any moment.

"Lose something?" The kid directed his words right at Ari,

and Maggie noted the tone was one of humor, with a touch of warmth and a total absence of bite.

Ari sucked in a breath, tried to blank her face, and turned. "Hi. I—I'm so sorry. My sister's turned into an escape artist." She reached for Bailey, who wound her arms around his neck. "Oh God. I...she. Bailey, let go."

Maggie hid her smile against Faith's head as she watched the drama unfold.

"Sorry. She's not normally this clingy. Bailey, come on, now."

Cullen whispered something in the little girl's ear. She giggled, pulling back to offer him a toothy grin. He grinned back and Ari's jaw went slack. Maggie couldn't blame her. The guy had one of those secret, lethal weapon smiles that transformed his serious face into something absolutely stunning.

Bailey unwound her arms and Cullen offered her to Ari. Wordlessly, she took her sister, automatically tucking her against her hip.

"See you around, Ari." With a nod acknowledging the rest of them, Cullen sauntered off.

"He knows my name?" Ari breathed.

Athena smirked. "Doe eyes much?"

"Shut up!"

"I mean, justified," Kennedy acknowledged. "He's hot."

"He seems sweet, and comfortable with small children." Pru scooped up Bailey, "The string bean likes him."

As Faith started to fuss, Maggie bounced and rubbed her back. "Good guy in bad boy wrapping paper. That one's going to be kryptonite."

Porter slipped an arm around Maggie's back. "I'm just glad that's Flynn's problem to worry about."

"Your time is coming, boyo," Flynn muttered darkly.

"Not for thirty more years," Porter insisted, dropping a kiss on Faith's head.

Logan boomed a laugh. "You keep thinking that, pal."

As the laughter died down, Pru jumped in, "Okay everybody is here. We're getting a full family picture by the tree." She reached out to snag Misty Pennebaker. "Can we trouble you to play photographer for a minute?"

"Of course."

They all set assorted bags to the side and jostled into formation. Misty raised the phone. "I'm gonna take a few, okay? Everybody smile."

Maggie grinned and waited while Misty snapped pictures, played with the camera settings, snapped a few more.

"These will be amazing," she told them. "You should get Troy to frame a print for you, to hang at the inn."

"Free of charge," Troy Cartwright said, slinging an arm around Misty's shoulders to look at the images. "The least I can do for what you all have done and will do for this town. That Joan Reynolds, she knew what she was doin', didn't she?"

"I'd say she did," Misty smiled at all of them. And, perhaps aware of the depth of feeling Troy's statement inspired, she linked her arm with his and turned him away from the group, as though to give them a moment to themselves. "Now don't run off, because I want to show you Denver's carvings. Here you go, honey." Misty handed the phone off to Ari, who immediately started thumbing through the pictures.

Maggie stood for a moment, savoring the memory of her mother and the warmth of the family she'd left for them to share. From the unusual quiet, and the looks on her sisters' faces, she knew they were doing the same.

It was Athena's voice that cut into their moment of silence. "Since we're all together, this seems a good enough time to make an announcement."

Maggie and her other sisters sucked in a collective breath.

"Are you pregnant?" Pru gasped.

"Are you kidding? Do I look like someone who needs to raise tiny humans? I am happy cuddling yours and giving them back." She chuckled. "I think I've always known that babyland is a place I like to visit, but I wouldn't want to live there."

All eyes swung to Logan. "And I'm good with that. We've got nieces aplenty, and the way y'all can't seem to keep your hands off each other..."

Xander caught Logan with a playful slap to the back of the head.

"Wait, so, what's the big announcement, then?" Kennedy wanted to know.

"Logan and I are adopting."

The family exploded with congratulations and hugs and questions.

"There are kids out there already who need a chance. Like we did. Who need a family—" Athena's voice cut off, uncharacteristically strained.

Logan stepped in, wrapping an arm around her. "We've found a pair of brothers, Eight and ten, who need us."

"And we want them. So much." Athena didn't try to hide the glistening in her eyes that was more than just excitement. "We're getting them just in time for Christmas."

"Oh honey," Pru wailed, throwing her arms around Athena, and catching Logan at the same time. "I am so proud of you right now."

Kennedy glommed on. "Those boys don't know how lucky they are. But they will."

Porter was already pulling Faith from her sling. Her husband knew she needed to get in on this.

"I can't wait to meet them," Maggie said. She wrapped her arms around all her sisters, and then said low, in a voice meant for them alone, "It's just what she would have wanted."

They held like that for a long moment. Then Maggie felt a

warm hand on her shoulder. She glanced over, expecting to see Porter, but there was no one there. She felt Kennedy start, then Pru, then Athena. One by one, the rest of her sisters straightened, and Maggie knew they'd felt it too.

Mom.

"Did you just feel—?" Kennedy asked.

"Like...a hug?" Athena asked.

"It's Mom," Pru whispered. "She's here."

"She always has been, hasn't she?" Maggie asked. In a moment, a reel of the years since Joan's death spun out in her mind, good and bad, but mostly so, so good. She thought about how they'd all tried to go their separate ways. Maybe they'd needed to do that, to become the amazing women they'd all grown up to be, to be able to have what they had now. Joan's death had brought them all together again, but it had taken more than that to finally bring them home. It had taken family. It had taken love.

The things that Joan had taught them. The things she had given them so freely. Her presence in the room was there, so real that Maggie almost thought she could smell her mother's perfume.

Kennedy squeezed her hand. "I think you're right."

"All right, that's enough mushy stuff," Ari declared, wading in and breaking the mood. "This calls for a party!"

And party they did.

Choose Your Next Romance

This concludes The Misfit Inn quartet! I hope you enjoyed getting to know the Reynolds sisters as much as I enjoyed writing them.

Now, I know you're curious what kind of secret Mia's hiding

and what the scoop is with her estranged husband. Now you can find out! Their prequel backstory *Rescued By a Bad Boy* is available now for FREE! And you won't want to miss out on their second chance romance, *Mixed Up With a Marine* Book 1 in the Bad Boy Bakers series. Keep turning the pages for a preview!

Or maybe you want to know about the Men of the Misfit Inn? The girls had a LOT of foster brothers! You can meet the first of them, Caleb Romero, in *Let It Be Me* . This book has the perfect caretaking unicorn hero, a friends to lovers, neighbor, age gap, firefighter romance with another precocious teen and a dog who totally thinks he's a cat.

Sneak Peek Rescued By a Bad Boy

Bad Boy Bakers Book 1

What's a little marriage between friends?

Mia has been Braxton's best friend for years. Even when they no longer lived in the same foster family, even after he'd aged out of the system, he'd continued look out for the one person who got under his skin and made him care.

For the last six years, Mia's been keeping her head down, putting one foot in front of the other, unable to trust anyone with her secrets—including the foster brother who's been the one bright spot in her life, as well as her secret crush.

Just one more day until Mia turns eighteen—a legal adult. Brax doesn't trust her foster father and wants her out of that house. Is proposing a marriage of convenience to your best friend a little drastic? Maybe so. But what Brax feels is so far beyond friendship. Is it possible Mia feels it, too?

Mia Torres snapped from sleep to wakefulness in a heartbeat, ears straining to analyze for threat before she opened her eyes or moved a muscle. A faint *scritch scritch* sounded at the window as the overgrown black hawthorn bush outside nodded in the wind. The clatter of breakfast dishes sounded from elsewhere in the house, but there was no squeak of floorboards, no sense of movement nearby. She cracked her eyes open and spotted her desk chair still wedged under the doorknob, exactly where she'd left it last night. Her paltry wooden sentry had done its job. Beneath the pillow, her hand relaxed, releasing the scissors she slept with. Flexing stiff fingers, she sat up and stretched. Her spine and shoulders popped.

One more day.

Less than twenty-four hours until she turned eighteen. They couldn't hold her after today. In truth, she really needed to make it through the end of the semester until graduation, but if worse came to worst and she ever had to use those scissors, she could leave tomorrow. The idea of it terrified her, but she'd figure it out. She was so over the foster system. It was supposed to keep her safe. For nearly six years, she'd bought into that, done everything she was told, kept her head down, stayed invisible. She was very, very good at being invisible. But this last placement had her questioning all the well-meaning adults who'd put her in this position, claiming it was for the best.

It hadn't been so bad when Lainey and Max had been here. But Lainey had been busted for drugs at Halloween, and Max was doing a stint in juvie for boosting some rich guy's sports car for a joy ride. For the past two months, it had been only Mia. Her foster mom, Darlene, wasn't so bad. She wasn't a warm woman, but she appreciated hard work and manners, something Mia's real mother had drilled into her from a young age. She'd held onto them after her mom died, feeling like it was a small way to honor her. But Darlene's husband, Wayne, made Mia nervous. He hadn't ever laid a hand on her, hadn't said anything outright threatening. He just watched her. Long, assessing gazes with those flat, watery blue eyes that Mia wasn't sure how to read. She didn't know if he'd stay content with only looking, and she wasn't taking any chances.

The oversized flannel shirt she dragged on over her henley hid the shape of her body. It was probably poor camouflage for the curves that had sprung up against all her hopes two years ago, but it made her feel more at ease. She'd use whatever flimsy armor she could manage. Working her long, thick sable hair into a braid, she peeked out the window at the gray January day. Freezing and gross but not actively snowing. It was as much of a win as she could expect in this part of Washington. She'd take it.

A glance at the clock told her she needed to get a move on, or she'd be late for school. The lace-up boots she'd found at a second-hand store for ten bucks would do good to make it the rest of the winter. Maybe she could shore up the inside seams with duct tape. Later. She added a second pair of socks before slipping them on and shrugging into her coat. Out of long-ingrained habit, she hauled the duffel bag out from under the bed and did a quick inventory of its contents. A few changes of clothes. Basic toiletries. The little Lego knight she'd been gifted in her first foster home by the boy who'd become her best friend. The sketch pad where she captured the dreams she didn't dare tell anyone about. A picture of her mother. The things she couldn't live without if she had to run. Satisfied all was as it should be, she shoved the go bag back in place and stuffed the last of her school-books in her backpack. There'd be a quiz in U.S. Government today, and she'd been up too late preparing. Quick and quiet, she removed the chair from beneath the knob, sliding it back in place beneath the boards laid over two battered file cabinets that served as her desk. One last look to make sure everything was in place.

The scissors. Pulling them out from beneath the pillow, she hid them under the mattress.

Time to go.

Wayne was at the kitchen table, lingering over a cup of coffee. A too large figure in a quilted flannel jacket, he seemed to take up half the room just by breathing. Mia's step hitched a fraction of a second at the sight of him. He'd normally be gone to his job at the steel mill by now. Ducking her head to avoid eye contact, she made a beeline for the cabinet to grab a pack of Pop Tarts for the walk to school.

"No greeting this morning?" His voice held a smoker's rasp and something slick and oily in the tone that automatically put her back up.

Smoothing her features, Mia turned in his direction and muttered, "Morning." Then she couldn't stop herself from asking, "Aren't you late?" She regretted the words as soon as they were out. They opened the door for conversation, which was the last thing she wanted.

"It's a service day. Line's down for repair."

She grunted an acknowledgment and headed for the door.

"In a hurry?"

Without looking back, she reached for the door. "I have a test this morning."

"Have a good day at school."

Uncertain what to do with that, she just kept going, straight out into the cold. The whip of winter wind helped clear her head. Her boots crunched on old snow as she strode down the driveway to the sidewalk. A figure melted out of the trees up near the corner. Stubble darkened the cheeks of the tall, rangy boy who was well on his way to manhood. At the sight of him, Mia felt the tension in her shoulders dissolve and her heart kick into high gear.

Braxton Whitmore was her lifeline. A former foster sibling,

he'd made the past six years tolerable. He'd befriended her when she'd had no one. Taught her how to fight, what to watch for. Kept her safe. And even though he'd aged out of the system last year, he was still looking out for her.

Was it any wonder she was in love with him?

Determined not to betray herself, Mia worked to control her features and hurried to meet him.

* * *

Brax hunched into the shearling-lined denim of his jacket, keeping his eyes on the house instead of the girl who'd done everything in her limited power to hide the fact that she was a woman. He'd had a lot of practice at trying not to notice those failed efforts. The baggy, shapeless clothes couldn't fully conceal that hourglass figure his fingers itched to touch. The total lack of makeup only served to draw attention to those striking, long-lashed coffee-colored eyes he wanted to drown in. As she neared, those unpainted lips curved into one of the hard-won smiles that fueled his days.

"Morning." Her breath puffed out in a cloud with the greeting.

Brax grunted an acknowledgement, his gaze shifting back to the single-story ranch where the blinds in one of the front windows twitched, as if someone were watching her. His eyes narrowed. "Wayne still home?"

"The line is down for repair, apparently."

This close, Brax could see the faint shadows beneath her eyes. "You didn't sleep well. Problem?" His gut tightened at the thought of everything that could happen to her in the night without him being there to stop it. He'd done his best to prepare her, but nothing changed the fact that she was small, and her foster father was a big son of a bitch, who could've played defensive line for the Seahawks.

Her shoulders jerked in a shrug, but she didn't avoid eye contact. "No more than usual. I'm just edgy."

So was Brax. "You're taking precautions?"

"Always."

Satisfied with her answer, he let the tension release and fell into step beside her for the trek to school, as he did every day, come rain, snow, or shine, before he went to the first of two jobs. What would she say if she knew he organized his entire work schedule around being able to see her to and from school? She'd probably be horrified by how many decisions he'd made with her in mind. He hadn't planned it that way. For so long, his focus had been on his own survival.

He'd been on the streets for nearly a year after his mother had ODed. A skinny, half-starved ten-year-old, who'd had more in common with the stray mongrels he'd sometimes emulated than the kids his age he'd seen in public. The restaurant owner who'd caught him foraging in the trash for food had lured him in with a hot meal while he called the cops who'd ultimately connected Brax with social services. It hadn't taken them long to figure out that he had no family and dumped him into the system. That had just been trading one kind of survival for another. He'd trusted no one and bounced through so many placements by the time he was thirteen, he'd earned the "problem child" label. He'd still been one step from feral when he'd landed in Mia's first foster home.

She'd been shell-shocked and so damned scared. When he'd heard her crying that first night, he'd sneaked into her room and curled up on the floor by her bed, close enough to reach up and brush her hand. It had been the first deliberate human contact he'd attempted. When she'd latched on, that little hand squeezing his, he hadn't pulled away. Thus had begun their unlikely friendship.

In her, he'd sensed the kind of gentleness that would get slaughtered by the harsh realities of the world they lived in. Some instinct he hadn't recognized had driven him to protect her. Maybe because he'd seen too much goodness broken to be able to stand by and watch as it happened to her. So he'd shaped up, because he'd known they'd ship him off somewhere else if he didn't. The social worker had been so impressed with his turn-around, she'd made sure he and Mia stayed together. At least until he'd aged out a little over a year ago. It was a minor miracle. The only good thing either of them had gotten out of foster care.

"You're thinking deep thoughts this morning." Her voice brought him back from his musings.

"Just thinking about tomorrow. It's the big one-eight."

Mia blew out a breath. "Yep."

They both knew the implications of this birthday.

"You given any more thought to what you wanna do?" He kept his voice easy, no pressure.

"Yeah. I'm gonna try to stick it out 'til graduation. If I go out on my own, I'd probably have to drop out to work enough to support myself. And even then, it probably wouldn't be enough to make it on my own."

Brax got that. He worked his ass off at two jobs so that he didn't have to depend on anyone else, and so he could put a little bit by each pay period in case of... In case. He wanted to tell her she wouldn't have to do it on her own. That she'd have him. But something held him back. Would she see the offer as friendship or a request for more? God knew he wanted more with her, but he'd never do anything to pressure her or risk destroying the trust she had in him. She was too important.

"Makes sense," he agreed equably. But he couldn't get the image of those blinds out of his mind. He wanted her out of that house, and he'd been considering extreme measures to accomplish it.

She opened a pack of Pop Tarts, passing him one, as she always did, for the last chunk of the walk. "One of these days, I'll be able to afford real pastries, like they have in the window of the bakery downtown. They always look so shiny and beautiful."

Understanding she wanted easier conversation, he followed her lead. "And what kind would you get?"

"Something raspberry. Maybe one of those tart things with all the pretty designs made out of dough. Or the pinwheels. Oh! Or those sort of swirly ones—what are they called?—palmiers."

"Why raspberry?"

"They were my mom's favorite. I don't think I've had one since she died."

Brax decided he'd move heaven and earth to get this girl something raspberry for her birthday.

At the dog groomer's across the street from the school grounds, they stopped, watching other students flowing into the two-story brick building.

"I gotta go. Test this morning."

Much as he'd hated everything about the restrictions of school, he wished he was going in there with her. He wasn't ready to walk away from her yet. He suspected he never would be. "You have time to come by my place after school?"

Her brows drew together. "Don't you have to work tonight?"

"Not until tomorrow night." He'd talk Jerry into trading shifts with him. "I have a surprise for your birthday." Or he would by the end of the day.

Her face twisted somewhere between suspicion and excitement. "Early?"

"Yes, early. I can't wait."

That earned him another of those smiles that warmed him up inside. "Then I can't either. See you after school!"

As he always did, Brax waited for her to get inside the building. The jingle of the shop bell behind him told him someone was coming out. He was unsurprised when Valentina, the tatted-up owner of Mudpuppies, strode out. She wore a hot pink bandana over her spiral curls and a smirk on her warm brown face as she looked across the school grounds. "When you gonna lock that down?"

"It's not like that, V."

"The hell it isn't. I been watching you walk her to and from school every day for the past... how many years? You are totally gone over that girl."

That was completely beside the point.

"I'm just looking out for her."

"Mmmhmm."

Brax met her skeptical gaze. "She's not ready for anything else."

Valentina crossed her arms and arched a perfectly manicured brow. "You actually asked her?" When he kept his mouth shut, she just shook her head. "That's what I thought. Boy, you're loyal as the day is long, but you sure are blind. She's crazy about you."

As the bell rang for the start of the school day, Brax glanced back at the school. Was she right? Did Mia feel more than he thought she did? Like most foster kids he knew, they both habitually played things close to the vest, masking their emotions because, in their world, feelings were weaknesses to be exploited. Was it worth the risk of finding out?

"Her birthday's tomorrow. Eighteen." He didn't know why he said it, except that it had been on his mind for weeks.

"That what you've been waiting for?"

Was it? Maybe on some level. He'd been very aware of their year and change age difference since he'd left the system, not wanting to do anything to rock the boat and put her at risk or give anyone ammunition to keep them apart.

But at eighteen, she got to make her own decisions. She'd have to fight for them, but she'd be a legal adult.

Maybe he'd talk to her about it. But he'd see how the birthday surprise went first.

"I gotta go. Lots to do today to surprise her."

Valentina grinned. "Good for you, honey."

* * *

Grab your copy of *Rescued By a Bad Boy* today for FREE! And don't miss out on Mia and Brax's second chance romance *Mixed Up With a Marine!*

Can a Marine turned baker and a jaded contractor find their way to a second chance?

Braxton Whitmore needs a change. After leaving the Marines, he's free to build a new life. But is he gonna be a baker? *Really?* When his buddy inherits a decrepit bar and proposes they partner up to turn it into a bakery, Brax figures why not? Until his ex comes walking in.

Mia Whitmore has built a new life for herself, far from the heartbreak and secrets that tore her marriage apart. The last thing she expects is for her estranged husband to be business partners with her latest client. Or for Brax to think they're already divorced.

As they're forced into proximity on the renovation, truths come to light, and Brax and Mia get a second chance. But when past secrets become present danger, Brax puts everything on the line to protect the woman who's always held his heart.

Other Books By Kait Nolan

A complete and up-to-date list of all my books can be found at https://kaitnolan.com.

GIBSON HOLLOW
SMALL TOWN SOUTHERN ROMANCE

- Hero After Midnight (prequel)
- Hero Ever After (Alia and Ramsey)
- Hero, Unexpected (Bodie and Emmaline)

KILTED HEARTS
SMALL TOWN CONTEMPORARY SCOTTISH ROMANCE

- *Jilting The Kilt* (prequel)
- *Cowboy in a Kilt* (Raleigh and Kyla)
- *Grump in a Kilt* (Malcolm and Charlotte)
- *Playboy in a Kilt* (Connor and Sophie)
- *Protector in a Kilt* (Ewan and Isobel)
- *Single Dad in a Kilt* (Hamish and Afton)

- *Kilty Pleasures* (Jason and Skye)

SPECIAL OPS SCOTS
SMALL TOWN MILITARY SCOTTISH ROMANCE

- *One Fine Night* (prequel)
- *Before Highland Sunset* (Alex and Ciara)
- *Beyond Highland Sunrise* (Callum and Parker)
- *Beneath Highland Stars* (Finley and Saoirse)

BAD BOY BAKERS
SMALL TOWN MILITARY ROMANCE

- *Rescued By a Bad Boy* (Brax and Mia prequel)
- *Mixed Up With a Marine* (Brax and Mia)
- *Wrapped Up with a Ranger* (Holt and Cayla)
- *Stirred Up by a SEAL* (Jonah and Rachel)
- *Hung Up on the Hacker* (Cash and Hadley)
- *Caught Up with the Captain* (Grey and Rebecca)

RESCUE MY HEART SERIES
SMALL TOWN MILITARY ROMANCE

- *Someone Like You* (Ivy and Harrison)
- *What I Like About You* (Laurel and Sebastian)
- *Bad Case of Loving You* (Paisley and Ty prequel)
  Included in *Made For Loving You* (Paisley and Ty)

THE MISFIT INN SERIES
SMALL TOWN FAMILY ROMANCE

- *When You Got A Good Thing* (Kennedy and Xander)
- *Til There Was You* (Misty and Denver)

- *Those Sweet Words* (Pru and Flynn)
- *Stay A Little Longer* (Athena and Logan)
- *Bring It On Home* (Maggie and Porter)
- *Come Away with Me* (Moses and Zuri)

MEN OF THE MISFIT INN
SMALL TOWN SOUTHERN ROMANCE

- *Let It Be Me* (Emerson and Caleb)
- *Our Kind of Love* (Abbey and Kyle)
- *Don't You Wanna Stay* (Deanna and Wyatt)
- *Until We Meet Again* (Samantha and Griffin prequel)
- *Come A Little Closer* (Samantha and Griffin)
- *Just Wanted You To Know* (Livia and Declan)
- *A Love Like You* (Juliette and Mick)

WISHFUL ROMANCE SERIES
SMALL TOWN SOUTHERN ROMANCE

- *To Get Me To You* (Cam and Norah)
- *Know Me Well* (Liam and Riley)
- *Be Careful, It's My Heart* (Brody and Tyler)
- *The Matchmaker Maneuver* (Myles and Piper prequel)
- *Just For This Moment* (Myles and Piper)
- *Wish I Might* (Reed and Cecily)
- *Turn My World Around* (Tucker and Corinne)
- *Dance Me A Dream* (Jace and Tara)
- *See You Again* (Trey and Sandy)
- *The Christmas Fountain* (Chad and Mary Alice)
- *You Were Meant For Me* (Mitch and Tess)
- *A Lot Like Christmas* (Ryan and Hannah)

- *Dancing Away With My Heart* (Zach and Lexi)

WISHFUL MOMENTS SERIES
BITE-SIZED WISHFUL ROMANCE

- *Once Upon A Coffee* (Avery and Dillon)
- *Once Upon A Rescue* (Brooke and Hayden)
- *Who I Am with You* (Dinah and Robert)

WISHING FOR A HERO SERIES (A WISHFUL SPINOFF SERIES)
SMALL TOWN ROMANTIC SUSPENSE

- *Make You Feel My Love* (Judd and Autumn)
- *Watch Over Me* (Nash and Rowan)
- *Can't Take My Eyes Off You* (Ethan and Miranda)
- *Burn For You* (Sean and Delaney)

MEET CUTE ROMANCE
SMALL TOWN SHORT ROMANCE

- *Once Upon A Snow Day*
- *Once Upon A New Year's Eve*
- *Once Upon An Heirloom*

SUMMER FLING TRILOGY
CONTEMPORARY ROMANCE

- *Second Chance Summer*
- *Summer Camp Secret*
- *The Summer Camp Swap*

About Kait

Kait is a Mississippi native, who often swears like a sailor, calls everyone sugar, honey, or darlin', and can wield a bless your heart like a saber or a Snuggie, depending on requirements.

You can find more information on this *USA Today* best selling and RITA ® Award-winning author and her books on her website http://kaitnolan.com.

Do you need more small town sass and spark? Sign up for <u>her newsletter</u> to hear about new releases, book deals, and exclusive content!